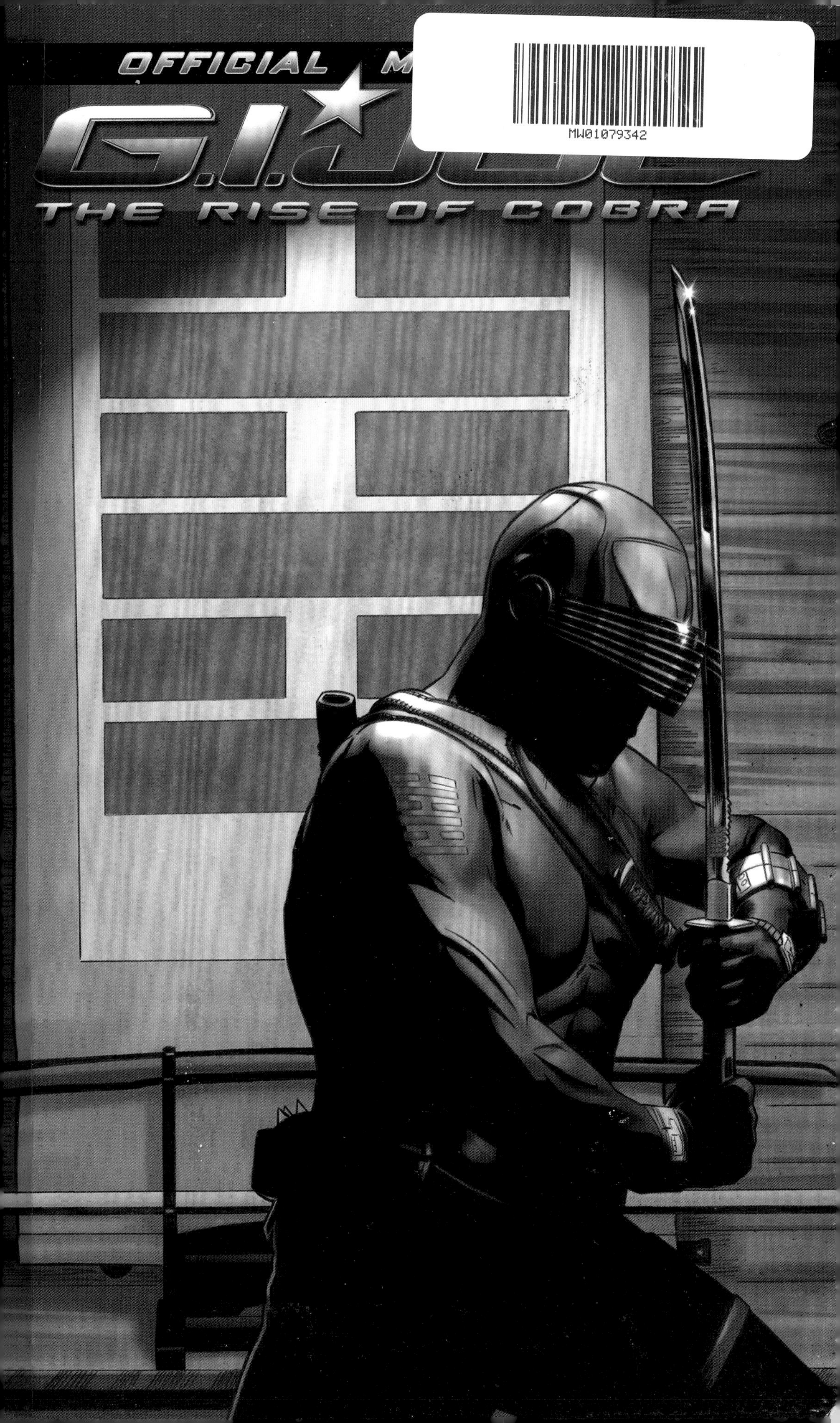
OFFICIAL
G.I.
THE RISE OF COBRA

OFFICIAL MOVIE PREQUEL
G.I. JOE
THE RISE OF COBRA

WRITTEN BY
CHUCK DIXON

ART BY
SL GALLANT

COLORS BY
ART LYON

LETTERS BY
ROBBIE ROBBINS AND CHRIS MOWRY

ORIGINAL SERIES EDITS BY
ANDY SCHMIDT

COLLECTION EDITS BY
JUSTIN EISINGER

EDITORIAL ASSISTANCE BY
MARIAH HUEHNER

COLLECTION DESIGN BY
CHRIS MOWRY

Special thanks to Hasbro's Aaron Archer, Michael Kelly, Amie Lozanski, Ed Lane, Joe Furfaro, Sarah Baskin, Jos Huxley, Michael Ritchie, Samantha Lomow, and Michael Verrecchia for their invaluable assistance.

ISBN: 978-1-60010-469-5
12 11 10 09   1 2 3 4

IDW Publishin
Operation
Ted Adams, Chief Executive Offic
Greg Goldstein, Chief Operating Offic
Matthew Ruzicka, CPA, Chief Financial Offic
Alan Payne, VP of Sal
Lorelei Bunjes, Dir. of Digital Servic
AnnaMaria White, Marketing & PR Manag
Marci Hubbard, Executive Assistai
Alonzo Simon, Shipping Manag
Editoria
Chris Ryall, Publisher/Editor-in-Chi
Scott Dunbier, Editor, Special Projec
Andy Schmidt, Senior Edit
Justin Eisinger, Edit
Kris Oprisko, Editor/Foreign Li
Denton J. Tipton, Edit
Tom Waltz, Edit
Mariah Huehner, Associate Edit
Desig
Robbie Robbins, EVP/Sr. Graphic Arti
Ben Templesmith, Artist/Design
Neil Uyetake, Art Direct
Chris Mowry, Graphic Arti
Amauri Osorio, Graphic Arti
Gilberto Lazcano, Production Assistai

CHAPTER ONE

ARTWORK BY
JOE CORRONEY

CODE NA
DUKE
FILE NAM
HAUSER,
PRIMAR
AIRF
SEC

ILE UM

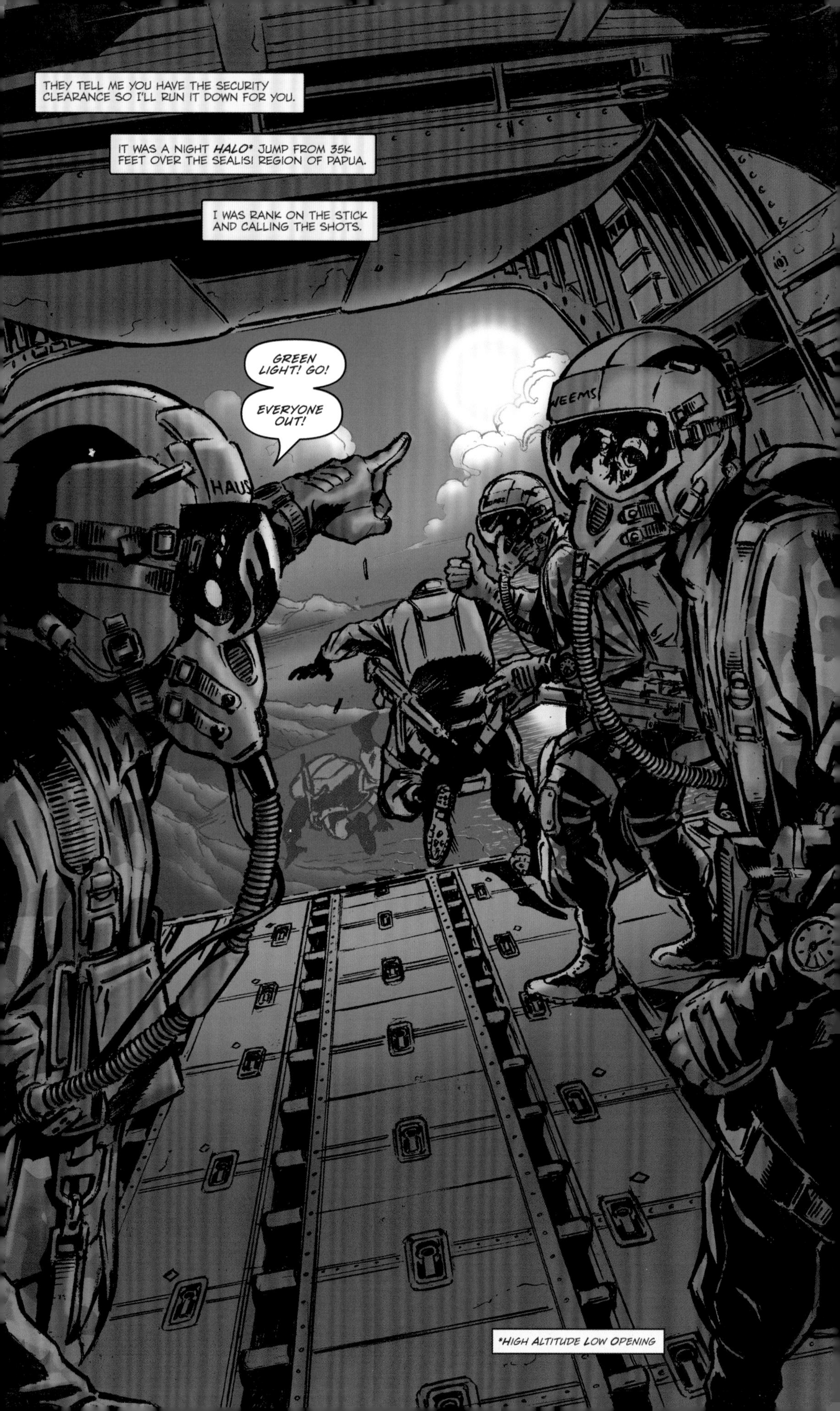
THEY TELL ME YOU HAVE THE SECURITY CLEARANCE SO I'LL RUN IT DOWN FOR YOU.
IT WAS A NIGHT HALO* JUMP FROM 35K FEET OVER THE SEALISI REGION OF PAPUA.
I WAS RANK ON THE STICK AND CALLING THE SHOTS.
GREEN LIGHT! GO!
EVERYONE OUT!
HAUS
WEEMS
*HIGH ALTITUDE LOW OPENING

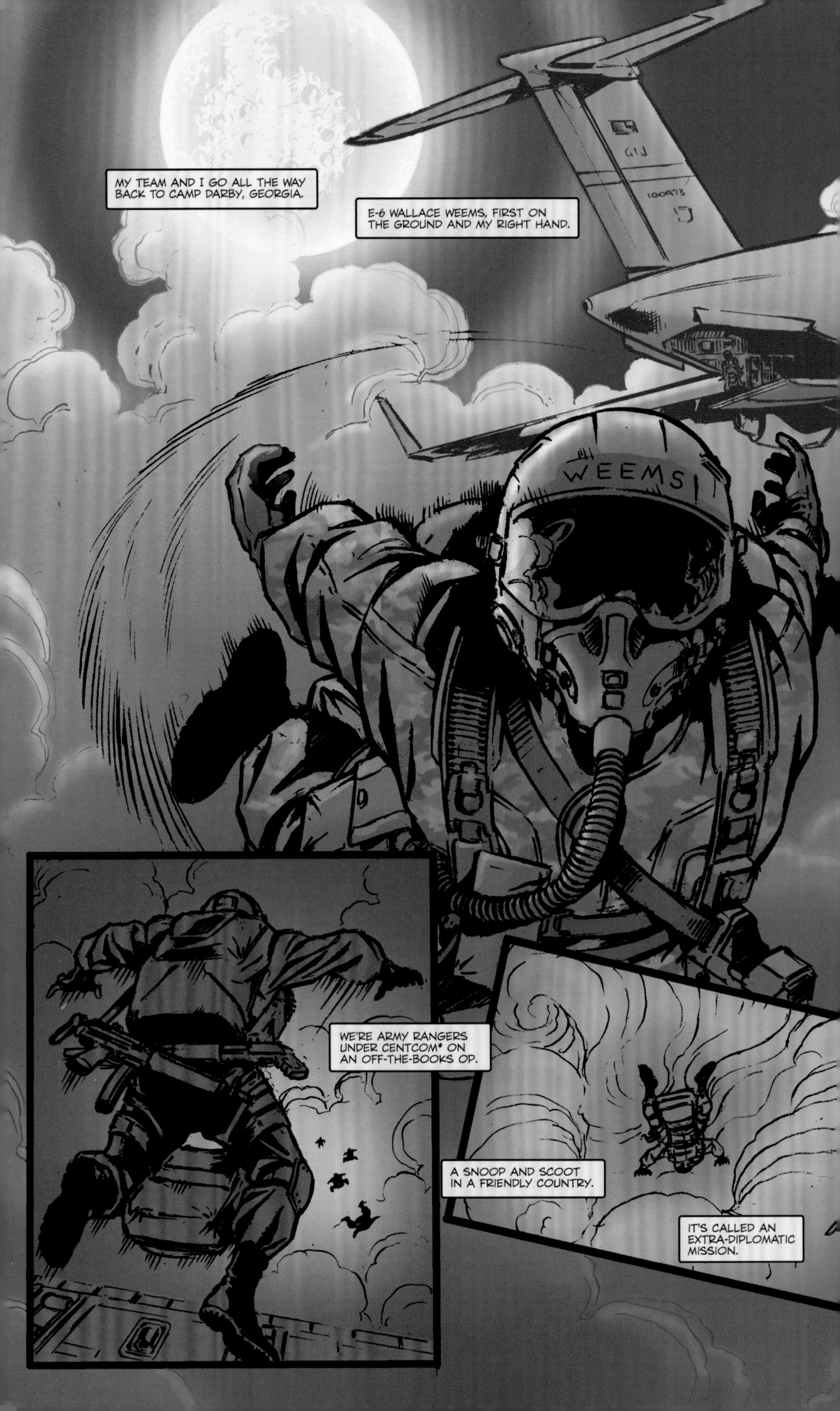
MY TEAM AND I GO ALL THE WAY BACK TO CAMP DARBY, GEORGIA.
E-6 WALLACE WEEMS, FIRST ON THE GROUND AND MY RIGHT HAND.
WEEMS
WE'RE ARMY RANGERS UNDER CENTCOM* ON AN OFF-THE-BOOKS OP.
A SNOOP AND SCOOT IN A FRIENDLY COUNTRY.
IT'S CALLED AN EXTRA-DIPLOMATIC MISSION.

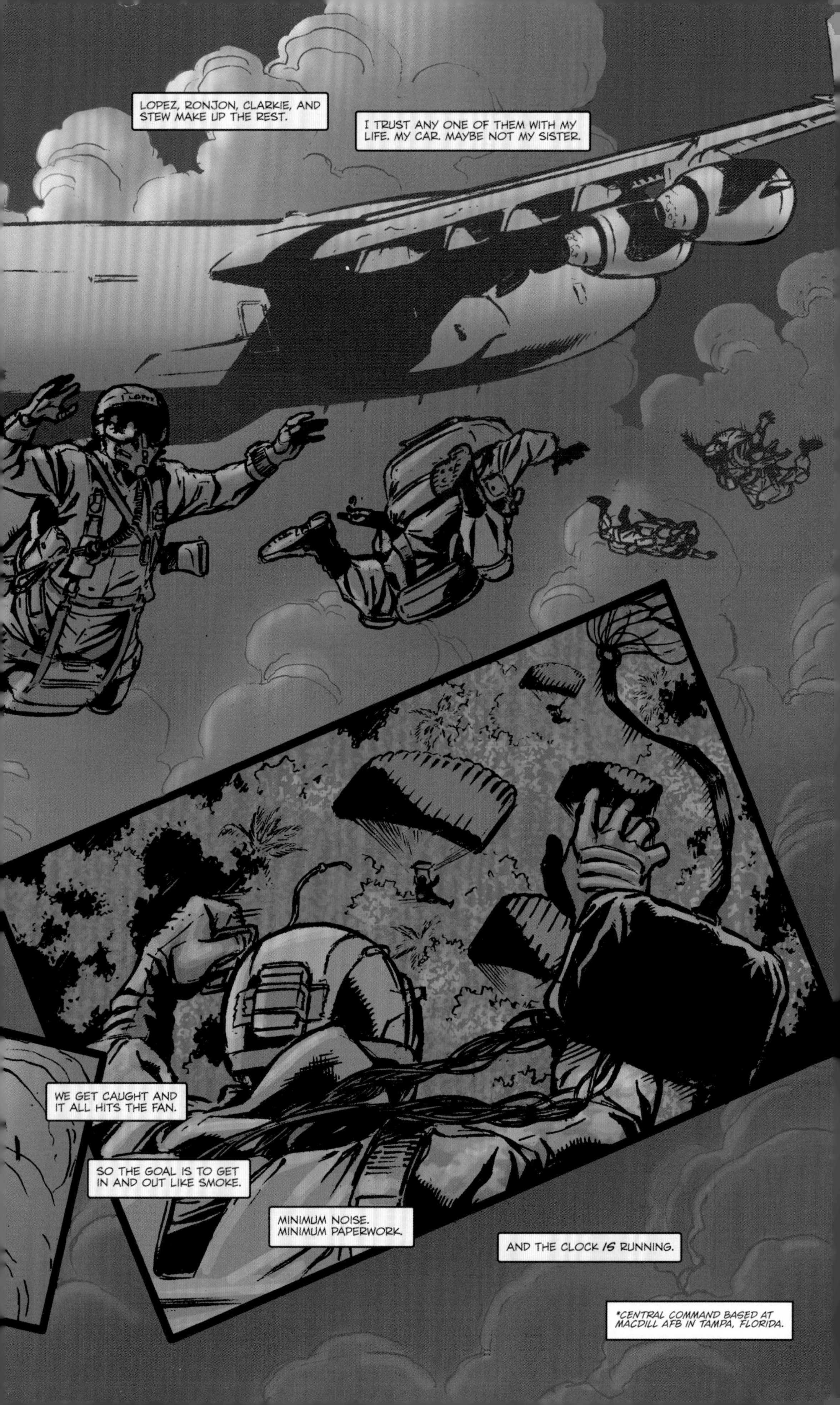
LOPEZ, RONJON, CLARKIE, AND STEW MAKE UP THE REST.
I TRUST ANY ONE OF THEM WITH MY LIFE. MY CAR. MAYBE NOT MY SISTER.
WE GET CAUGHT AND IT ALL HITS THE FAN.
SO THE GOAL IS TO GET IN AND OUT LIKE SMOKE.
MINIMUM NOISE. MINIMUM PAPERWORK.
AND THE CLOCK IS RUNNING.
*CENTRAL COMMAND BASED AT MACDILL AFB IN TAMPA, FLORIDA.

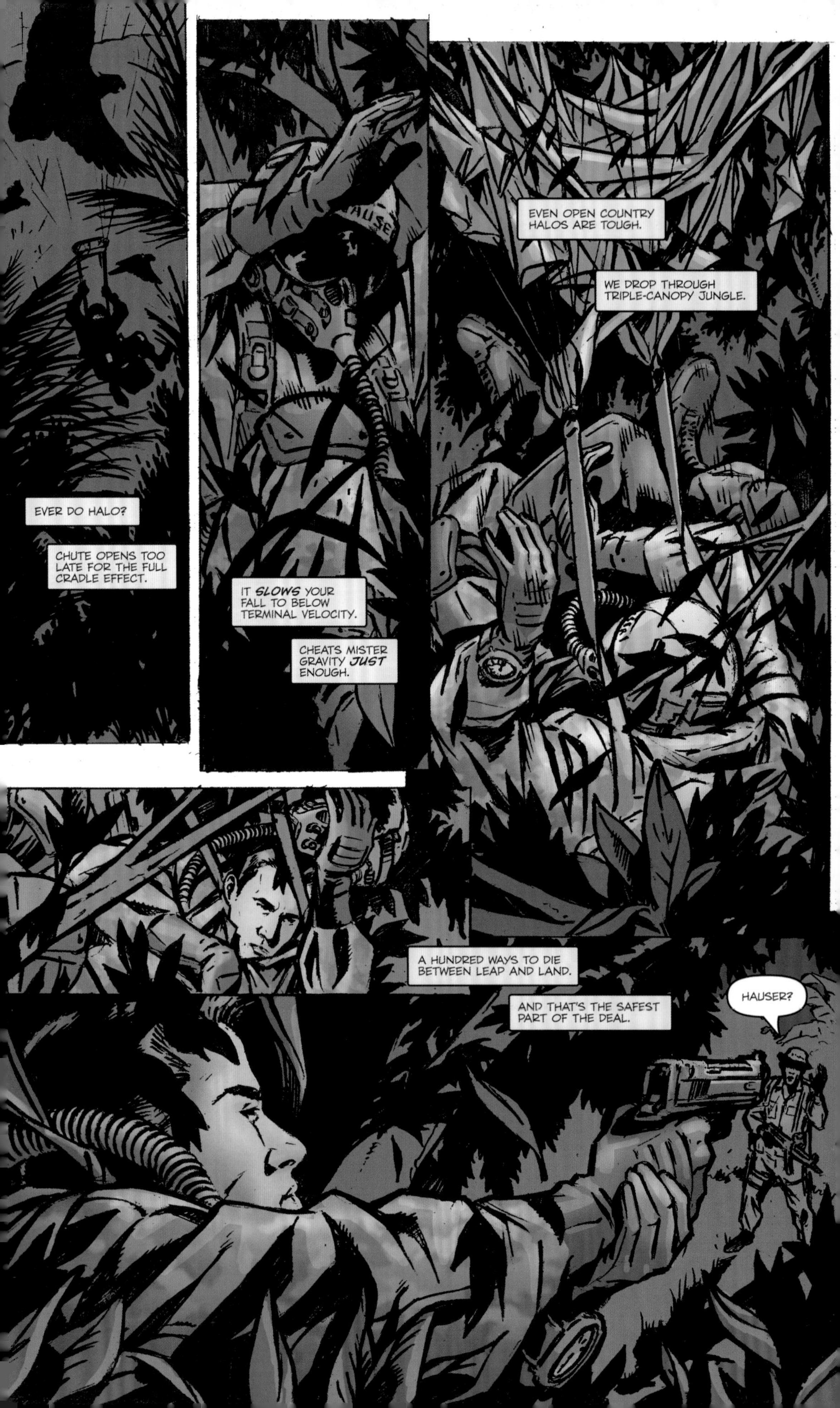

EVER DO HALO?
CHUTE OPENS TOO LATE FOR THE FULL CRADLE EFFECT.
IT SLOWS YOUR FALL TO BELOW TERMINAL VELOCITY.
CHEATS MISTER GRAVITY JUST ENOUGH.
EVEN OPEN COUNTRY HALOS ARE TOUGH.
WE DROP THROUGH TRIPLE-CANOPY JUNGLE.
A HUNDRED WAYS TO DIE BETWEEN LEAP AND LAND.
AND THAT'S THE SAFEST PART OF THE DEAL.
HAUSER?

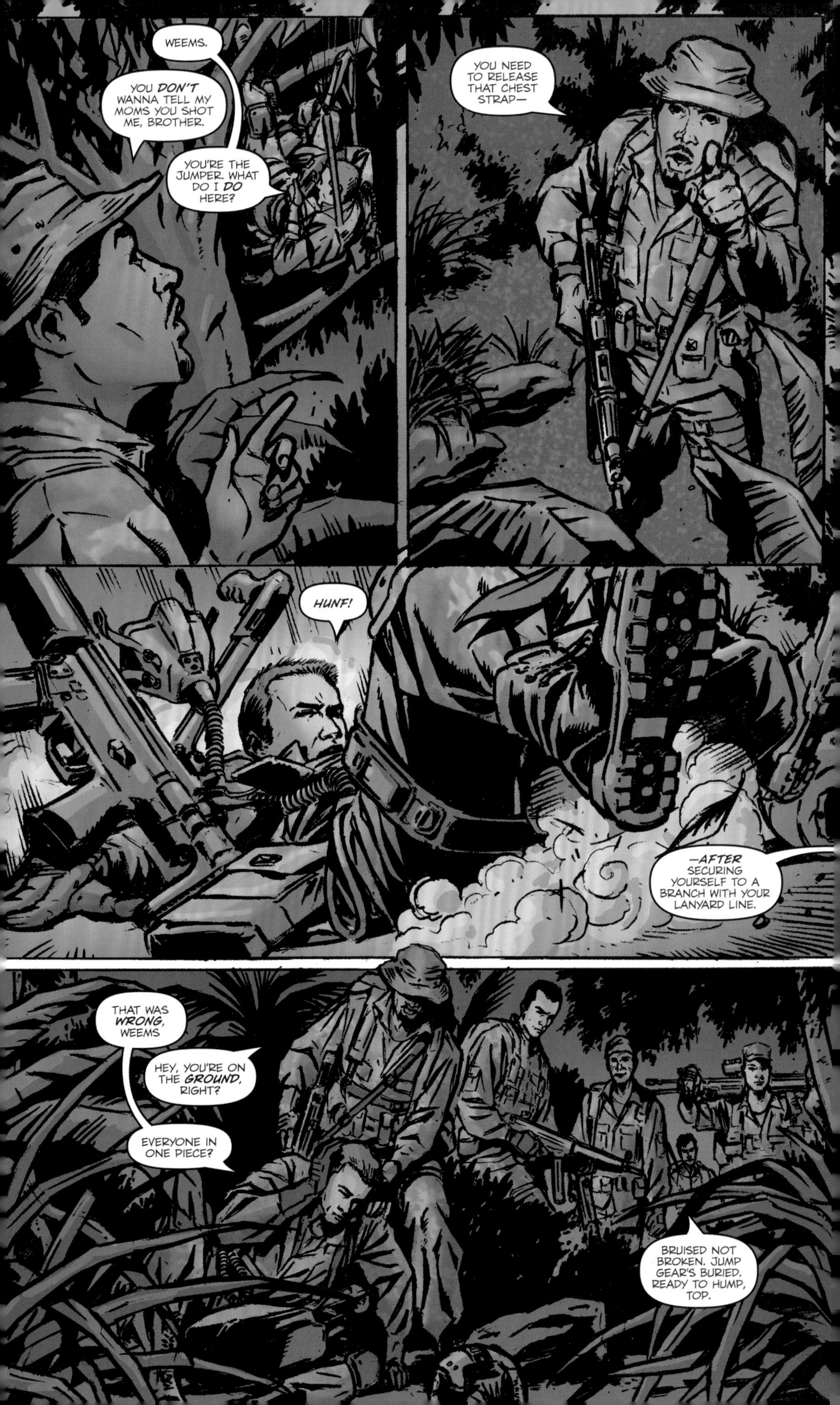
WEEMS.
YOU *DON'T* WANNA TELL MY MOMS YOU SHOT ME, BROTHER.
YOU'RE THE JUMPER. WHAT DO I *DO* HERE?
YOU NEED TO RELEASE THAT CHEST STRAP—
HUNF!
—*AFTER* SECURING YOURSELF TO A BRANCH WITH YOUR LANYARD LINE.
THAT WAS *WRONG*, WEEMS
HEY, YOU'RE ON THE *GROUND*, RIGHT?
EVERYONE IN ONE PIECE?
BRUISED NOT BROKEN. JUMP GEAR'S BURIED. READY TO HUMP, TOP.

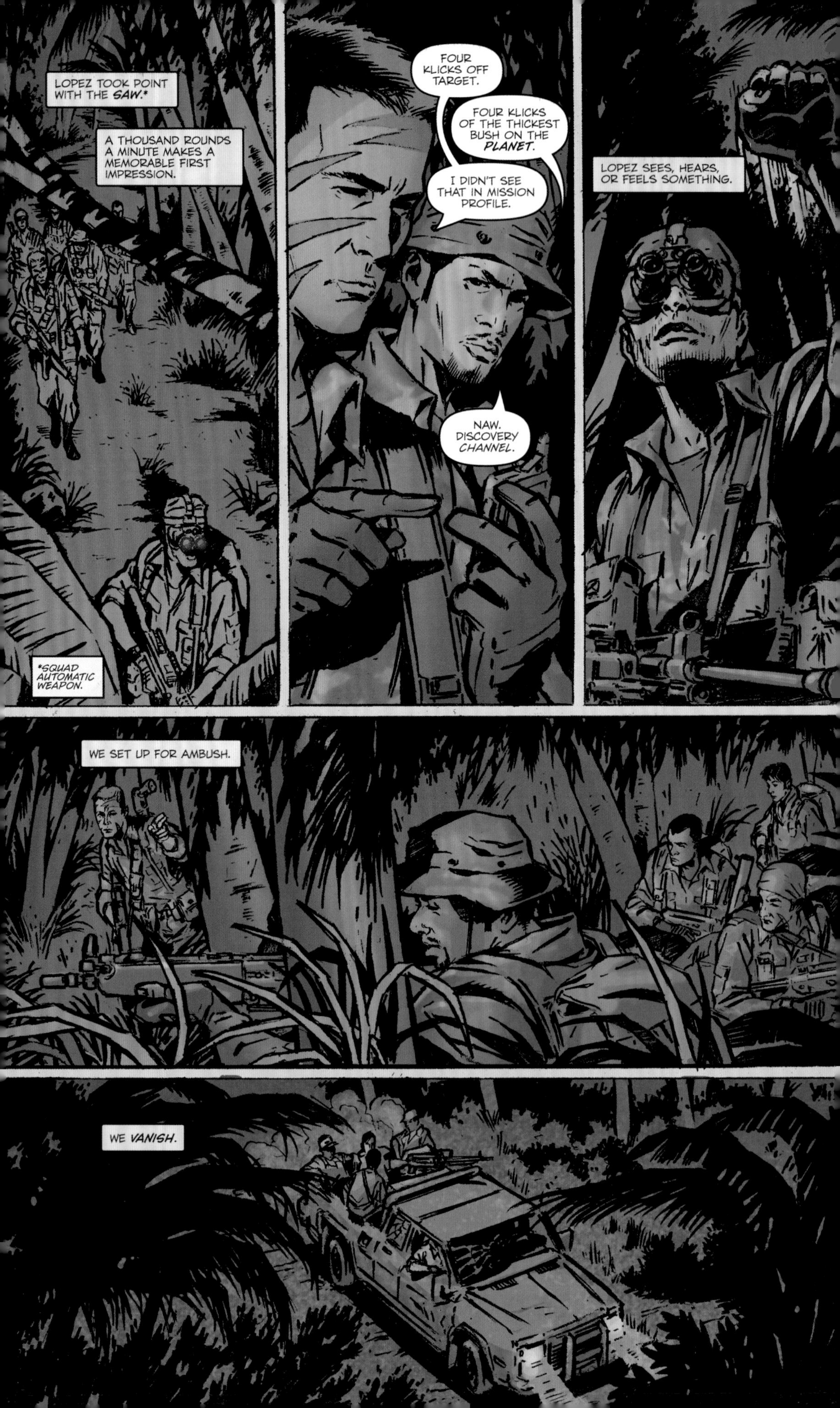

LOPEZ TOOK POINT WITH THE *SAW.**
A THOUSAND ROUNDS A MINUTE MAKES A MEMORABLE FIRST IMPRESSION.
*SQUAD AUTOMATIC WEAPON.
FOUR KLICKS OFF TARGET.
FOUR KLICKS OF THE THICKEST BUSH ON THE *PLANET*.
I DIDN'T SEE THAT IN MISSION PROFILE.
NAW. DISCOVERY *CHANNEL*.
LOPEZ SEES, HEARS, OR FEELS SOMETHING.
WE SET UP FOR AMBUSH.
WE *VANISH*.

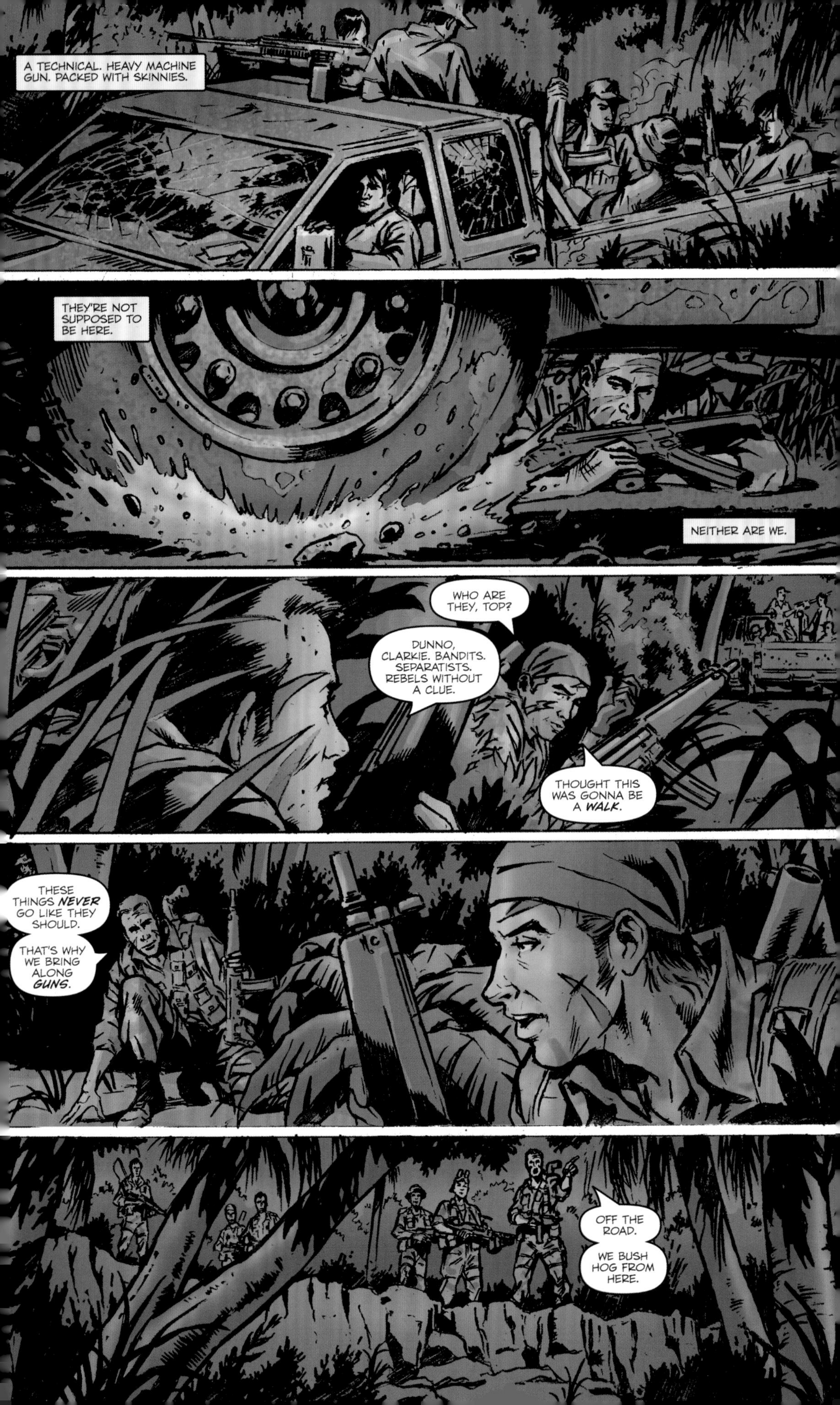
A TECHNICAL. HEAVY MACHINE GUN. PACKED WITH SKINNIES.
THEY'RE NOT SUPPOSED TO BE HERE.
NEITHER ARE WE.
WHO ARE THEY, TOP?
DUNNO, CLARKIE. BANDITS. SEPARATISTS. REBELS WITHOUT A CLUE.
THOUGHT THIS WAS GONNA BE A *WALK*.
THESE THINGS *NEVER* GO LIKE THEY SHOULD.
THAT'S WHY WE BRING ALONG *GUNS*.
OFF THE ROAD.
WE BUSH HOG FROM HERE.

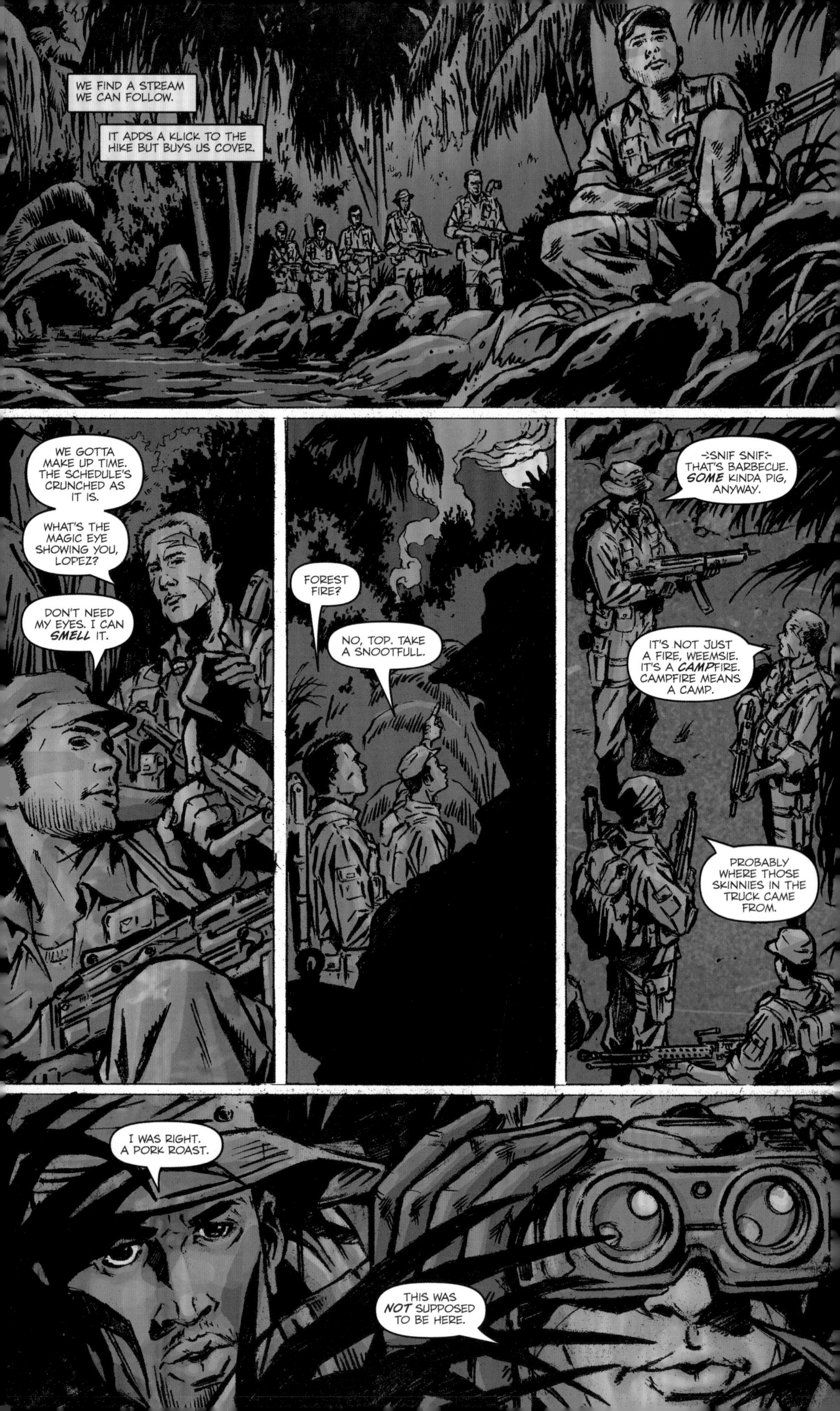

WE FIND A STREAM WE CAN FOLLOW.
IT ADDS A KLICK TO THE HIKE BUT BUYS US COVER.
WE GOTTA MAKE UP TIME. THE SCHEDULE'S CRUNCHED AS IT IS.
WHAT'S THE MAGIC EYE SHOWING YOU, LOPEZ?
DON'T NEED MY EYES. I CAN SMELL IT.
FOREST FIRE?
NO, TOP. TAKE A SNOOTFULL.
-SNIF SNIF- THAT'S BARBECUE. SOME KINDA PIG, ANYWAY.
IT'S NOT JUST A FIRE, WEEMSIE. IT'S A CAMPFIRE. CAMPFIRE MEANS A CAMP.
PROBABLY WHERE THOSE SKINNIES IN THE TRUCK CAME FROM.
I WAS RIGHT. A PORK ROAST.
THIS WAS NOT SUPPOSED TO BE HERE.

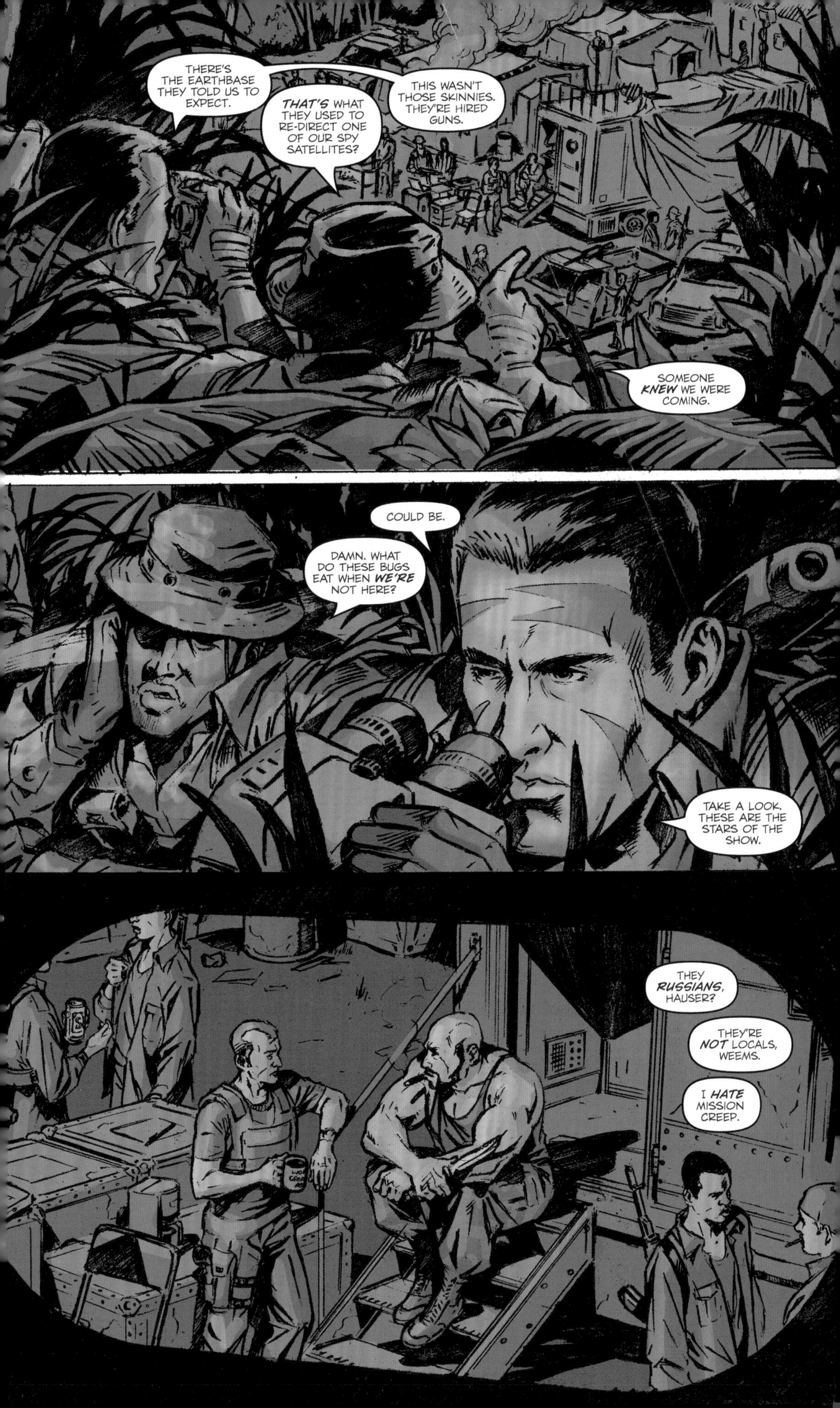
THERE'S THE EARTHBASE THEY TOLD US TO EXPECT.
THIS WASN'T THOSE SKINNIES. THEY'RE HIRED GUNS.
THAT'S WHAT THEY USED TO RE-DIRECT ONE OF OUR SPY SATELLITES?
SOMEONE KNEW WE WERE COMING.
COULD BE.
DAMN. WHAT DO THESE BUGS EAT WHEN WE'RE NOT HERE?
TAKE A LOOK. THESE ARE THE STARS OF THE SHOW.
THEY RUSSIANS, HAUSER?
THEY'RE NOT LOCALS, WEEMS.
I HATE MISSION CREEP.

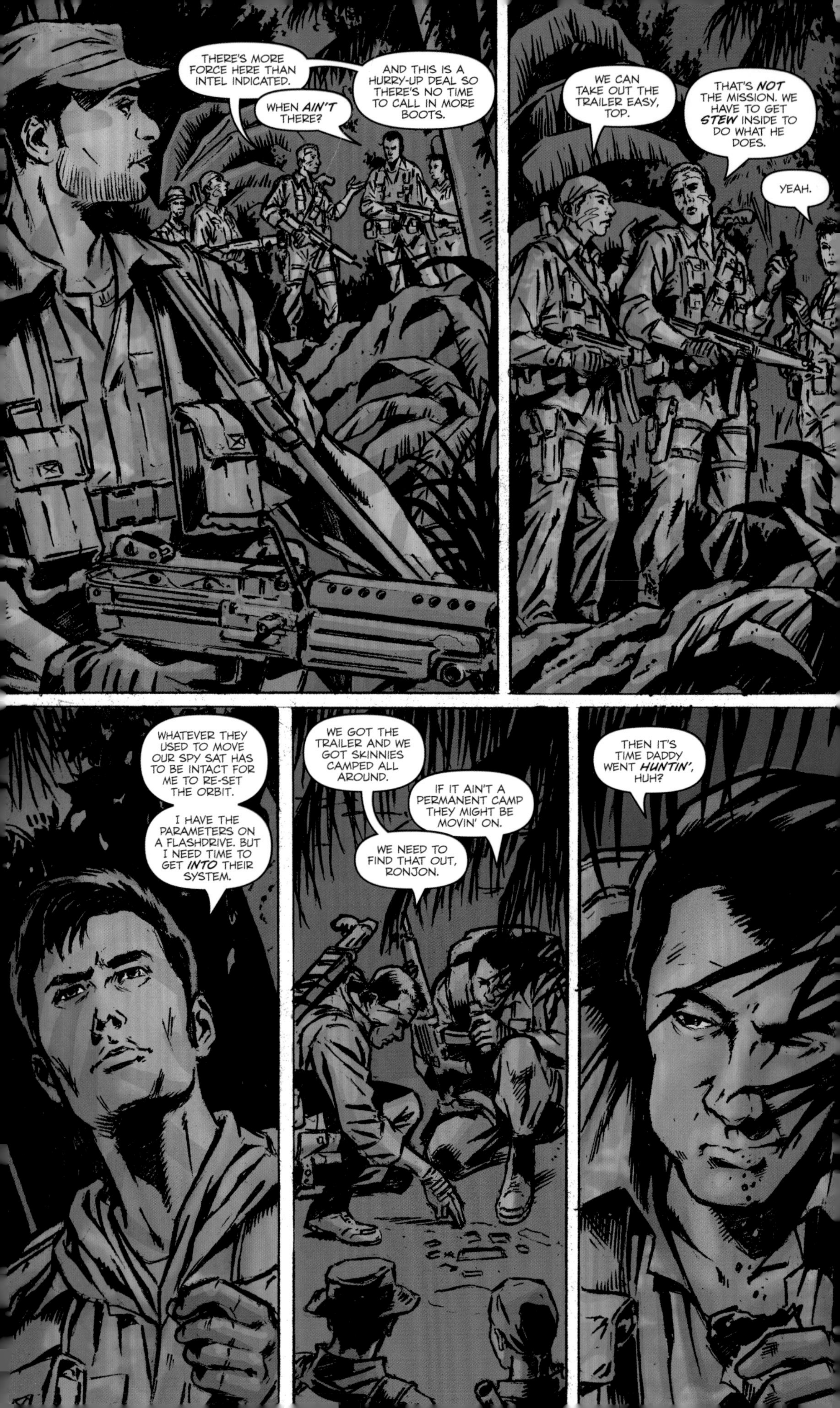

THERE'S MORE FORCE HERE THAN INTEL INDICATED.
WHEN AIN'T THERE?
AND THIS IS A HURRY-UP DEAL SO THERE'S NO TIME TO CALL IN MORE BOOTS.
WE CAN TAKE OUT THE TRAILER EASY, TOP.
THAT'S NOT THE MISSION. WE HAVE TO GET STEW INSIDE TO DO WHAT HE DOES.
YEAH.
WHATEVER THEY USED TO MOVE OUR SPY SAT HAS TO BE INTACT FOR ME TO RE-SET THE ORBIT.
I HAVE THE PARAMETERS ON A FLASHDRIVE. BUT I NEED TIME TO GET INTO THEIR SYSTEM.
WE GOT THE TRAILER AND WE GOT SKINNIES CAMPED ALL AROUND.
IF IT AIN'T A PERMANENT CAMP THEY MIGHT BE MOVIN' ON.
WE NEED TO FIND THAT OUT, RONJON.
THEN IT'S TIME DADDY WENT HUNTIN', HUH?

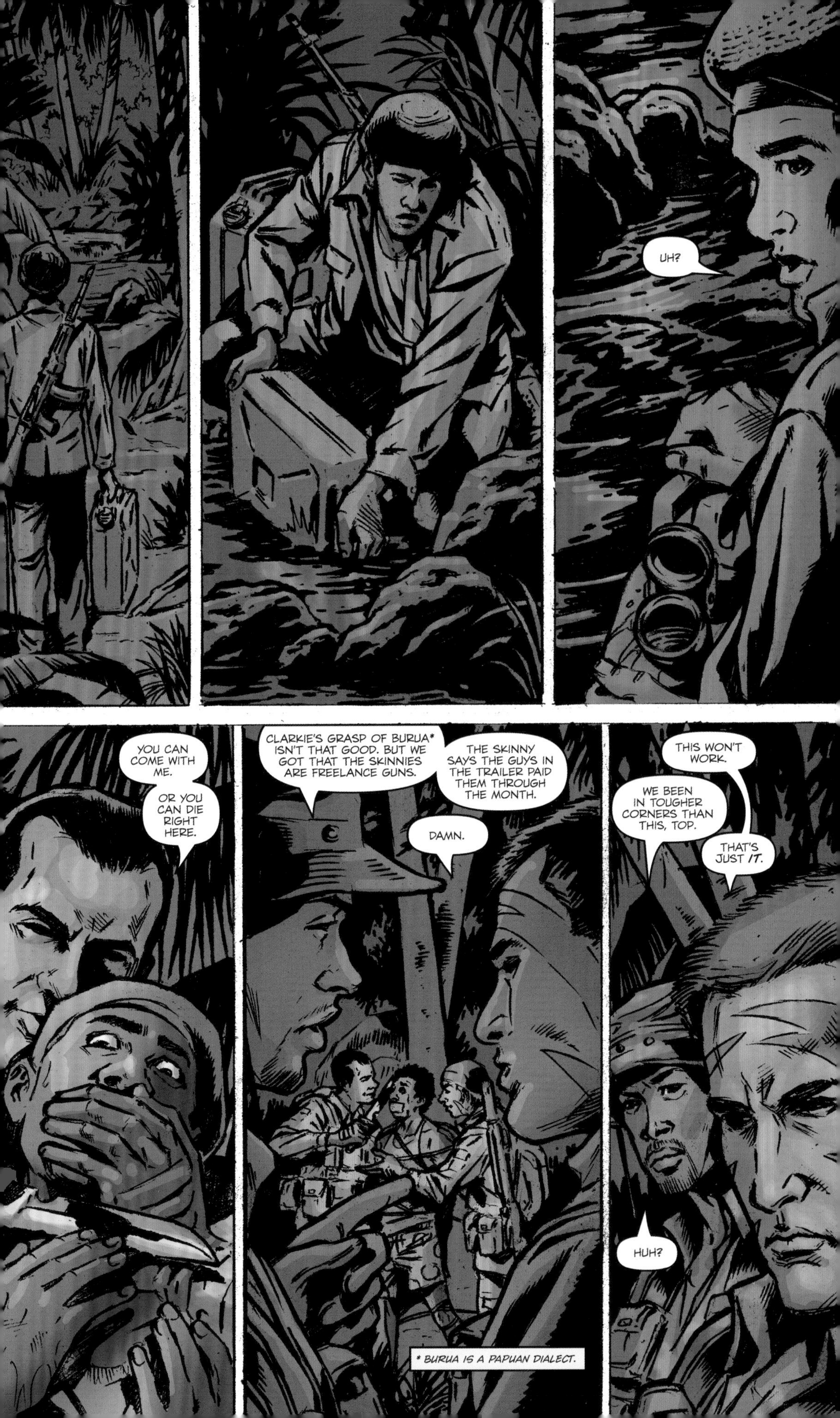
UH?
YOU CAN COME WITH ME.
OR YOU CAN DIE RIGHT HERE.
CLARKIE'S GRASP OF BURUA* ISN'T THAT GOOD. BUT WE GOT THAT THE SKINNIES ARE FREELANCE GUNS.
THE SKINNY SAYS THE GUYS IN THE TRAILER PAID THEM THROUGH THE MONTH.
DAMN.
* BURUA IS A PAPUAN DIALECT.
THIS WON'T WORK.
WE BEEN IN TOUGHER CORNERS THAN THIS, TOP.
THAT'S JUST *IT*.
HUH?

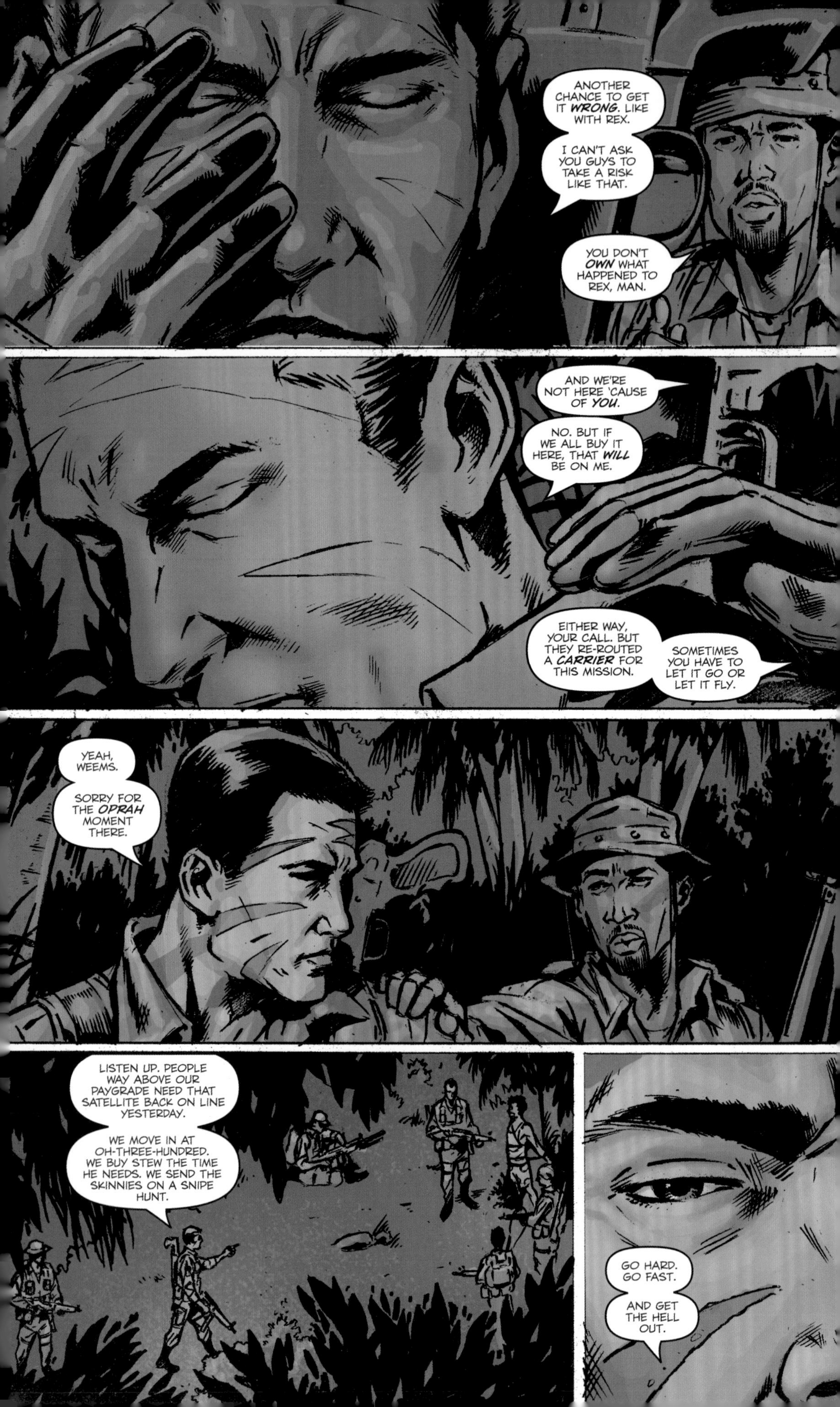

ANOTHER CHANCE TO GET IT WRONG. LIKE WITH REX.
I CAN'T ASK YOU GUYS TO TAKE A RISK LIKE THAT.
YOU DON'T OWN WHAT HAPPENED TO REX, MAN.
AND WE'RE NOT HERE 'CAUSE OF YOU.
NO. BUT IF WE ALL BUY IT HERE, THAT WILL BE ON ME.
EITHER WAY, YOUR CALL. BUT THEY RE-ROUTED A CARRIER FOR THIS MISSION.
SOMETIMES YOU HAVE TO LET IT GO OR LET IT FLY.
YEAH, WEEMS.
SORRY FOR THE OPRAH MOMENT THERE.
LISTEN UP. PEOPLE WAY ABOVE OUR PAYGRADE NEED THAT SATELLITE BACK ON LINE YESTERDAY.
WE MOVE IN AT OH-THREE-HUNDRED. WE BUY STEW THE TIME HE NEEDS. WE SEND THE SKINNIES ON A SNIPE HUNT.
GO HARD. GO FAST.
AND GET THE HELL OUT.

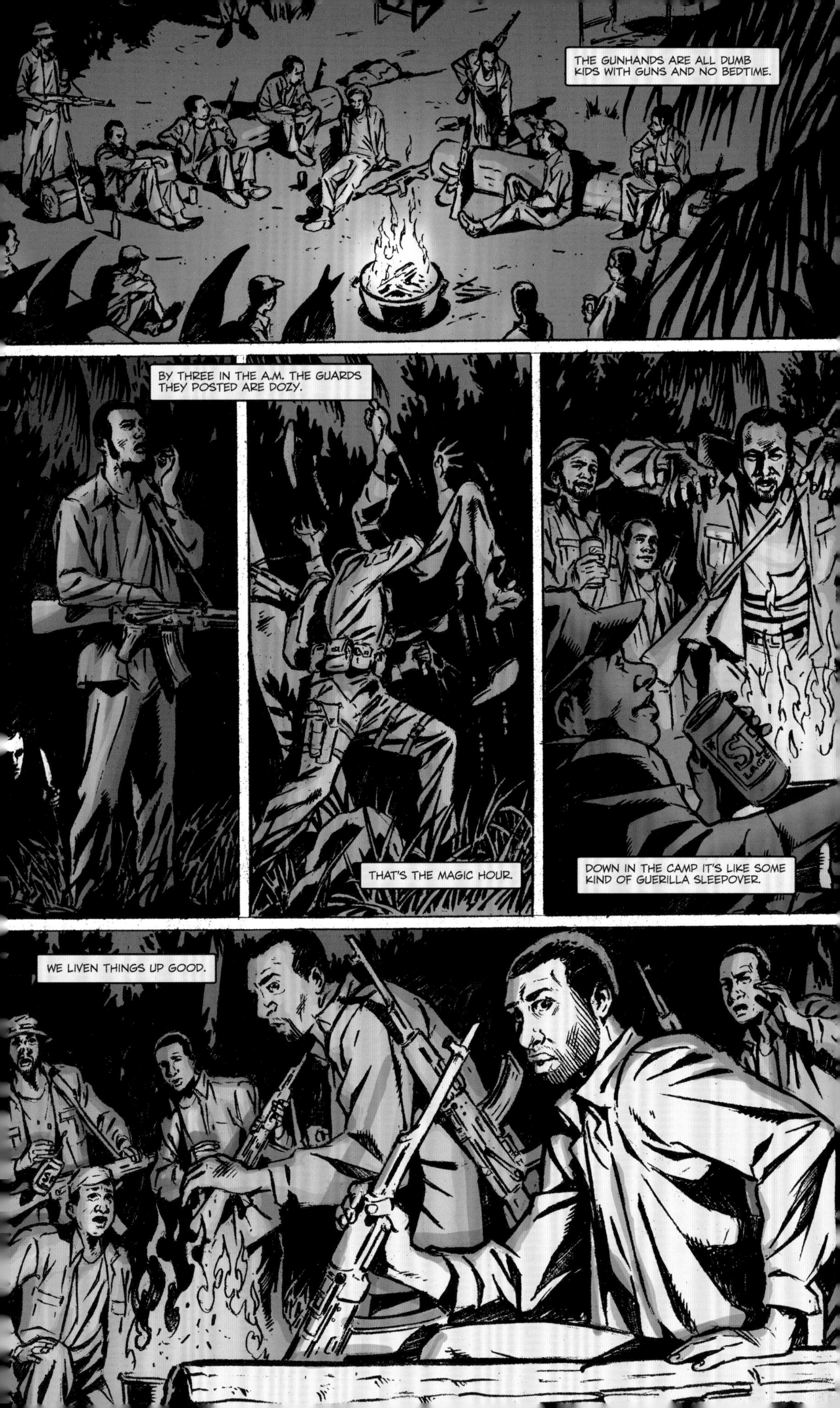
THE GUNHANDS ARE ALL DUMB KIDS WITH GUNS AND NO BEDTIME.
BY THREE IN THE A.M. THE GUARDS THEY POSTED ARE DOZY.
THAT'S THE MAGIC HOUR.
DOWN IN THE CAMP IT'S LIKE SOME KIND OF GUERILLA SLEEPOVER.
WE LIVEN THINGS UP GOOD.

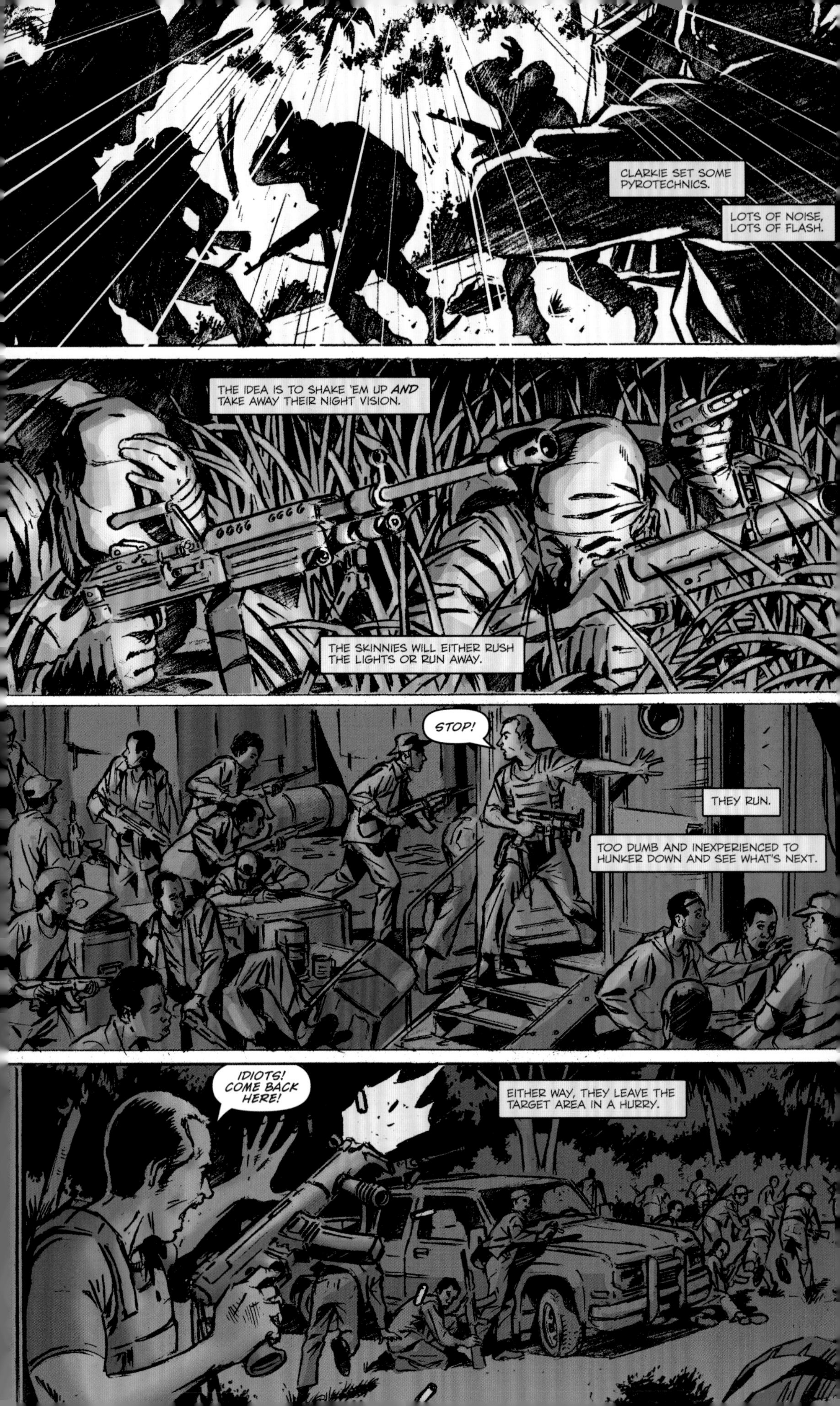
CLARKIE SET SOME PYROTECHNICS.
LOTS OF NOISE, LOTS OF FLASH.
THE IDEA IS TO SHAKE 'EM UP *AND* TAKE AWAY THEIR NIGHT VISION.
THE SKINNIES WILL EITHER RUSH THE LIGHTS OR RUN AWAY.
STOP!
THEY RUN.
TOO DUMB AND INEXPERIENCED TO HUNKER DOWN AND SEE WHAT'S NEXT.
IDIOTS! COME BACK HERE!
EITHER WAY, THEY LEAVE THE TARGET AREA IN A HURRY.

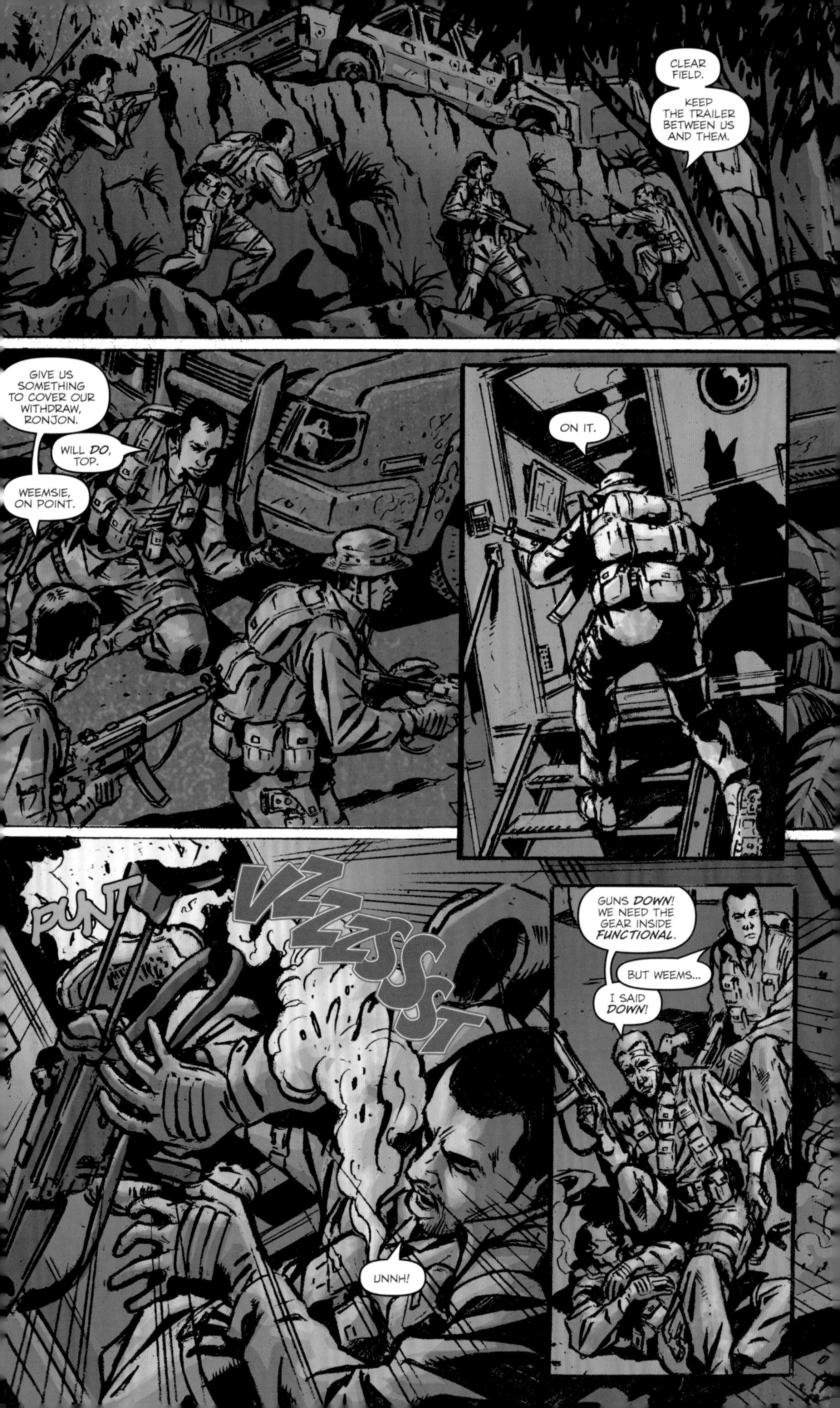

CLEAR FIELD.
KEEP THE TRAILER BETWEEN US AND THEM.
GIVE US SOMETHING TO COVER OUR WITHDRAW, RONJON.
WILL *DO*, TOP.
WEEMSIE, ON POINT.
ON IT.
PUNT
VZZSSST
UNNH!
GUNS *DOWN*! WE NEED THE GEAR INSIDE ***FUNCTIONAL***.
BUT WEEMS...
I SAID *DOWN*!

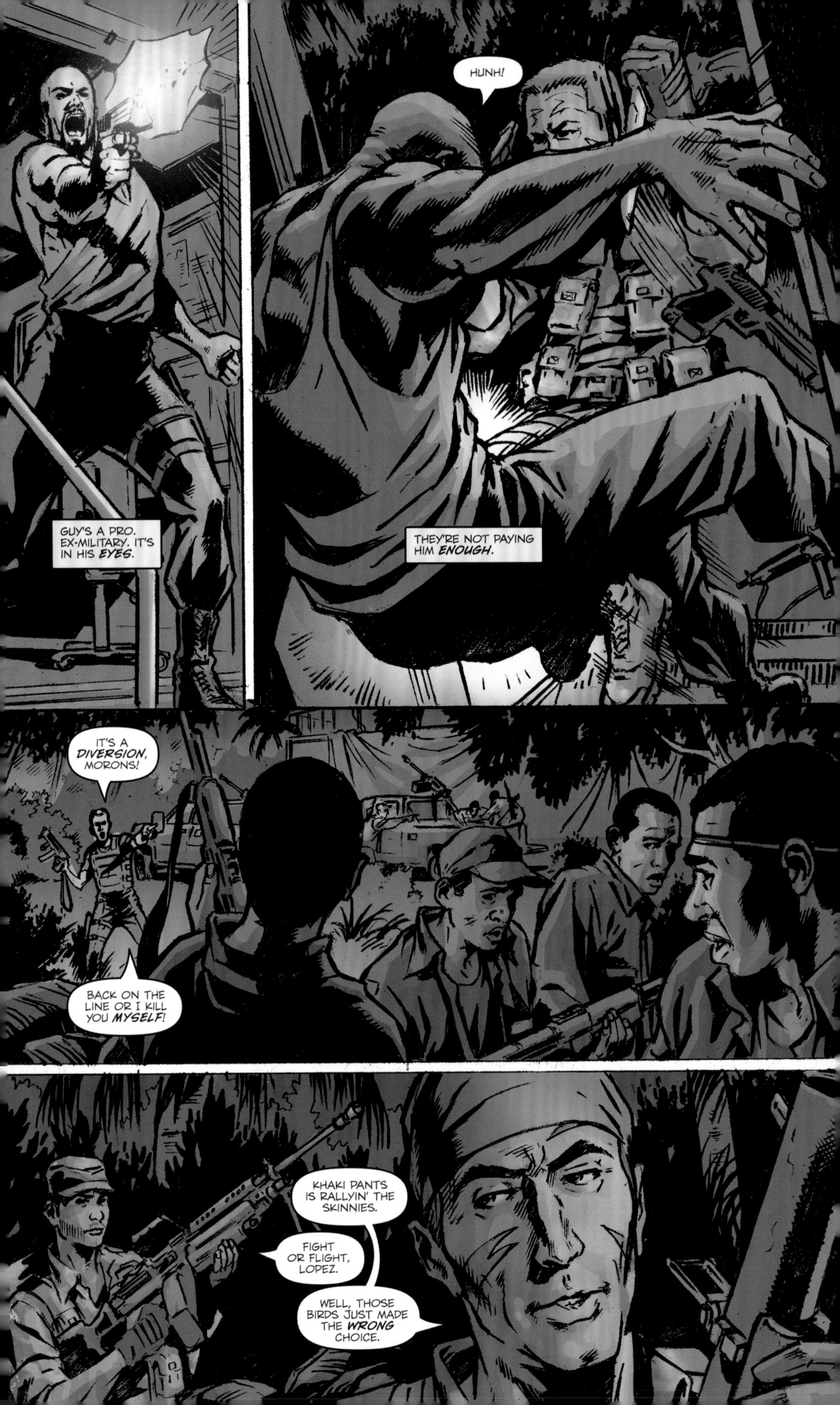
GUY'S A PRO. EX-MILITARY. IT'S IN HIS EYES.
HUNH!
THEY'RE NOT PAYING HIM ENOUGH.
IT'S A DIVERSION, MORONS!
BACK ON THE LINE OR I KILL YOU MYSELF!
KHAKI PANTS IS RALLYIN' THE SKINNIES.
FIGHT OR FLIGHT, LOPEZ.
WELL, THOSE BIRDS JUST MADE THE WRONG CHOICE.

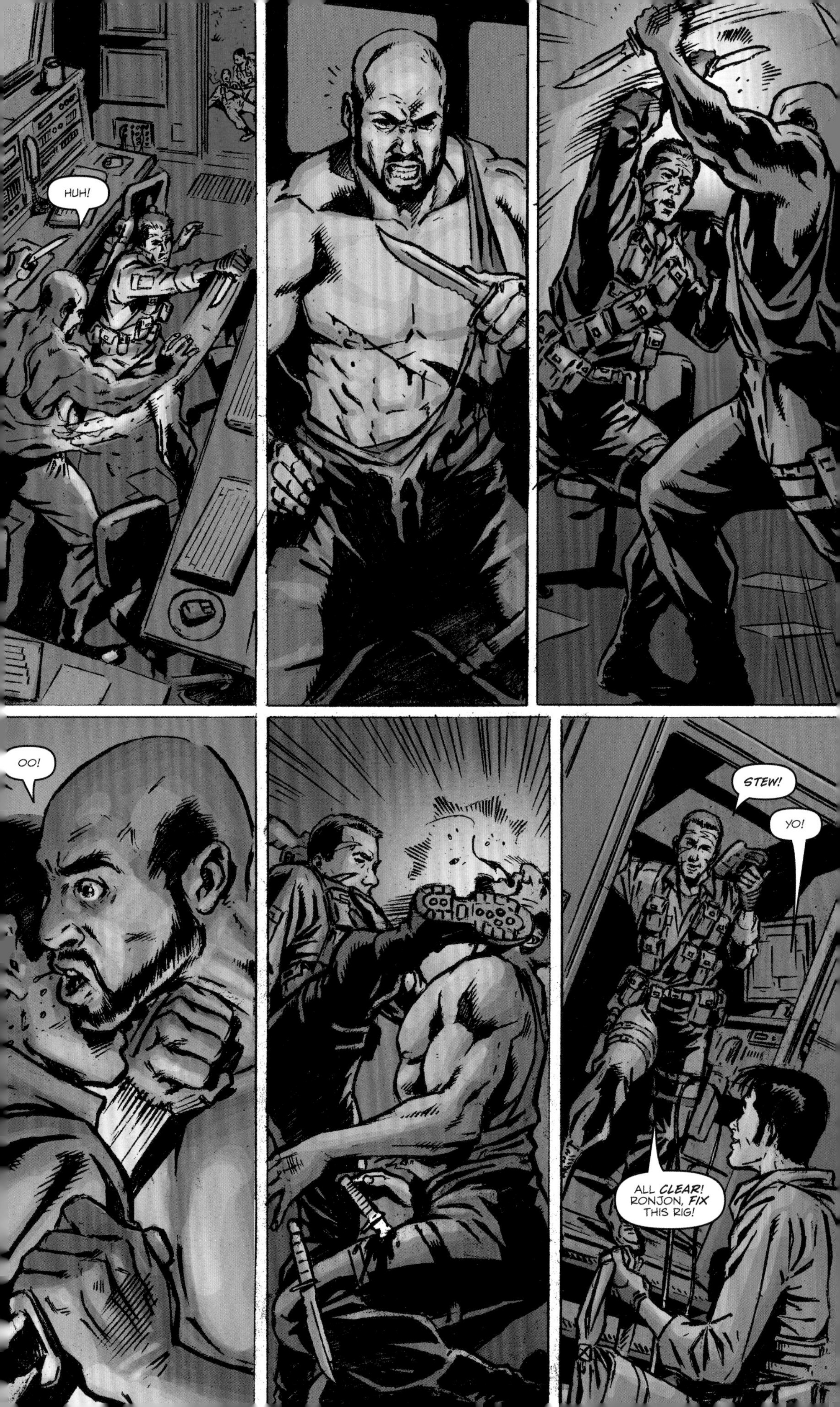
HUH!
OO!
STEW!
YO!
ALL CLEAR! RONJON, FIX THIS RIG!

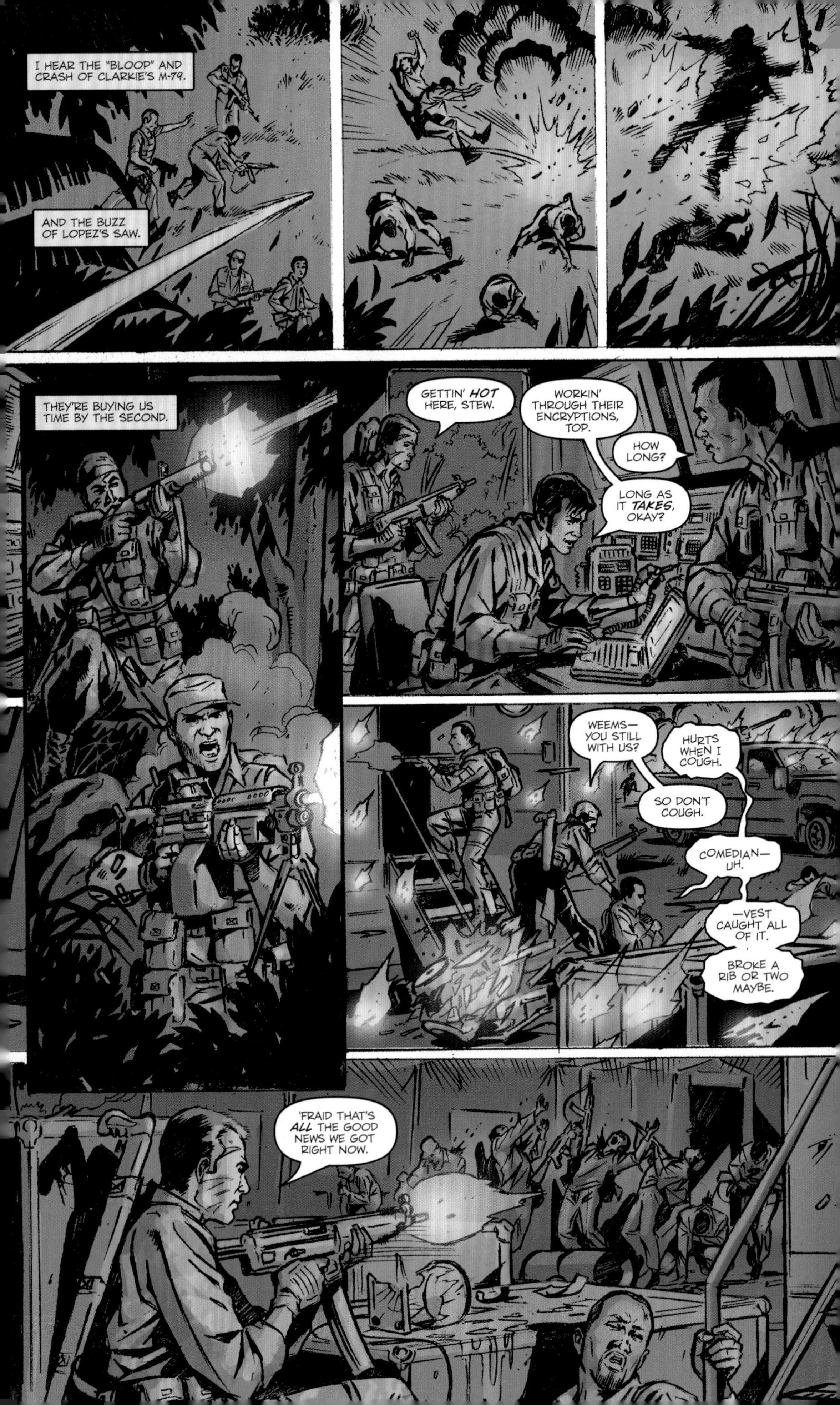

I HEAR THE "BLOOP" AND CRASH OF CLARKIE'S M-79.
AND THE BUZZ OF LOPEZ'S SAW.
THEY'RE BUYING US TIME BY THE SECOND.
GETTIN' *HOT* HERE, STEW.
WORKIN' THROUGH THEIR ENCRYPTIONS, TOP.
HOW LONG?
LONG AS IT *TAKES*, OKAY?
WEEMS— YOU STILL WITH US?
HURTS WHEN I COUGH.
SO DON'T COUGH.
COMEDIAN— UH.
—VEST CAUGHT ALL OF IT.
BROKE A RIB OR TWO MAYBE.
'FRAID THAT'S *ALL* THE GOOD NEWS WE GOT RIGHT NOW.

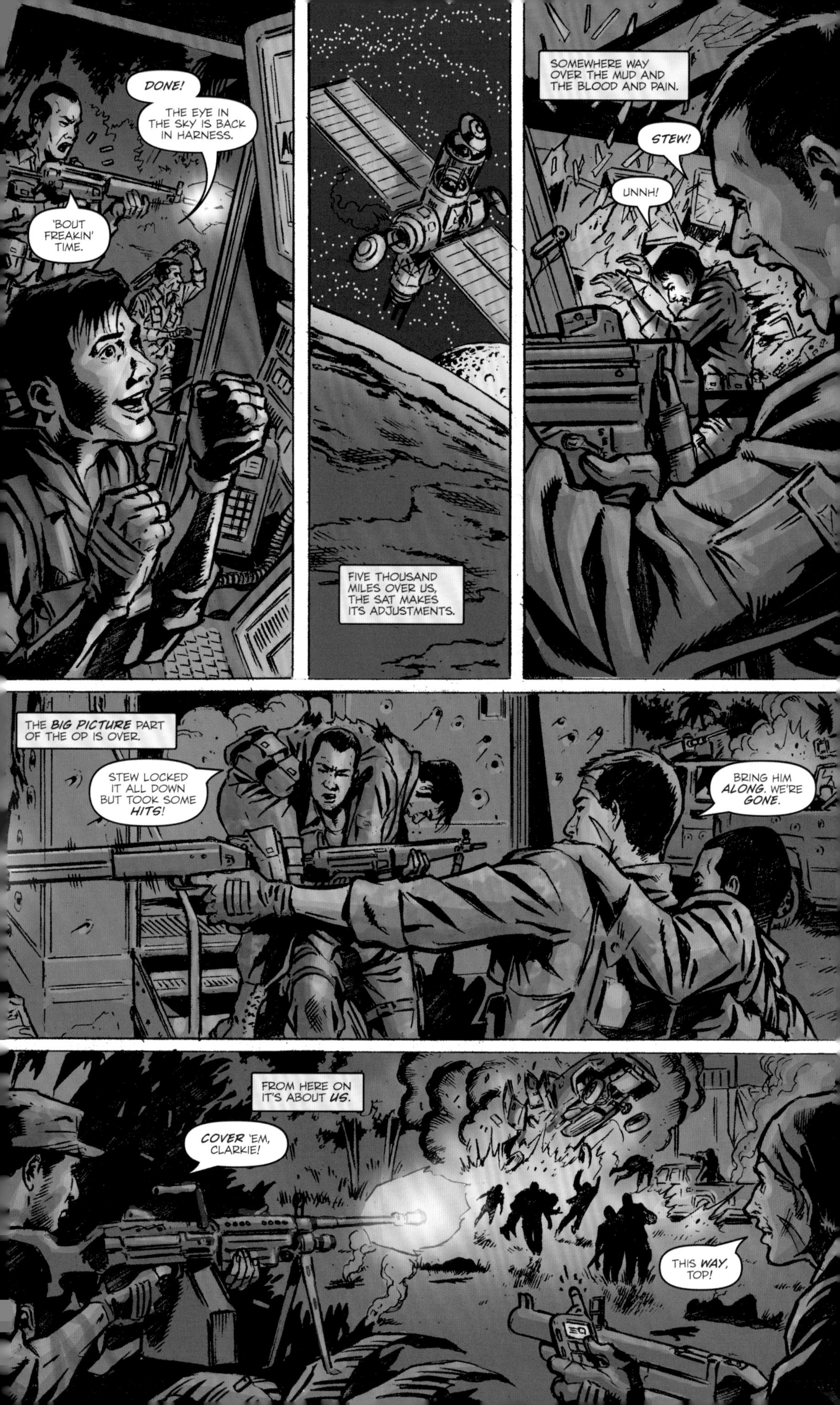
DONE!
THE EYE IN THE SKY IS BACK IN HARNESS.
'BOUT FREAKIN' TIME.
FIVE THOUSAND MILES OVER US, THE SAT MAKES ITS ADJUSTMENTS.
SOMEWHERE WAY OVER THE MUD AND THE BLOOD AND PAIN.
STEW!
UNNH!
THE BIG PICTURE PART OF THE OP IS OVER.
STEW LOCKED IT ALL DOWN BUT TOOK SOME HITS!
BRING HIM ALONG. WE'RE GONE.
FROM HERE ON IT'S ABOUT US.
COVER 'EM, CLARKIE!
THIS WAY, TOP!

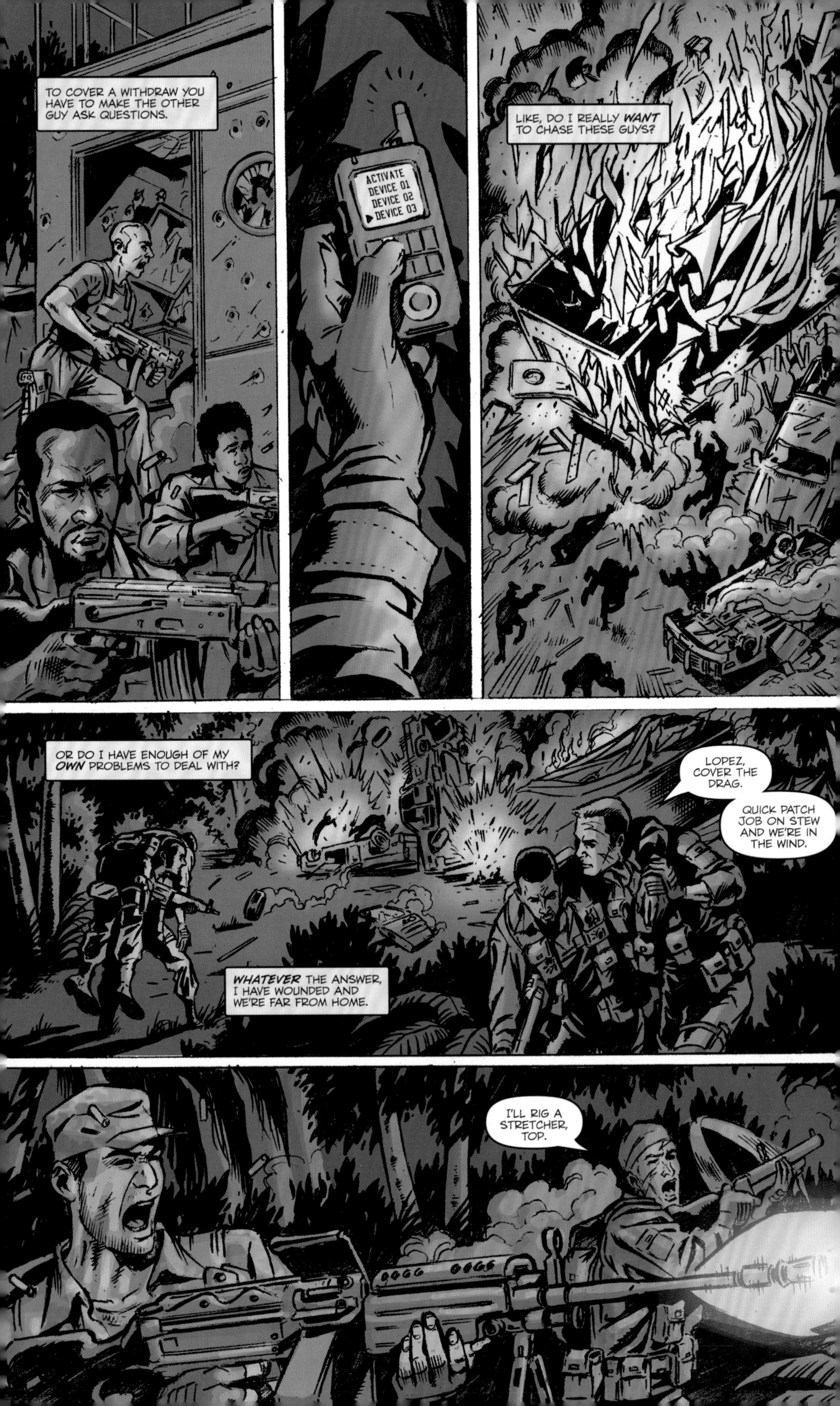
TO COVER A WITHDRAW YOU HAVE TO MAKE THE OTHER GUY ASK QUESTIONS.
ACTIVATE
DEVICE 01
DEVICE 02
DEVICE 03
LIKE, DO I REALLY WANT TO CHASE THESE GUYS?
OR DO I HAVE ENOUGH OF MY OWN PROBLEMS TO DEAL WITH?
LOPEZ, COVER THE DRAG.
QUICK PATCH JOB ON STEW AND WE'RE IN THE WIND.
WHATEVER THE ANSWER, I HAVE WOUNDED AND WE'RE FAR FROM HOME.
I'LL RIG A STRETCHER, TOP.

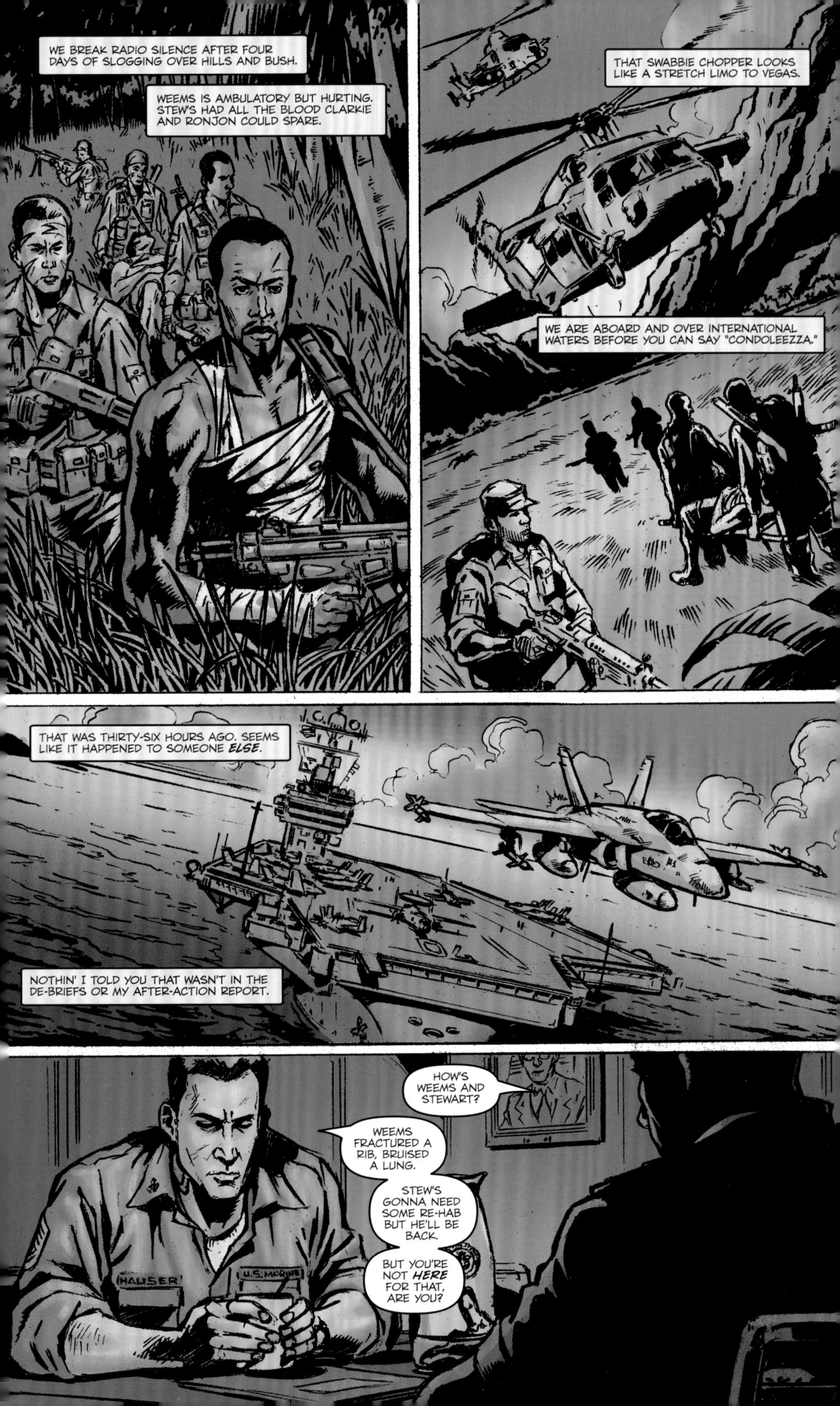
WE BREAK RADIO SILENCE AFTER FOUR DAYS OF SLOGGING OVER HILLS AND BUSH.
WEEMS IS AMBULATORY BUT HURTING. STEW'S HAD ALL THE BLOOD CLARKIE AND RONJON COULD SPARE.
THAT SWABBIE CHOPPER LOOKS LIKE A STRETCH LIMO TO VEGAS.
WE ARE ABOARD AND OVER INTERNATIONAL WATERS BEFORE YOU CAN SAY "CONDOLEEZZA."
THAT WAS THIRTY-SIX HOURS AGO. SEEMS LIKE IT HAPPENED TO SOMEONE *ELSE*.
NOTHIN' I TOLD YOU THAT WASN'T IN THE DE-BRIEFS OR MY AFTER-ACTION REPORT.
HOW'S WEEMS AND STEWART?
WEEMS FRACTURED A RIB, BRUISED A LUNG.
STEW'S GONNA NEED SOME RE-HAB BUT HE'LL BE BACK.
BUT YOU'RE NOT ***HERE*** FOR THAT, ARE YOU?
HAUSER
U.S. MARINE

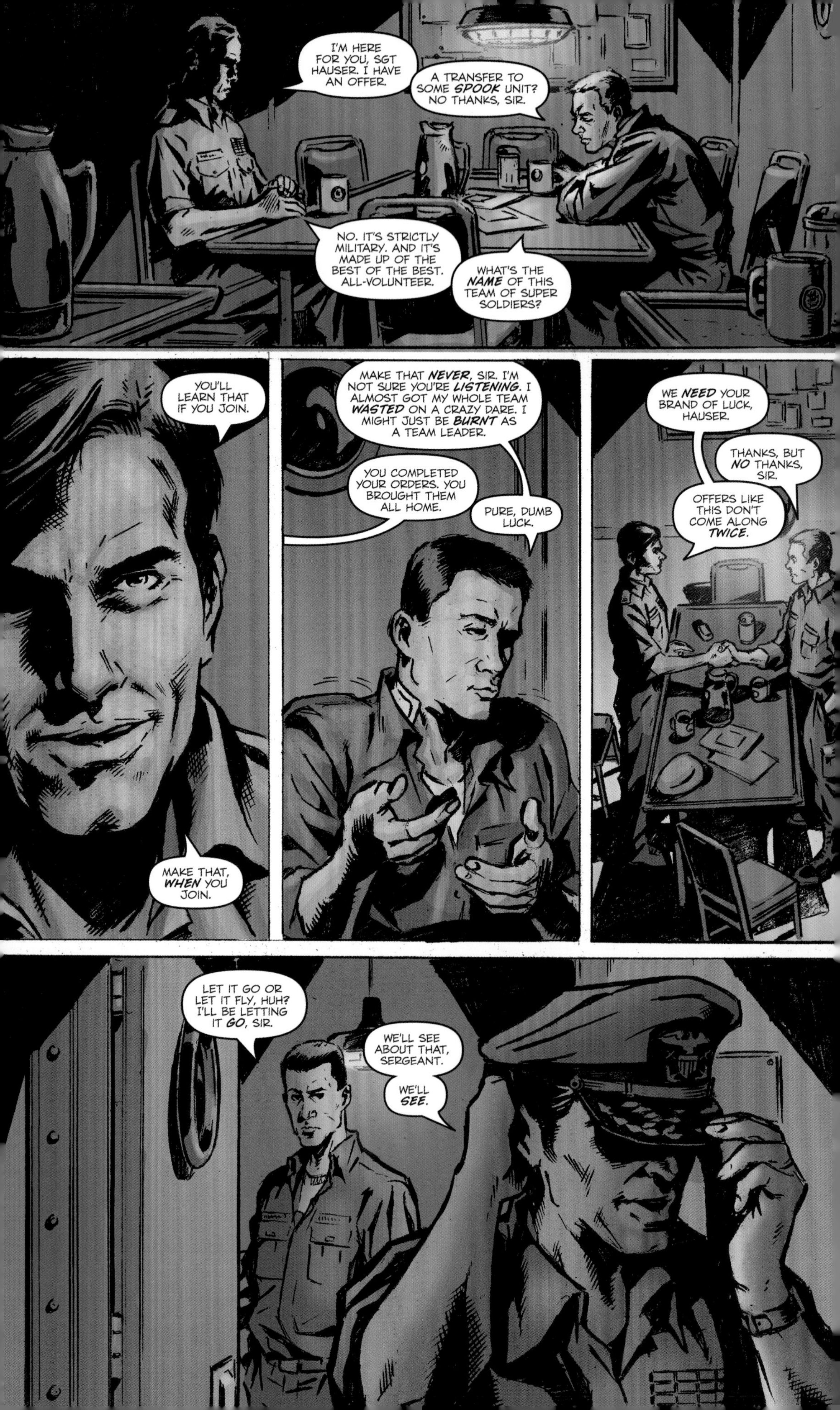
I'M HERE FOR YOU, SGT HAUSER. I HAVE AN OFFER.
A TRANSFER TO SOME SPOOK UNIT? NO THANKS, SIR.
NO. IT'S STRICTLY MILITARY. AND IT'S MADE UP OF THE BEST OF THE BEST. ALL-VOLUNTEER.
WHAT'S THE NAME OF THIS TEAM OF SUPER SOLDIERS?
YOU'LL LEARN THAT IF YOU JOIN.
MAKE THAT, WHEN YOU JOIN.
MAKE THAT NEVER, SIR. I'M NOT SURE YOU'RE LISTENING. I ALMOST GOT MY WHOLE TEAM WASTED ON A CRAZY DARE. I MIGHT JUST BE BURNT AS A TEAM LEADER.
YOU COMPLETED YOUR ORDERS. YOU BROUGHT THEM ALL HOME.
PURE, DUMB LUCK.
WE NEED YOUR BRAND OF LUCK, HAUSER.
THANKS, BUT NO THANKS, SIR.
OFFERS LIKE THIS DON'T COME ALONG TWICE.
LET IT GO OR LET IT FLY, HUH? I'LL BE LETTING IT GO, SIR.
WE'LL SEE ABOUT THAT, SERGEANT.
WE'LL SEE.

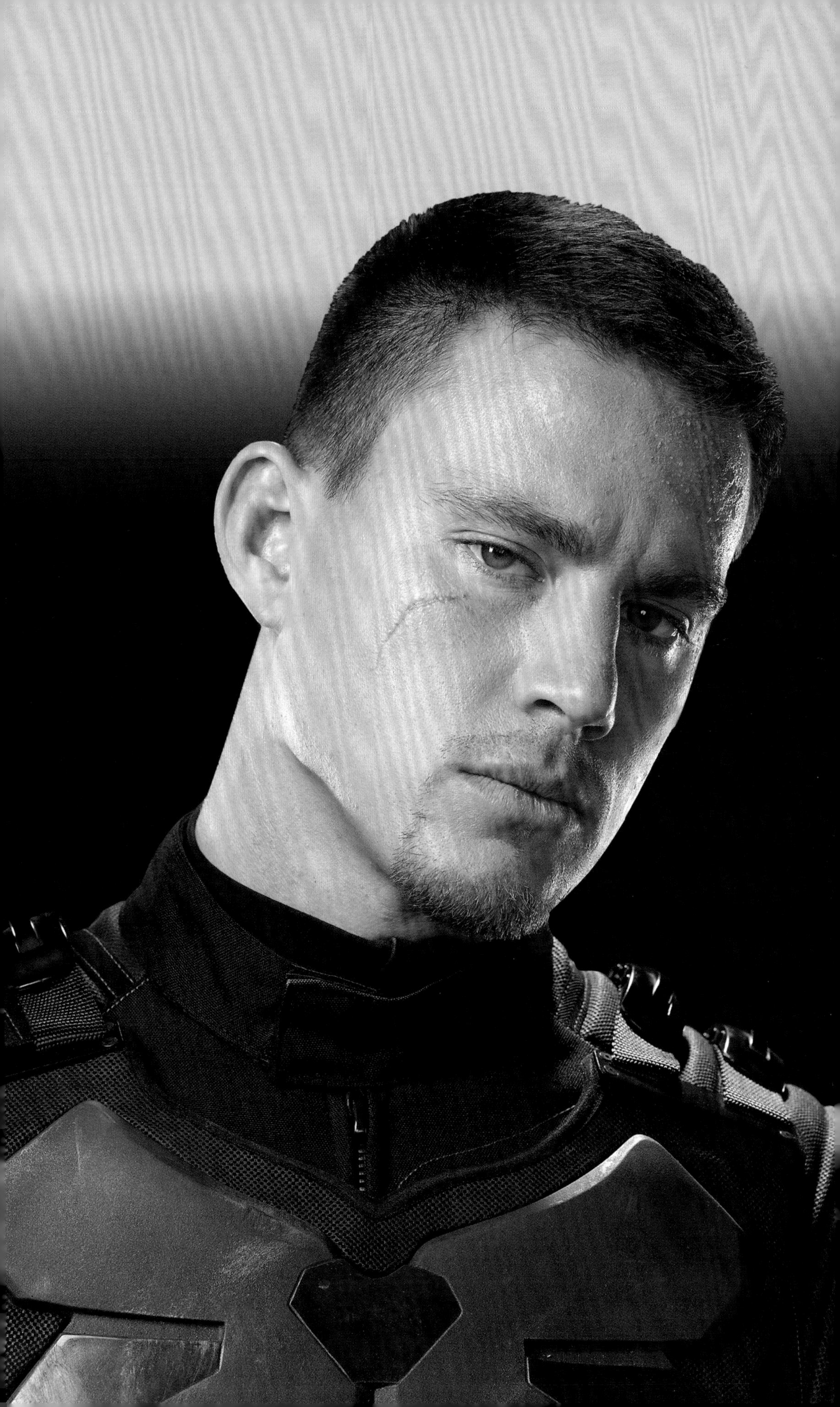

CHAPTER TWO

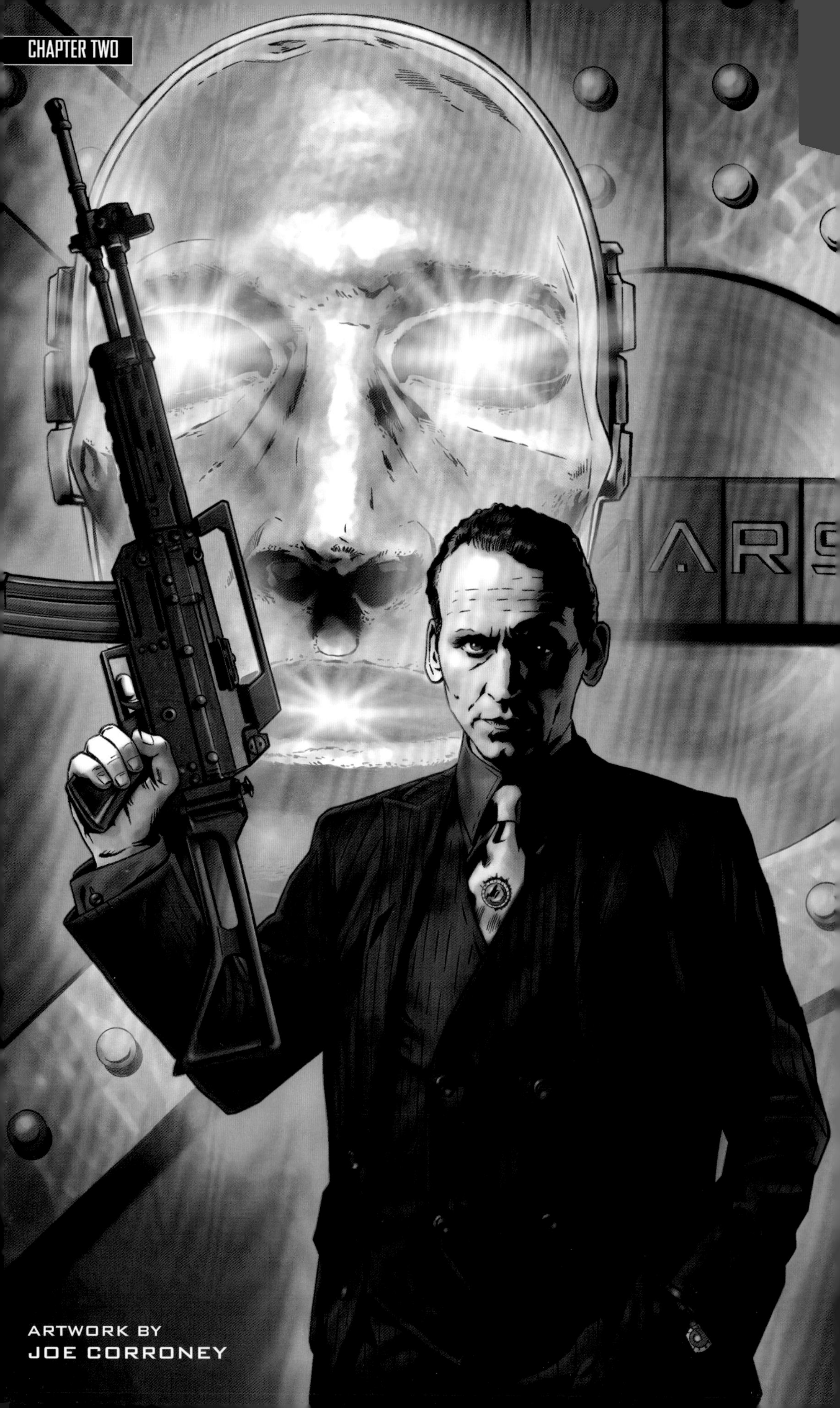

ARTWORK BY
JOE CORRONEY

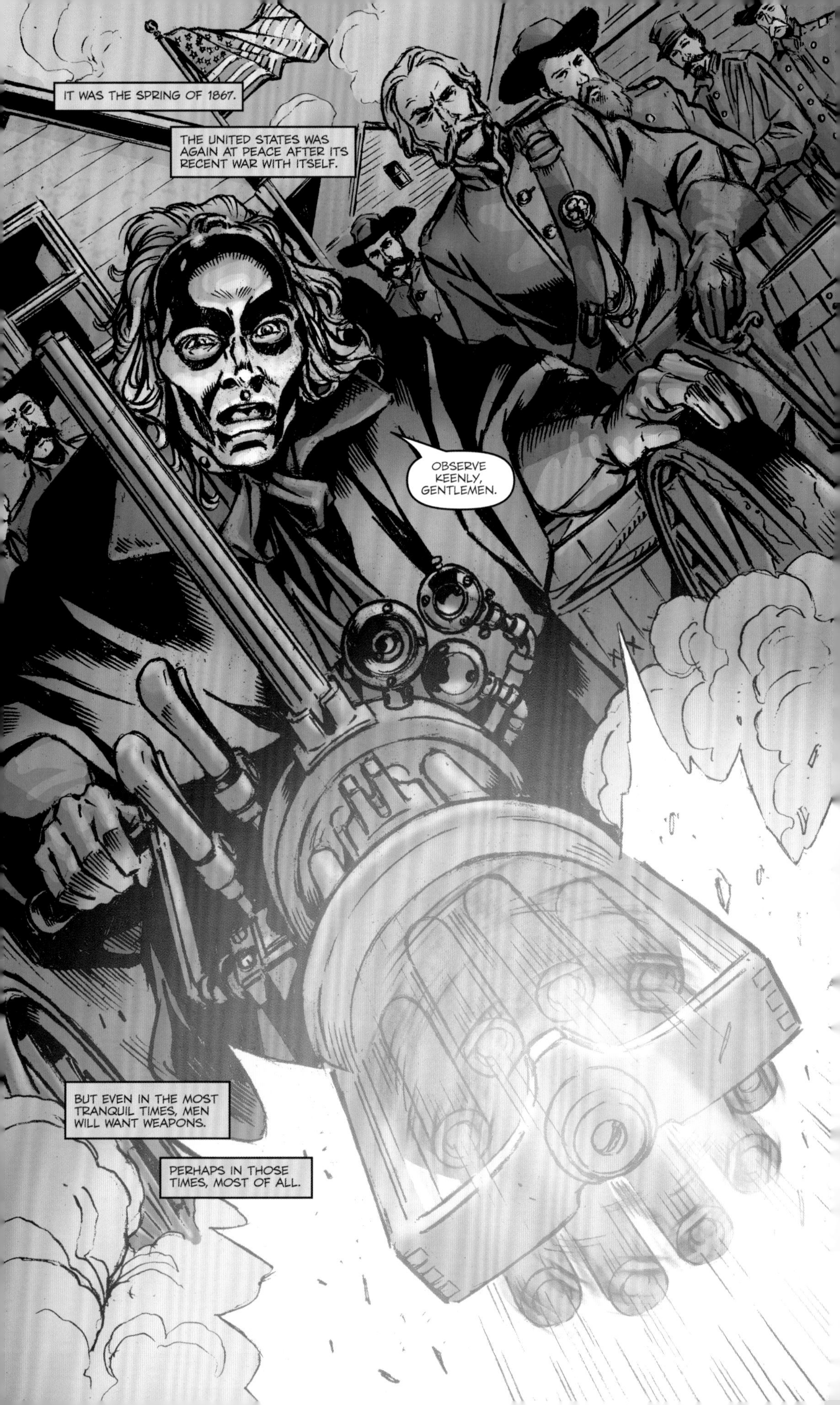
IT WAS THE SPRING OF 1867.
THE UNITED STATES WAS AGAIN AT PEACE AFTER ITS RECENT WAR WITH ITSELF.
OBSERVE KEENLY, GENTLEMEN.
BUT EVEN IN THE MOST TRANQUIL TIMES, MEN WILL WANT WEAPONS.
PERHAPS IN THOSE TIMES, MOST OF ALL.

FORMER CONFEDERATE SOLDIERS AND EXPATRIATE IRISH WERE PREPARING AN INVASION OF CANADA.

THEY CALLED THEMSELVES THE FENIAN BROTHERHOOD.

MADNESS, AYE. BUT A GUNSELLER NEVER JUDGES HIS CLIENTS.

THERE YOU HAVE IT, LADS. THREE HUNDRED ROUNDS A MINUTE.

AN *ENTIRE* RIFLE BATTALION ON WHEELS.

AN IMPRESSIVE *DISPLAY*, SIR.

SHOULD BRING DEATH AND CONFUSION TO THE REDCOATS, EH?

FOR THE TACTICAL ADVANTAGE THIS WEAPON OFFERS, IT'S WORTH THE COST.

WE'LL TAKE *TEN* OF THEM. AND A HUNDRED THOUSAND ROUNDS.

PAY THE MAN, SGT CARMODY.

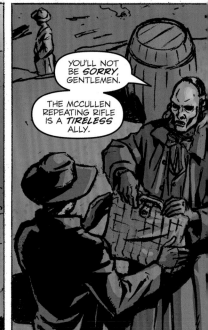

YOU'LL NOT BE *SORRY*, GENTLEMEN.

THE MCCULLEN REPEATING RIFLE IS A *TIRELESS* ALLY.

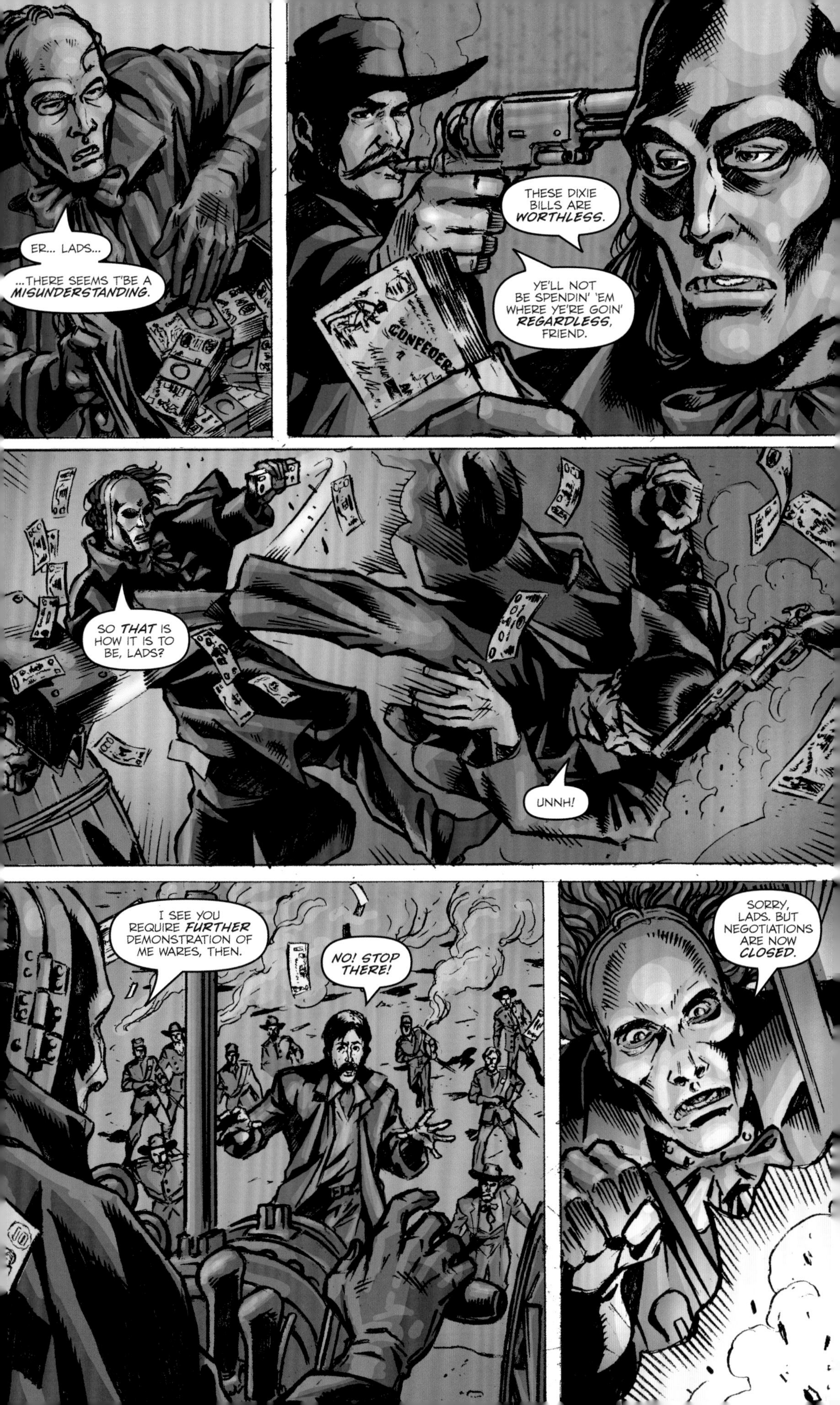
ER... LADS...
...THERE SEEMS T'BE A MISUNDERSTANDING.
THESE DIXIE BILLS ARE WORTHLESS.
YE'LL NOT BE SPENDIN' 'EM WHERE YE'RE GOIN' REGARDLESS, FRIEND.
SO THAT IS HOW IT IS TO BE, LADS?
UNNH!
I SEE YOU REQUIRE FURTHER DEMONSTRATION OF ME WARES, THEN.
NO! STOP THERE!
SORRY, LADS. BUT NEGOTIATIONS ARE NOW CLOSED.

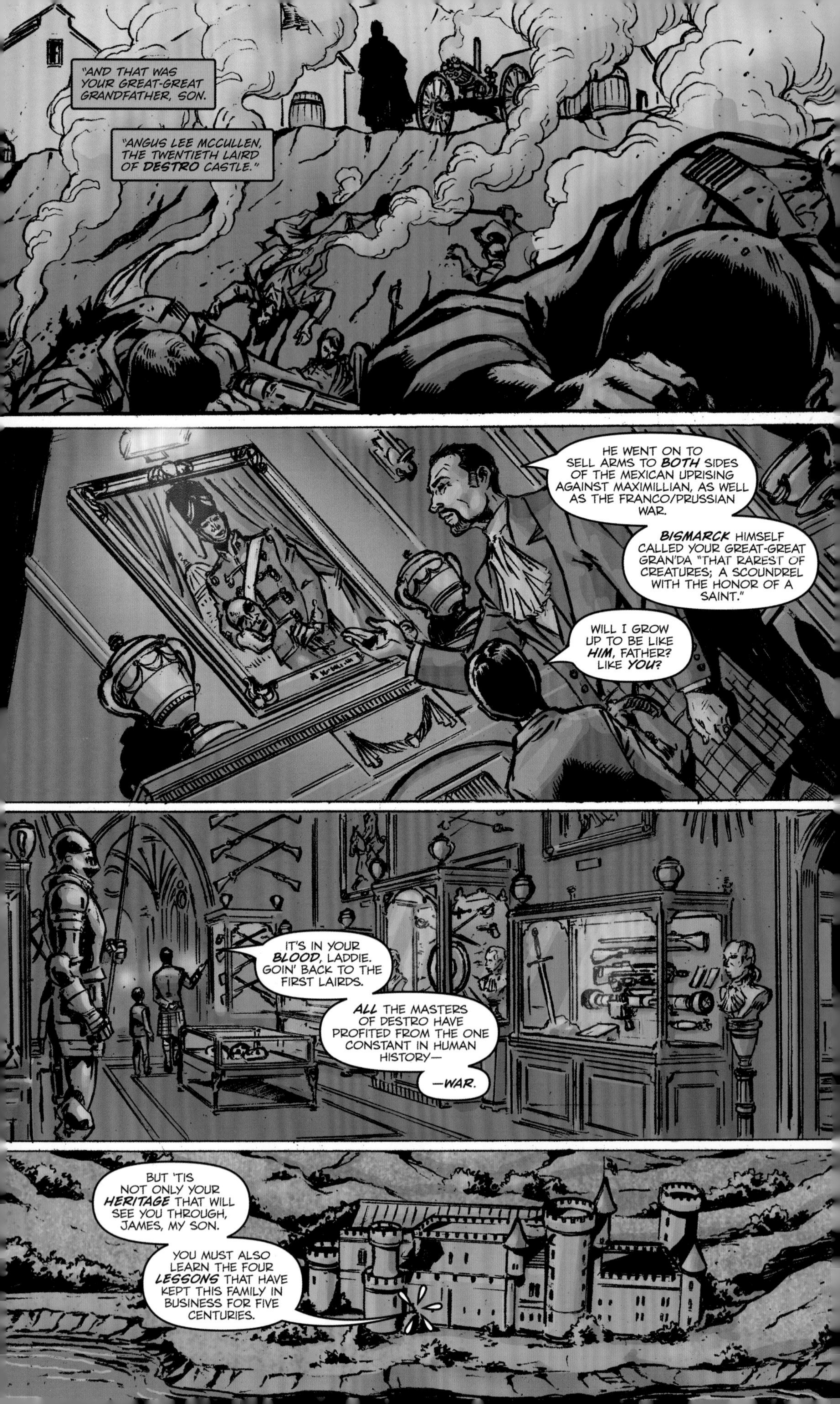
"AND THAT WAS YOUR GREAT-GREAT GRANDFATHER, SON.
"ANGUS LEE MCCULLEN, THE TWENTIETH LAIRD OF DESTRO CASTLE."
HE WENT ON TO SELL ARMS TO BOTH SIDES OF THE MEXICAN UPRISING AGAINST MAXIMILLIAN, AS WELL AS THE FRANCO/PRUSSIAN WAR.
BISMARCK HIMSELF CALLED YOUR GREAT-GREAT GRAN'DA "THAT RAREST OF CREATURES; A SCOUNDREL WITH THE HONOR OF A SAINT."
WILL I GROW UP TO BE LIKE HIM, FATHER? LIKE YOU?
IT'S IN YOUR BLOOD, LADDIE. GOIN' BACK TO THE FIRST LAIRDS.
ALL THE MASTERS OF DESTRO HAVE PROFITED FROM THE ONE CONSTANT IN HUMAN HISTORY—
—WAR.
BUT 'TIS NOT ONLY YOUR HERITAGE THAT WILL SEE YOU THROUGH, JAMES, MY SON.
YOU MUST ALSO LEARN THE FOUR LESSONS THAT HAVE KEPT THIS FAMILY IN BUSINESS FOR FIVE CENTURIES.

MONDAY

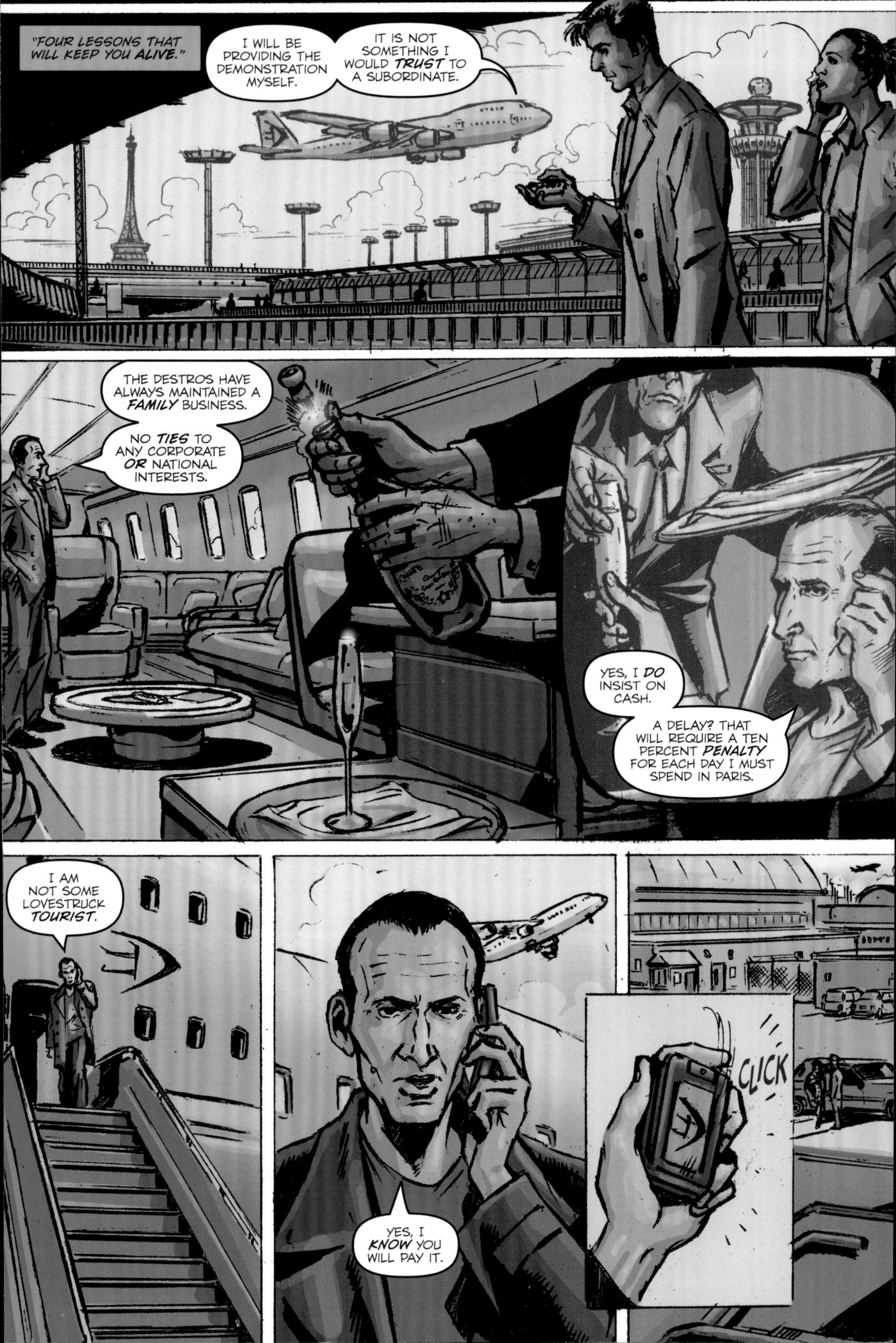
"FOUR LESSONS THAT WILL KEEP YOU ALIVE."
I WILL BE PROVIDING THE DEMONSTRATION MYSELF.
IT IS NOT SOMETHING I WOULD TRUST TO A SUBORDINATE.
THE DESTROS HAVE ALWAYS MAINTAINED A FAMILY BUSINESS.
NO TIES TO ANY CORPORATE OR NATIONAL INTERESTS.
YES, I DO INSIST ON CASH.
A DELAY? THAT WILL REQUIRE A TEN PERCENT PENALTY FOR EACH DAY I MUST SPEND IN PARIS.
I AM NOT SOME LOVESTRUCK TOURIST.
YES, I KNOW YOU WILL PAY IT.
CLICK

TUESDAY

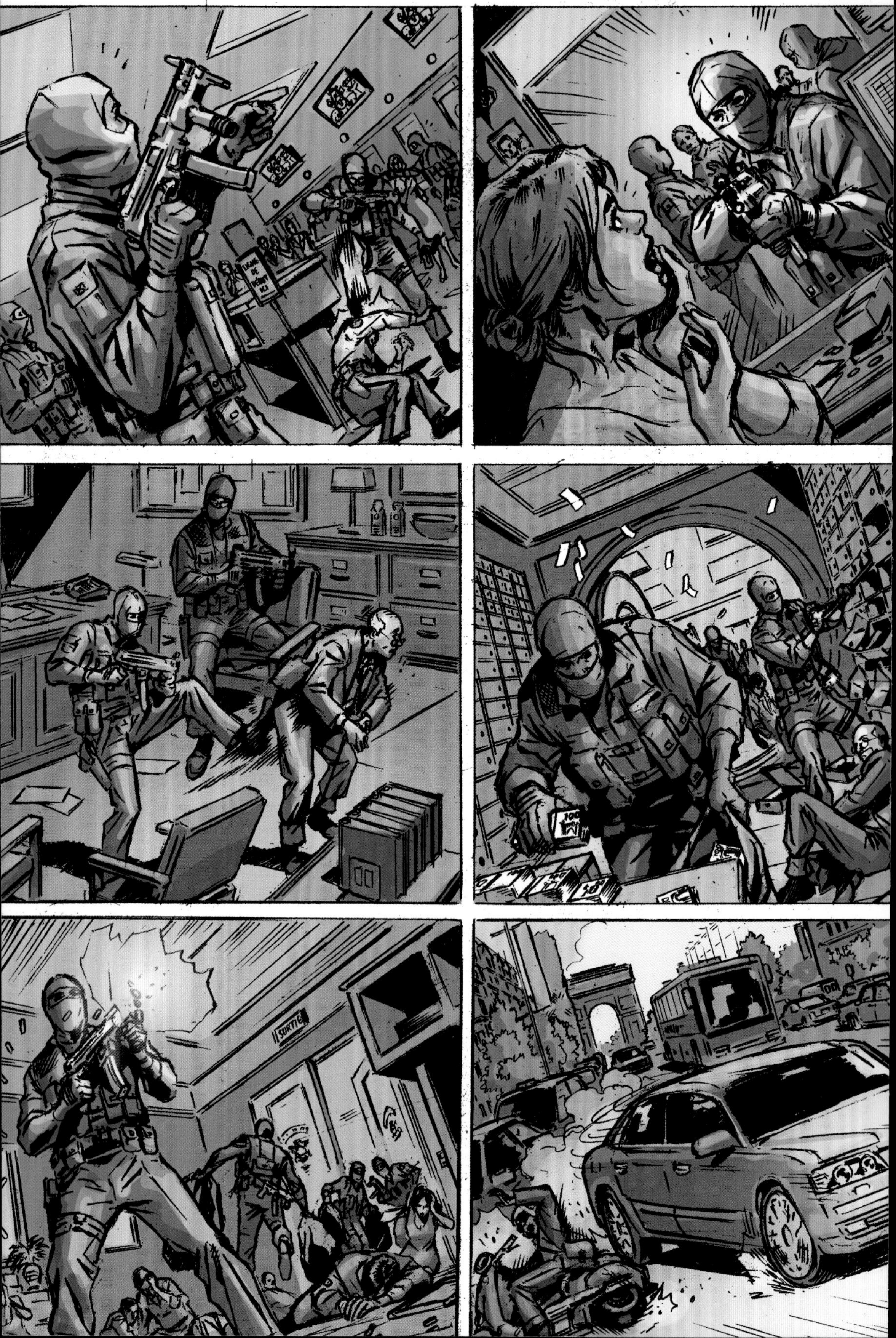
SORTIE

WEDNESDAY

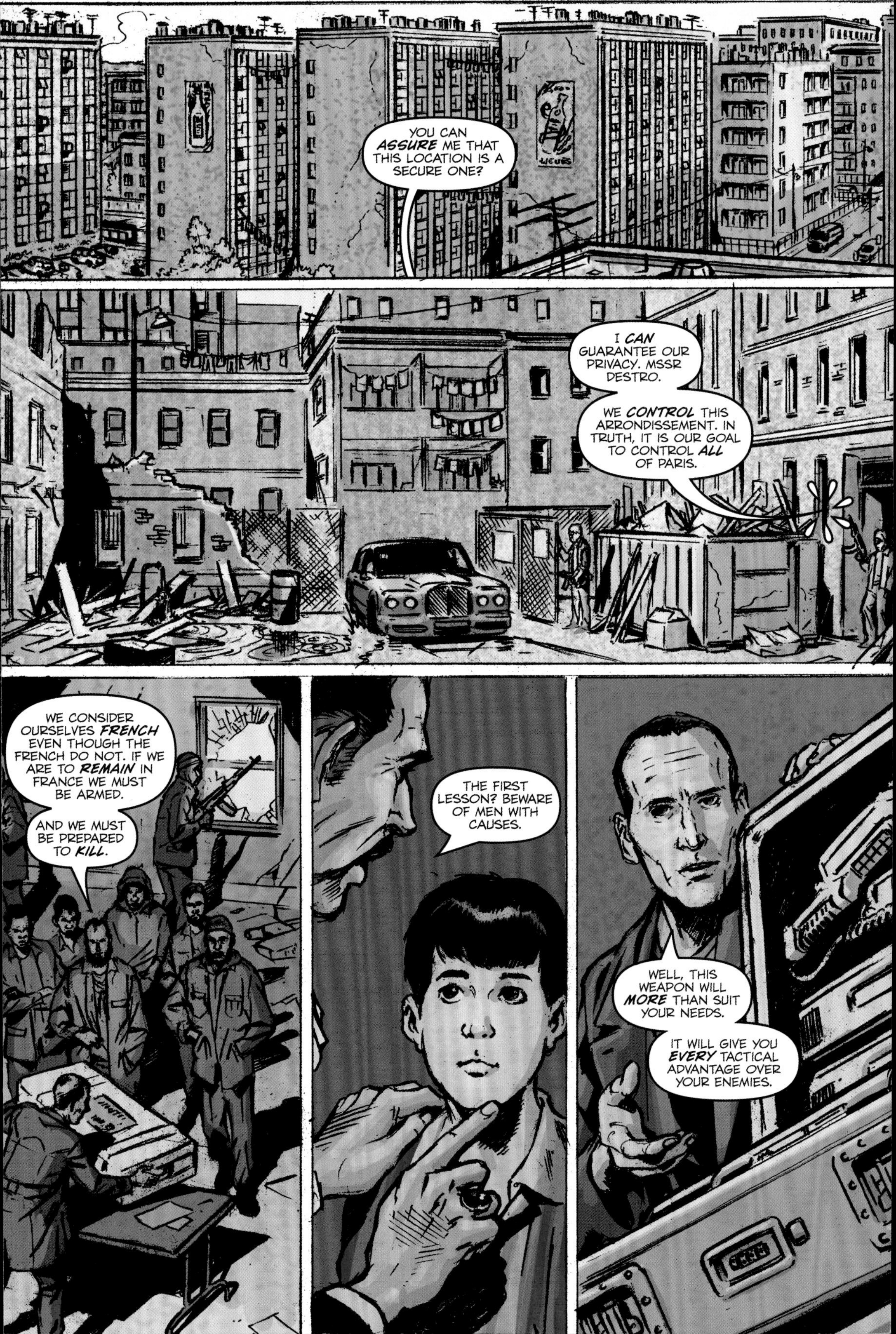

YOU CAN ASSURE ME THAT THIS LOCATION IS A SECURE ONE?
I CAN GUARANTEE OUR PRIVACY. MSSR DESTRO.
WE CONTROL THIS ARRONDISSEMENT. IN TRUTH, IT IS OUR GOAL TO CONTROL ALL OF PARIS.
WE CONSIDER OURSELVES FRENCH EVEN THOUGH THE FRENCH DO NOT. IF WE ARE TO REMAIN IN FRANCE WE MUST BE ARMED.
AND WE MUST BE PREPARED TO KILL.
THE FIRST LESSON? BEWARE OF MEN WITH CAUSES.
WELL, THIS WEAPON WILL MORE THAN SUIT YOUR NEEDS.
IT WILL GIVE YOU EVERY TACTICAL ADVANTAGE OVER YOUR ENEMIES.

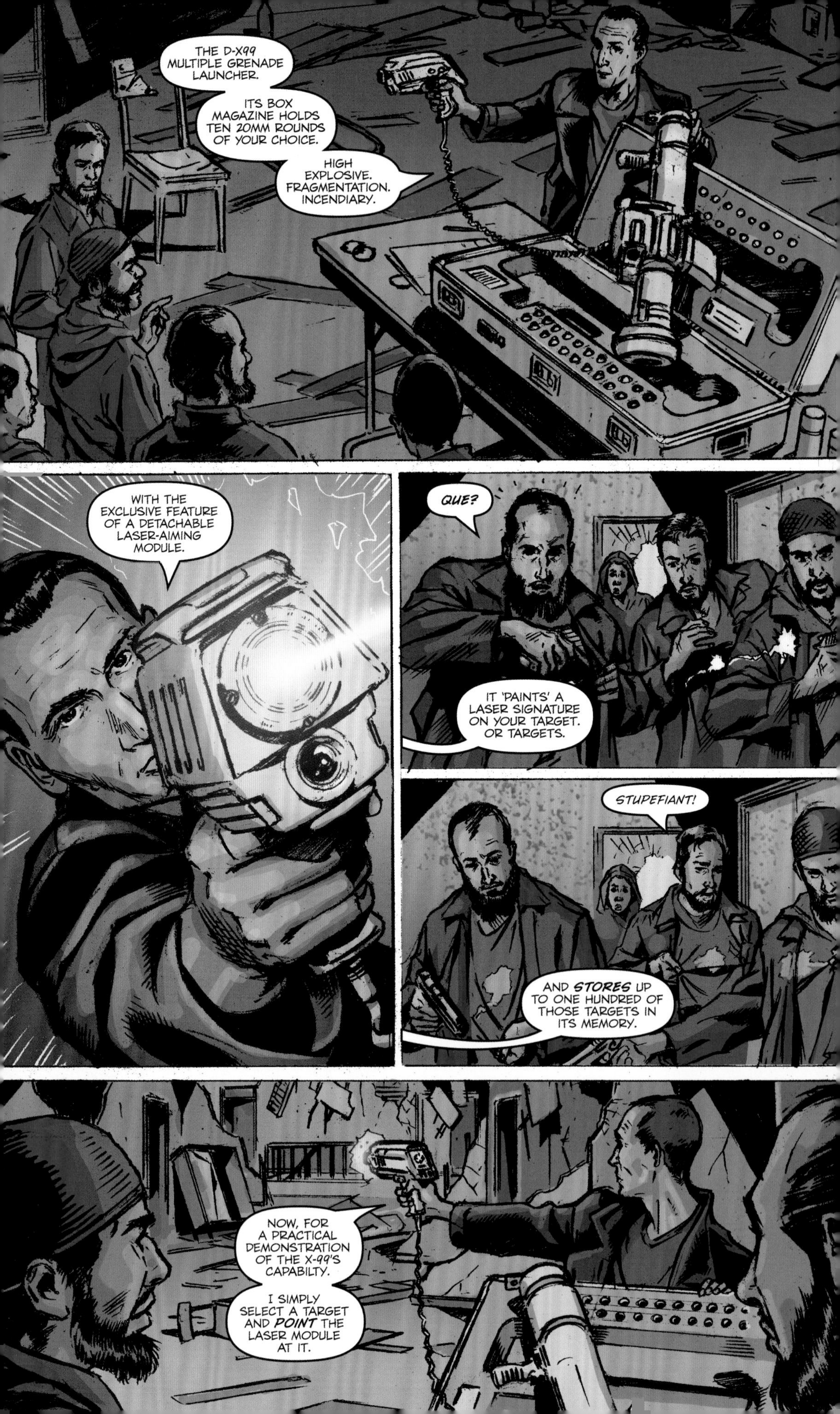
THE D-X99 MULTIPLE GRENADE LAUNCHER.
ITS BOX MAGAZINE HOLDS TEN 20MM ROUNDS OF YOUR CHOICE.
HIGH EXPLOSIVE. FRAGMENTATION. INCENDIARY.
WITH THE EXCLUSIVE FEATURE OF A DETACHABLE LASER-AIMING MODULE.
QUE?
IT 'PAINTS' A LASER SIGNATURE ON YOUR TARGET. OR TARGETS.
STUPEFIANT!
AND STORES UP TO ONE HUNDRED OF THOSE TARGETS IN ITS MEMORY.
NOW, FOR A PRACTICAL DEMONSTRATION OF THE X-99'S CAPABILTY.
I SIMPLY SELECT A TARGET AND POINT THE LASER MODULE AT IT.

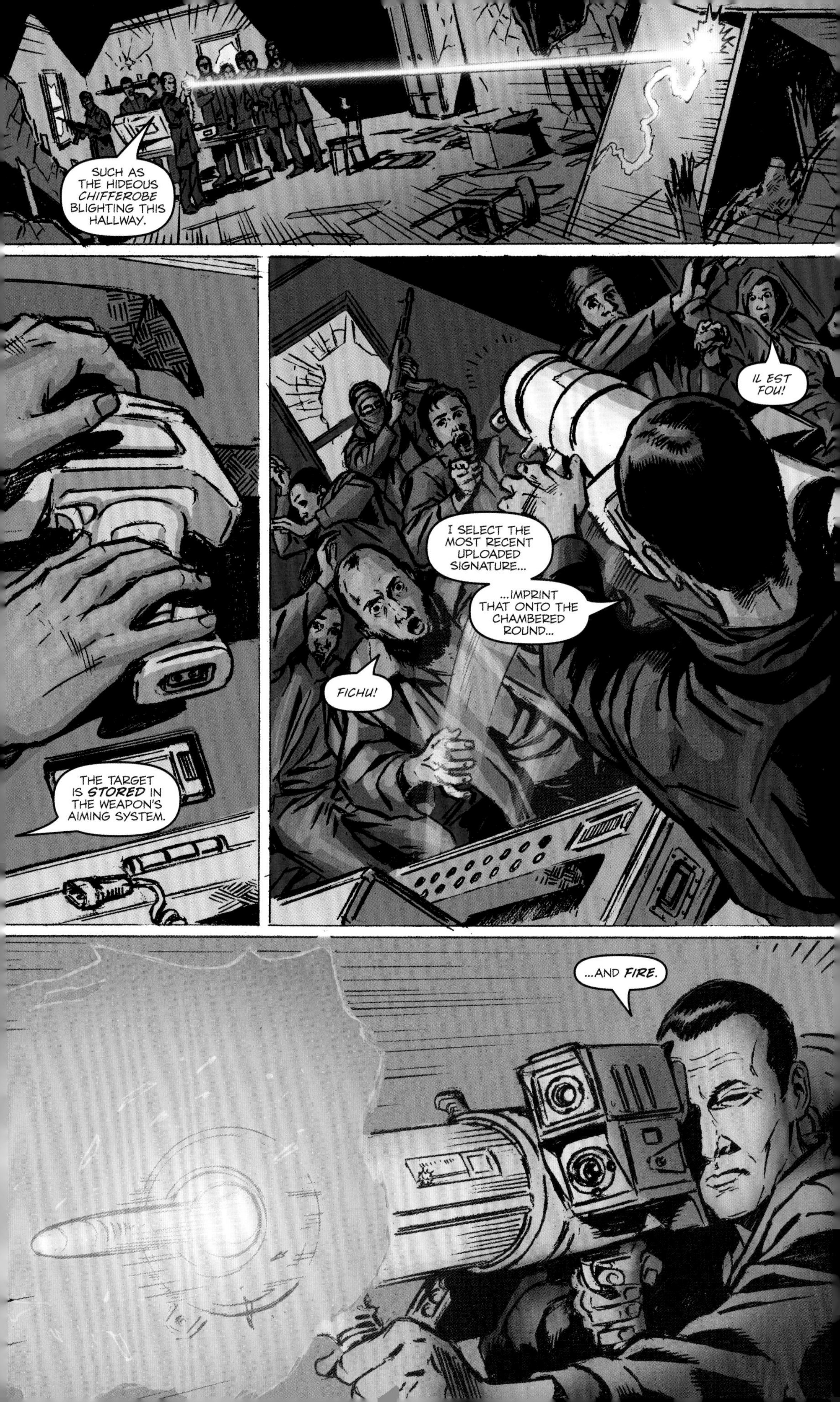
SUCH AS THE HIDEOUS CHIFFEROBE BLIGHTING THIS HALLWAY.
THE TARGET IS STORED IN THE WEAPON'S AIMING SYSTEM.
I SELECT THE MOST RECENT UPLOADED SIGNATURE...
...IMPRINT THAT ONTO THE CHAMBERED ROUND...
IL EST FOU!
FICHU!
...AND FIRE.

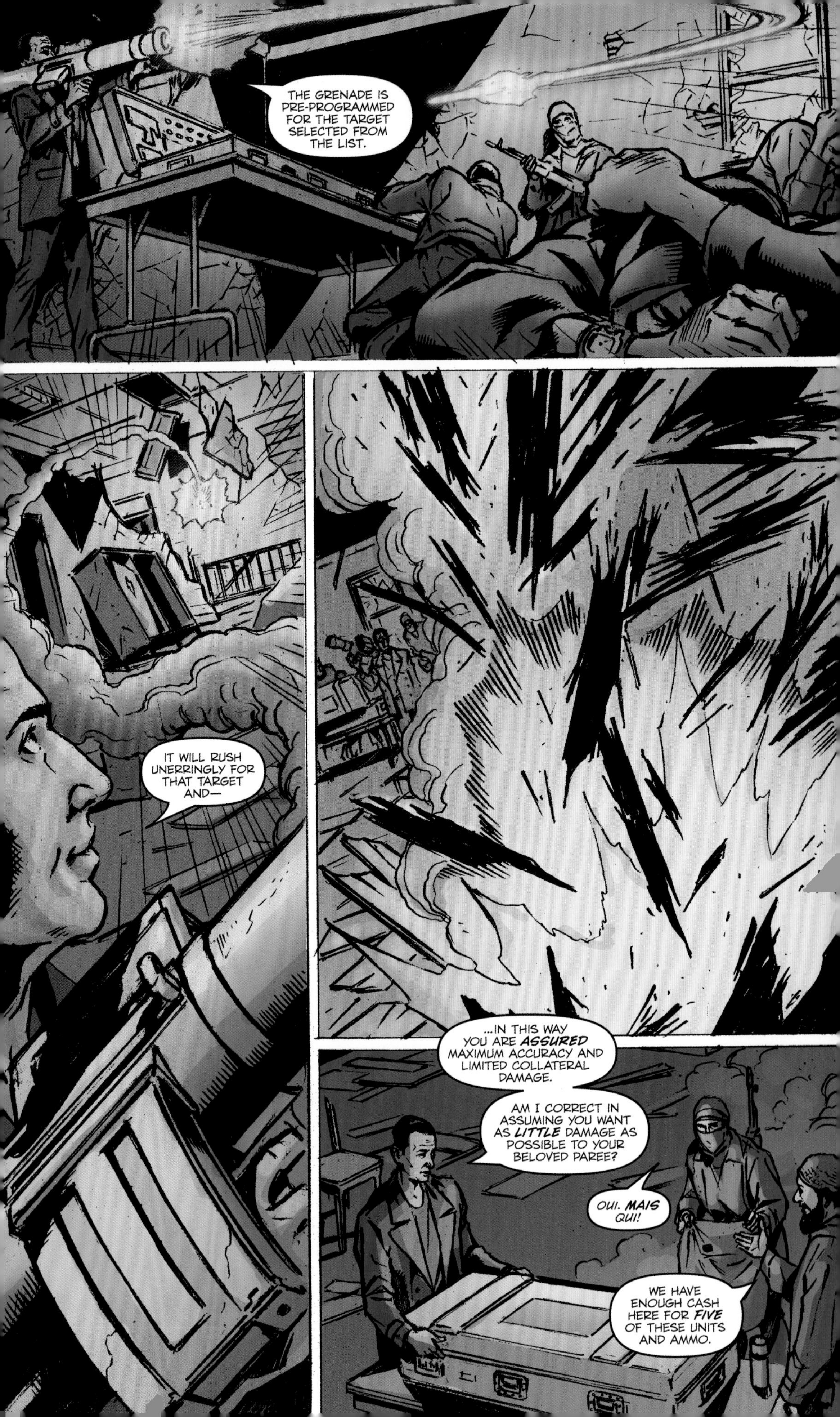
THE GRENADE IS PRE-PROGRAMMED FOR THE TARGET SELECTED FROM THE LIST.
IT WILL RUSH UNERRINGLY FOR THAT TARGET AND—
...IN THIS WAY YOU ARE ASSURED MAXIMUM ACCURACY AND LIMITED COLLATERAL DAMAGE.
AM I CORRECT IN ASSUMING YOU WANT AS LITTLE DAMAGE AS POSSIBLE TO YOUR BELOVED PAREE?
OUI. MAIS OUI!
WE HAVE ENOUGH CASH HERE FOR FIVE OF THESE UNITS AND AMMO.

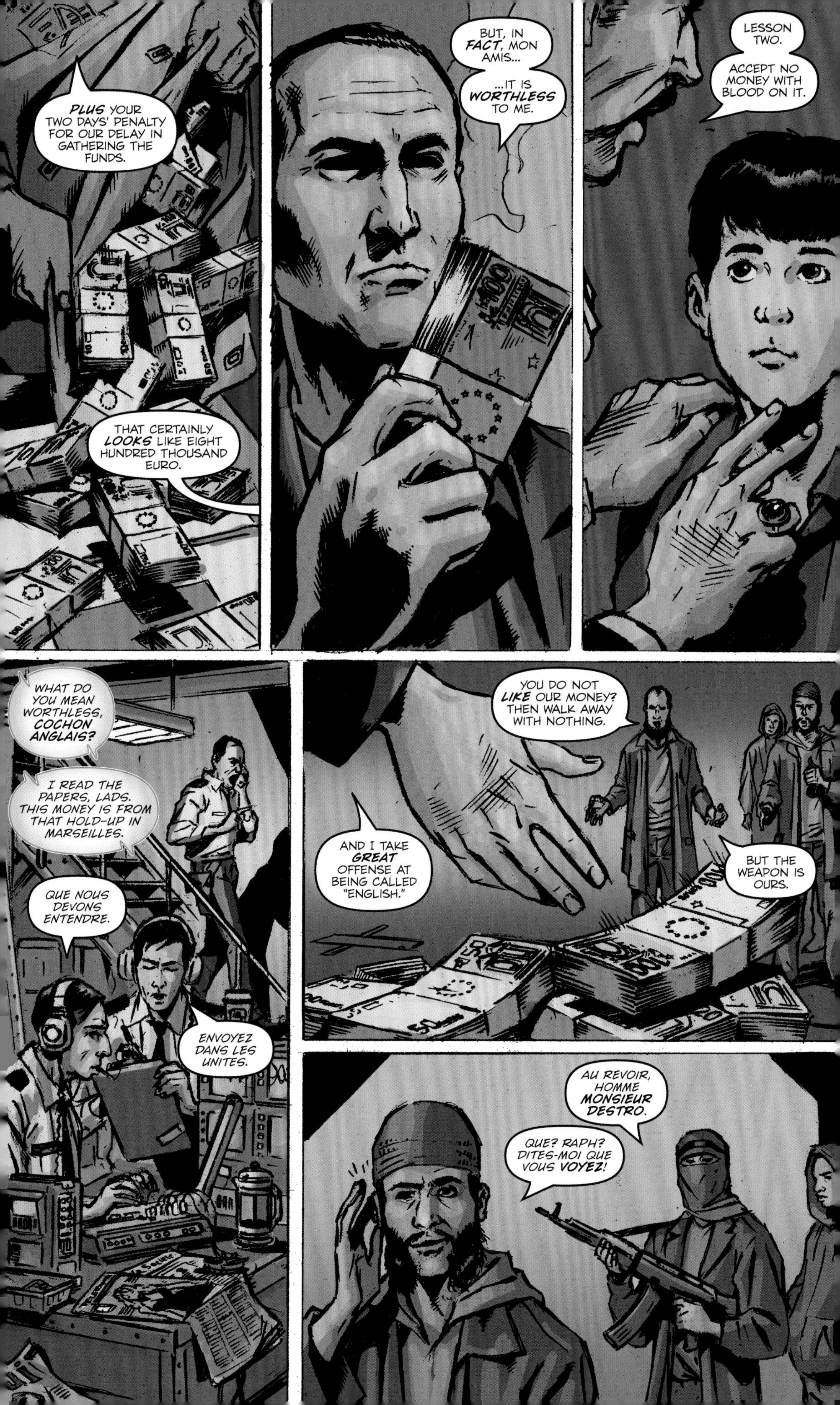
PLUS YOUR TWO DAYS' PENALTY FOR OUR DELAY IN GATHERING THE FUNDS.
THAT CERTAINLY LOOKS LIKE EIGHT HUNDRED THOUSAND EURO.
BUT, IN FACT, MON AMIS...
...IT IS WORTHLESS TO ME.
LESSON TWO.
ACCEPT NO MONEY WITH BLOOD ON IT.
WHAT DO YOU MEAN WORTHLESS, COCHON ANGLAIS?
I READ THE PAPERS, LADS. THIS MONEY IS FROM THAT HOLD-UP IN MARSEILLES.
QUE NOUS DEVONS ENTENDRE.
ENVOYEZ DANS LES UNITES.
YOU DO NOT LIKE OUR MONEY? THEN WALK AWAY WITH NOTHING.
AND I TAKE GREAT OFFENSE AT BEING CALLED "ENGLISH."
BUT THE WEAPON IS OURS.
AU REVOIR, HOMME MONSIEUR DESTRO.
QUE? RAPH? DITES-MOI QUE VOUS VOYEZ!

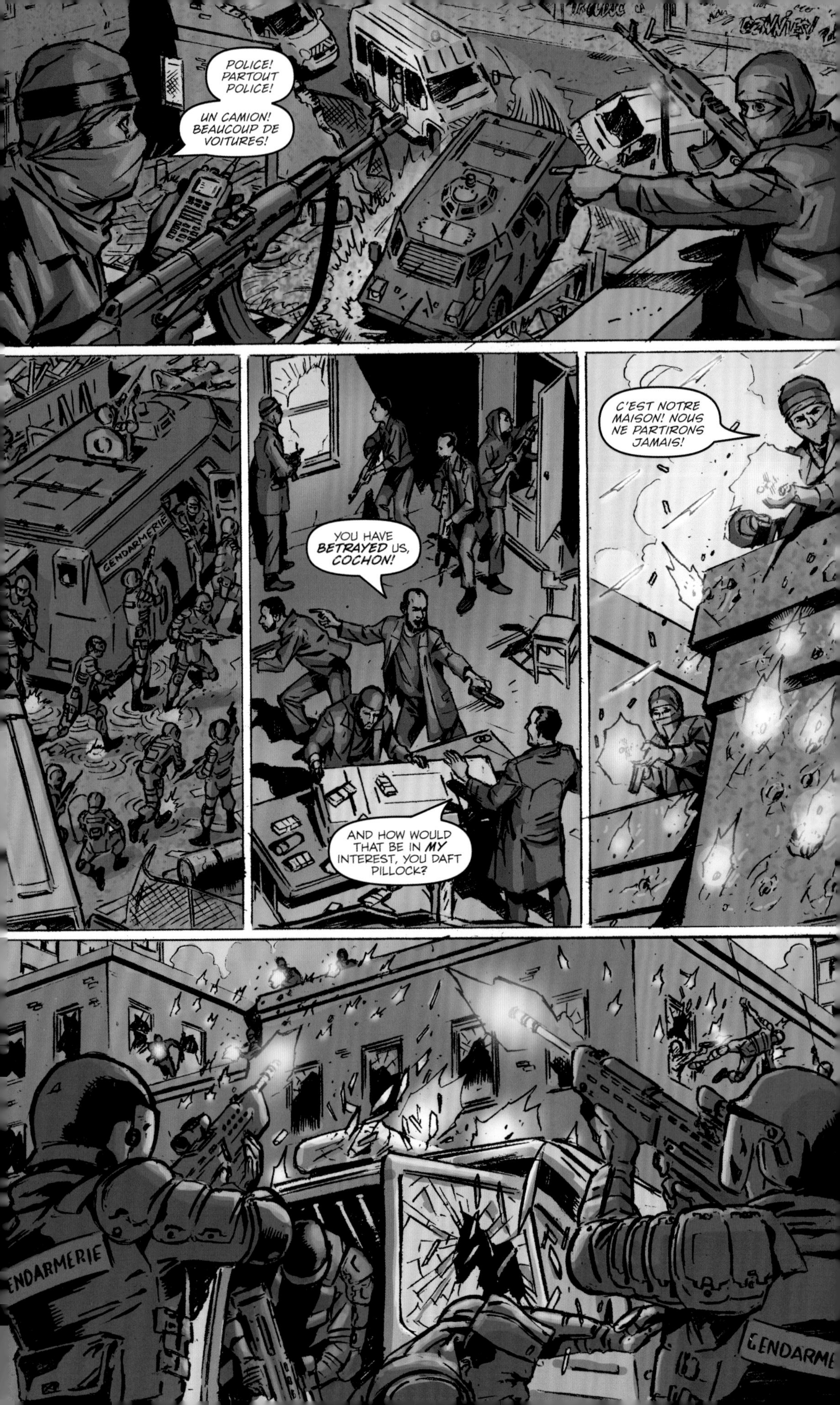
POLICE! PARTOUT POLICE!
UN CAMION! BEAUCOUP DE VOITURES!
GENDARMERIE
YOU HAVE BETRAYED US, COCHON!
AND HOW WOULD THAT BE IN MY INTEREST, YOU DAFT PILLOCK?
C'EST NOTRE MAISON! NOUS NE PARTIRONS JAMAIS!
GENDARMERIE
GENDARME

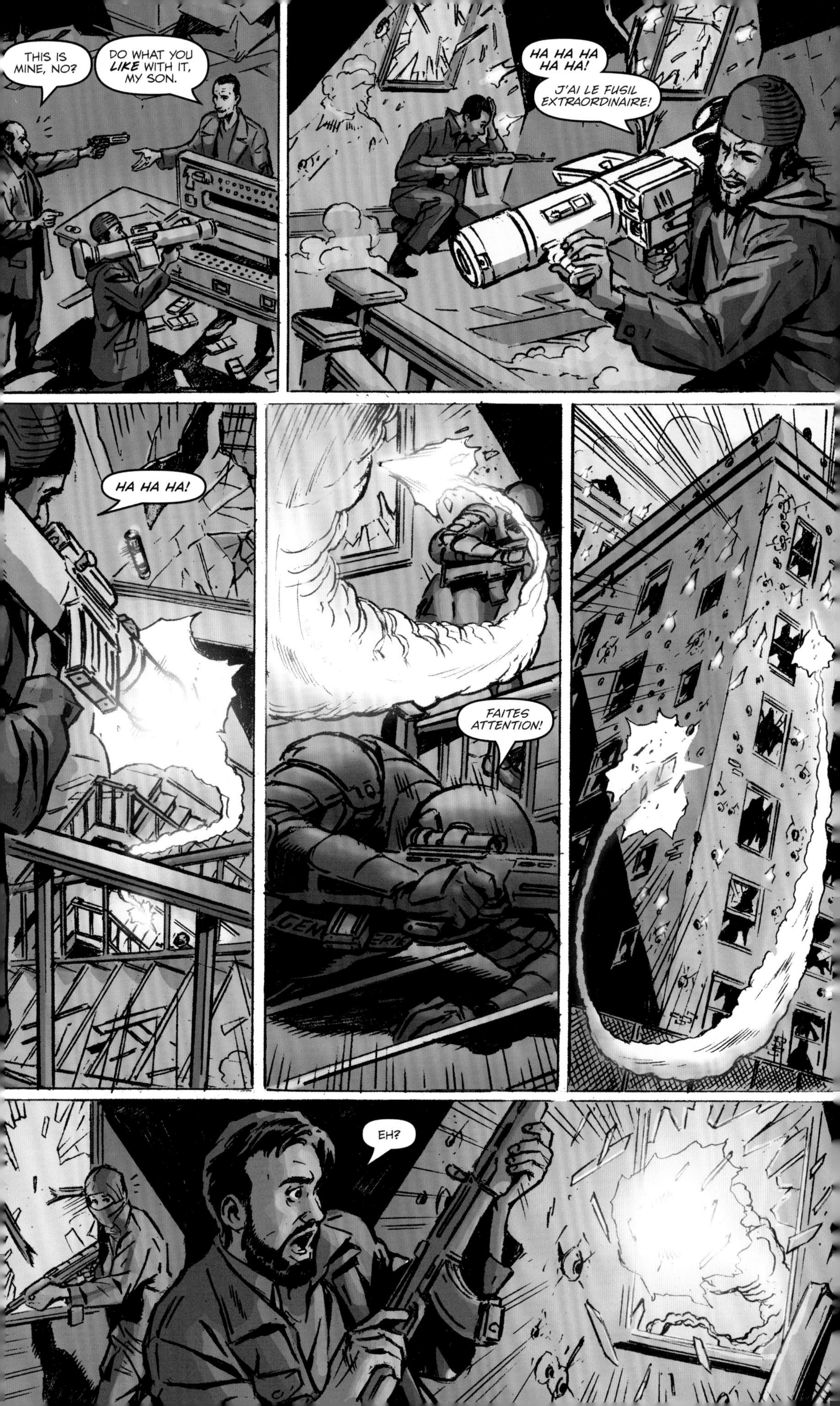
THIS IS MINE, NO?
DO WHAT YOU LIKE WITH IT, MY SON.
HA HA HA HA HA!
J'AI LE FUSIL EXTRAORDINAIRE!
HA HA HA!
FAITES ATTENTION!
EH?

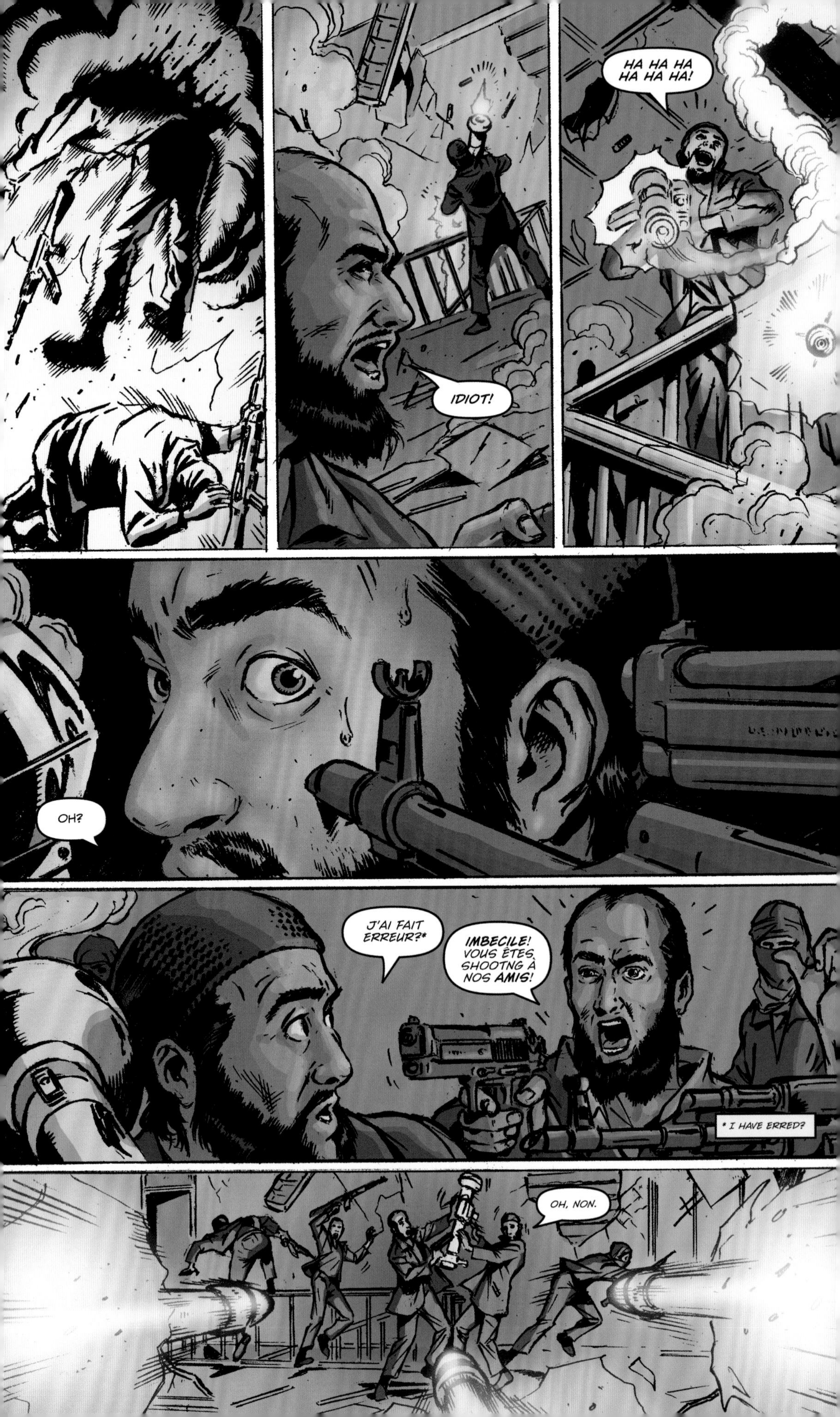
IDIOT!
HA HA HA
HA HA HA!
OH?
J'AI FAIT
ERREUR?*
IMBECILE!
VOUS ÊTES
SHOOTNG À
NOS AMIS!
* I HAVE ERRED?
OH, NON.

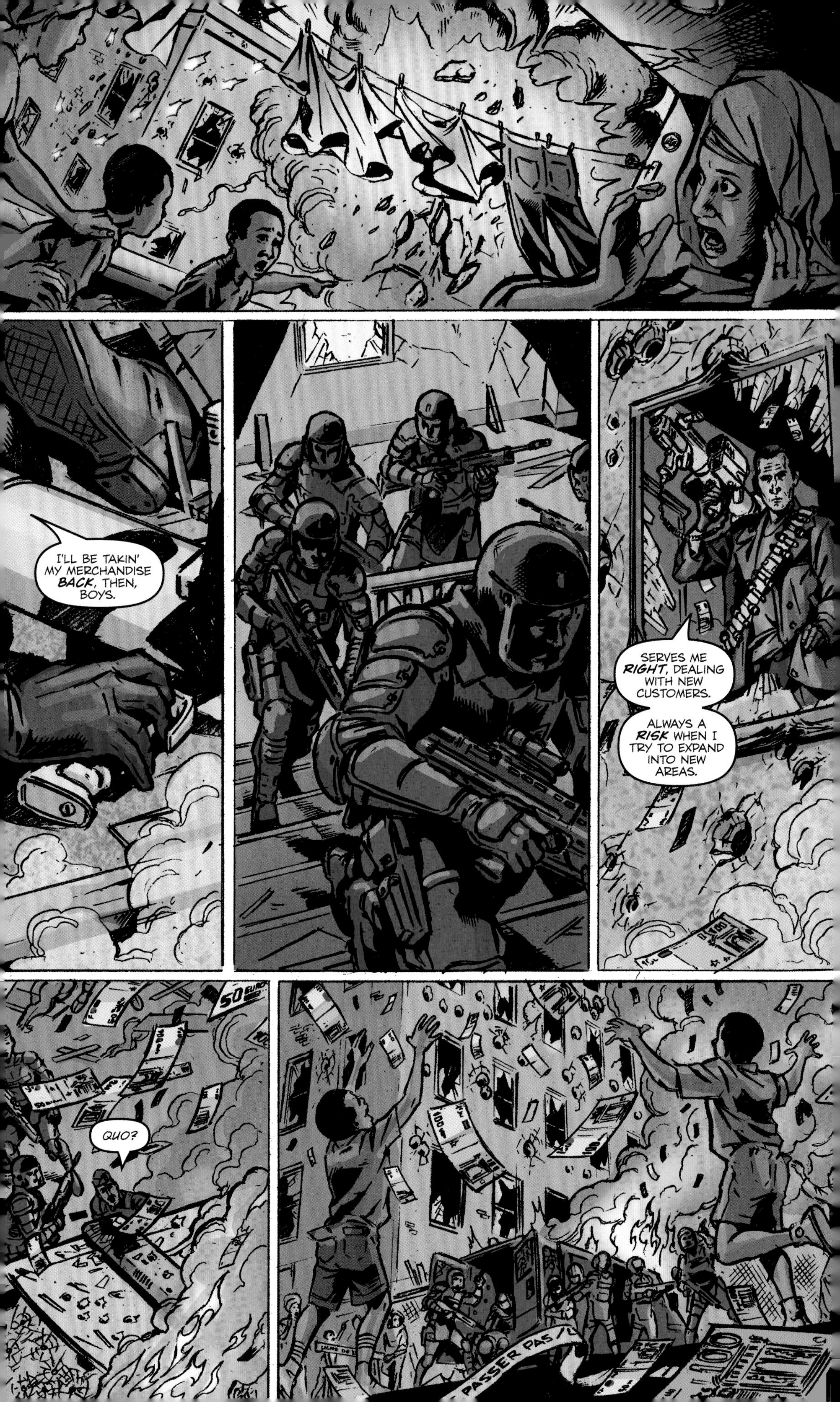
I'LL BE TAKIN' MY MERCHANDISE BACK, THEN, BOYS.
SERVES ME RIGHT, DEALING WITH NEW CUSTOMERS.
ALWAYS A RISK WHEN I TRY TO EXPAND INTO NEW AREAS.
QUO?
PASSER PAS

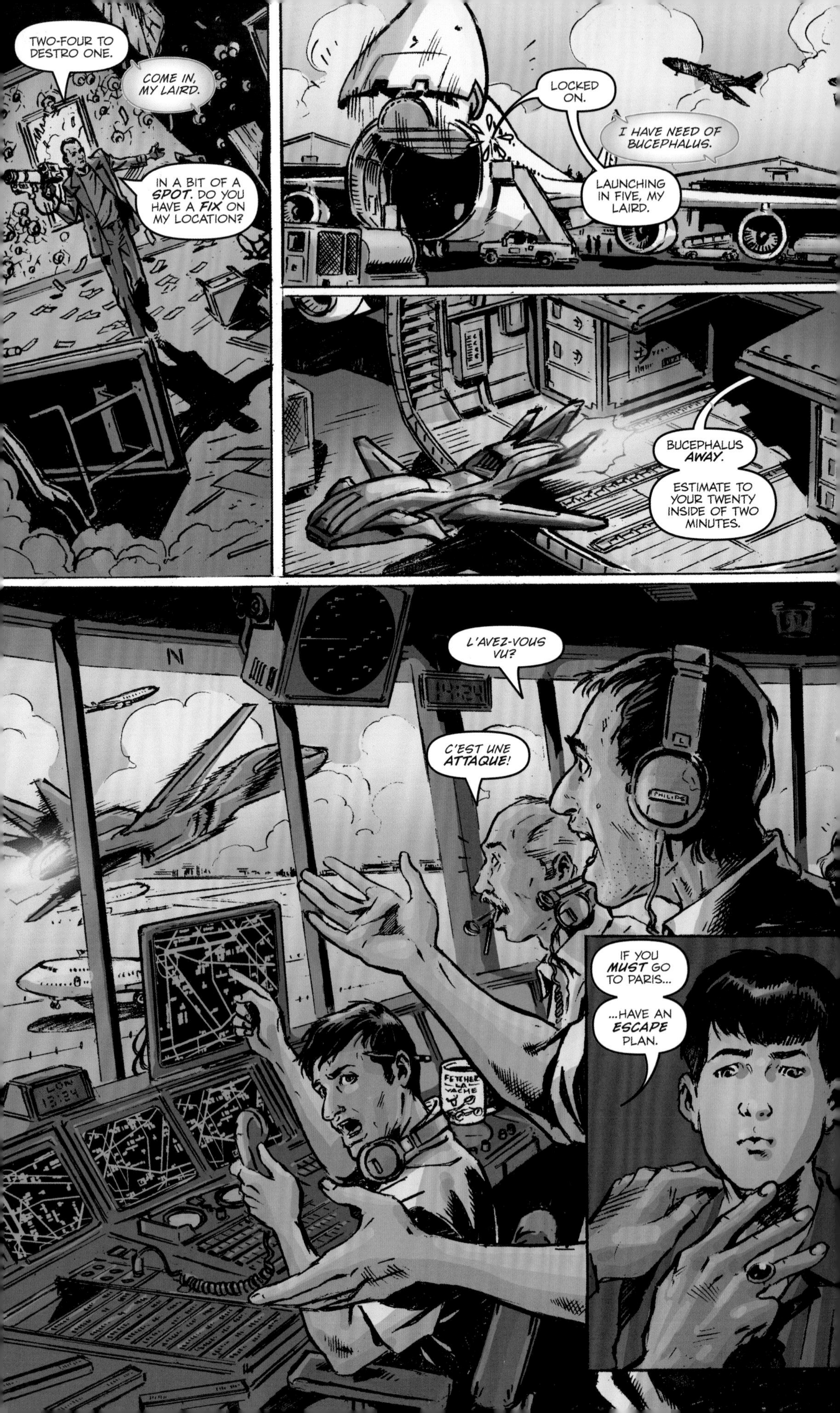
TWO-FOUR TO DESTRO ONE.
COME IN, MY LAIRD.
IN A BIT OF A SPOT. DO YOU HAVE A FIX ON MY LOCATION?
LOCKED ON.
I HAVE NEED OF BUCEPHALUS.
LAUNCHING IN FIVE, MY LAIRD.
BUCEPHALUS AWAY.
ESTIMATE TO YOUR TWENTY INSIDE OF TWO MINUTES.
L'AVEZ-VOUS VU?
C'EST UNE ATTAQUE!
IF YOU MUST GO TO PARIS...
...HAVE AN ESCAPE PLAN.

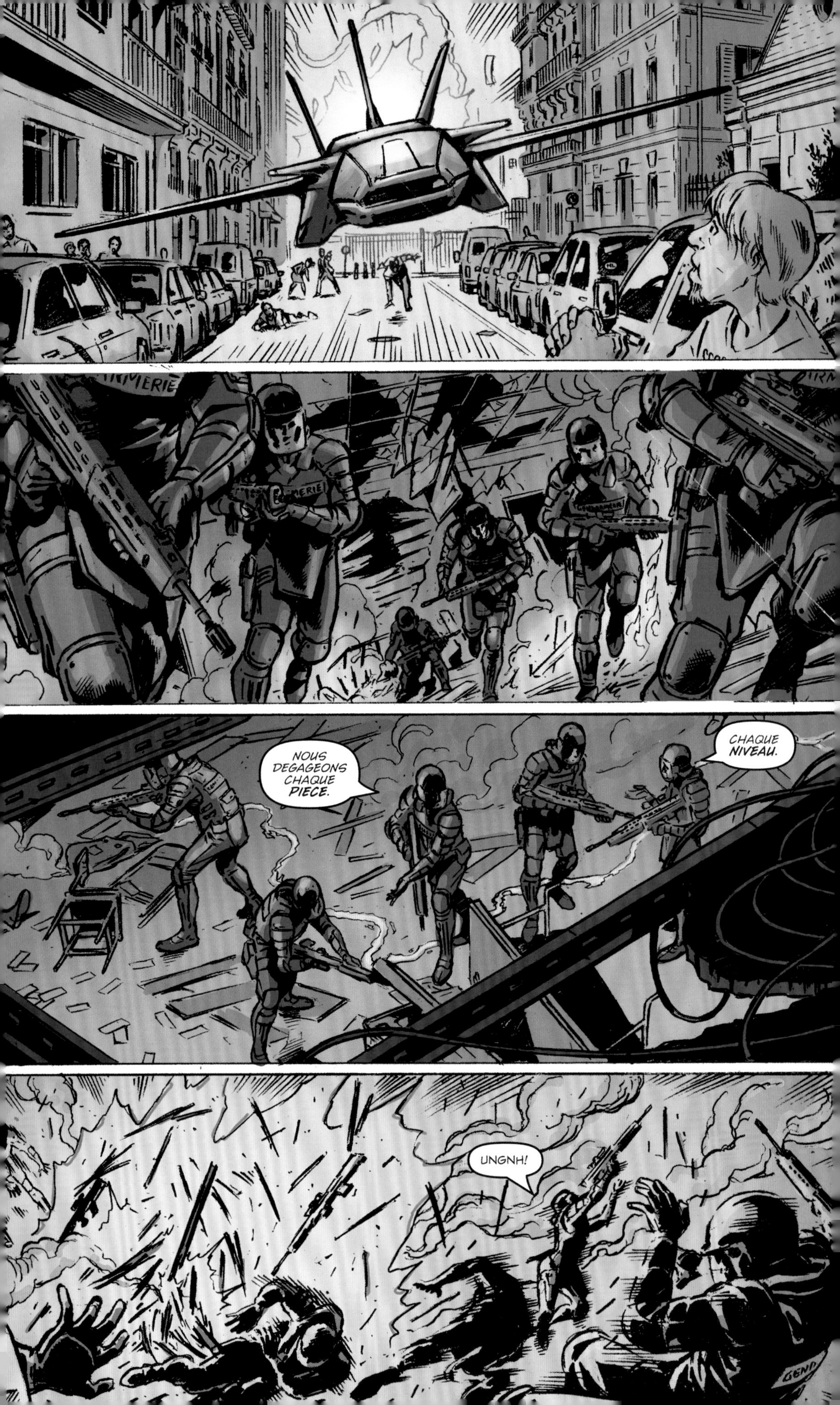
NOUS DEGAGEONS CHAQUE PIECE.
CHAQUE NIVEAU.
UNGNH!

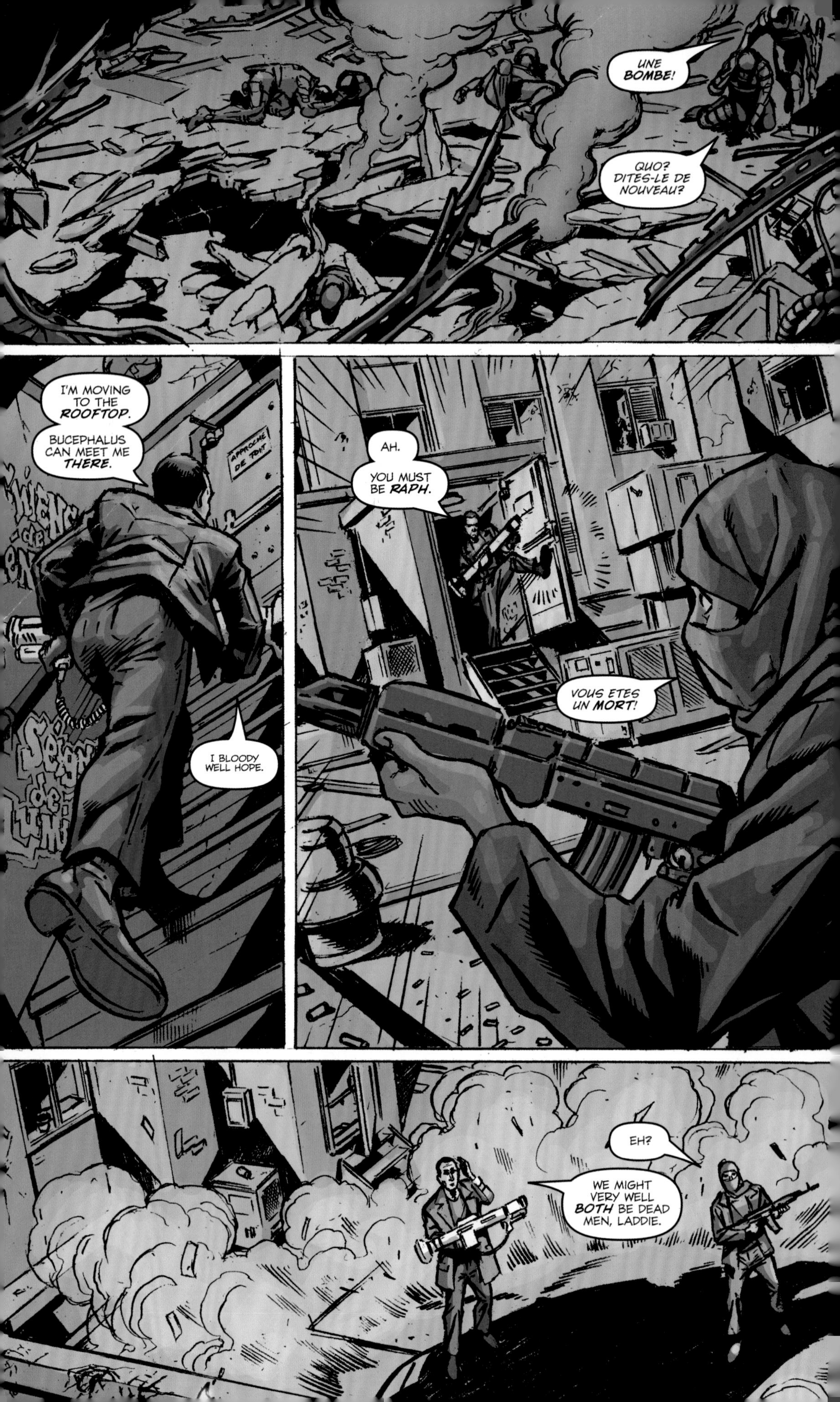
UNE BOMBE!
QUO? DITES-LE DE NOUVEAU?
I'M MOVING TO THE ROOFTOP.
BUCEPHALUS CAN MEET ME THERE.
I BLOODY WELL HOPE.
AH.
YOU MUST BE RAPH.
VOUS ETES UN MORT!
EH?
WE MIGHT VERY WELL BOTH BE DEAD MEN, LADDIE.

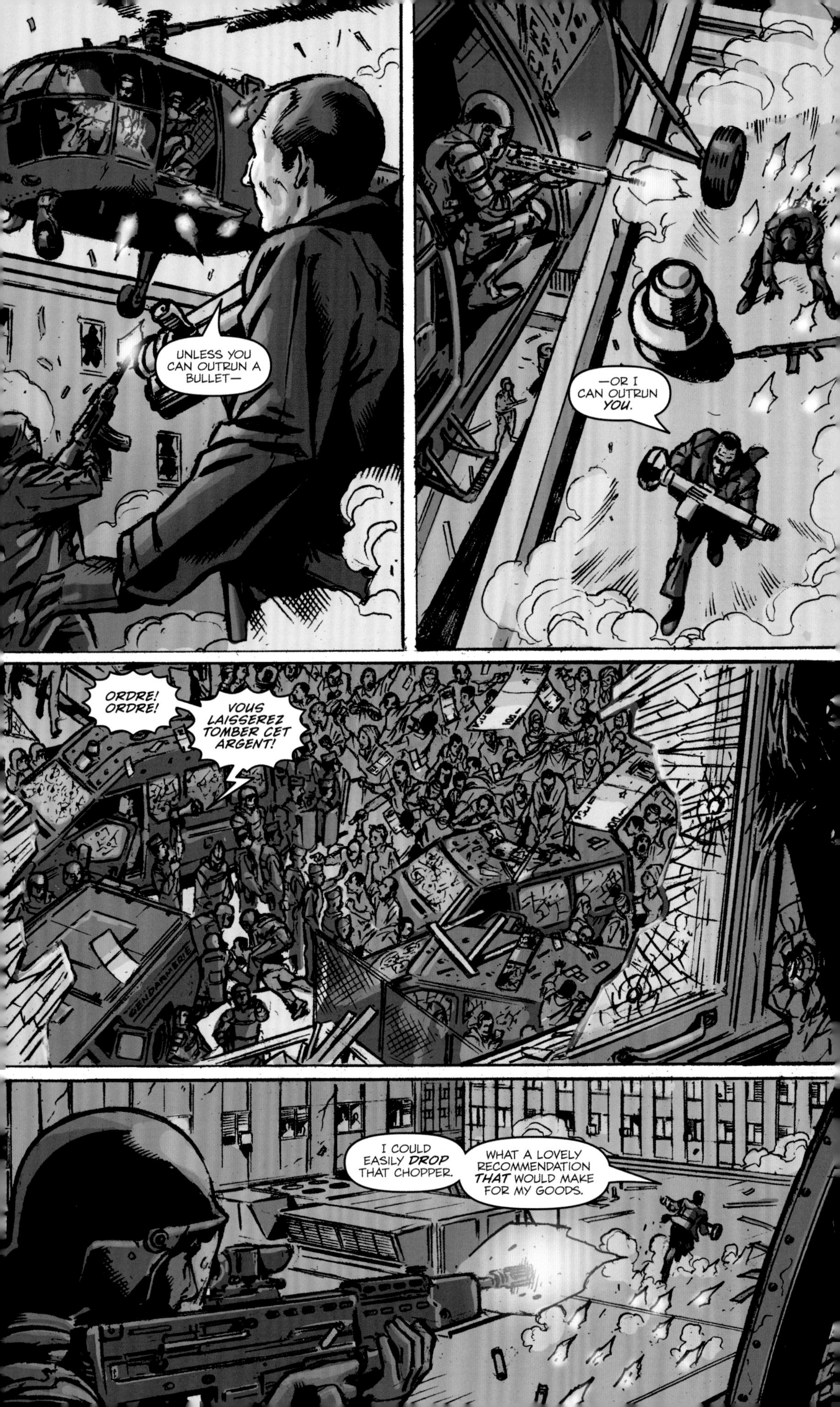
UNLESS YOU CAN OUTRUN A BULLET—
—OR I CAN OUTRUN *YOU*.
ORDRE! ORDRE!
VOUS LAISSEREZ TOMBER CET ARGENT!
I COULD EASILY ***DROP*** THAT CHOPPER.
WHAT A LOVELY RECOMMENDATION ***THAT*** WOULD MAKE FOR MY GOODS.

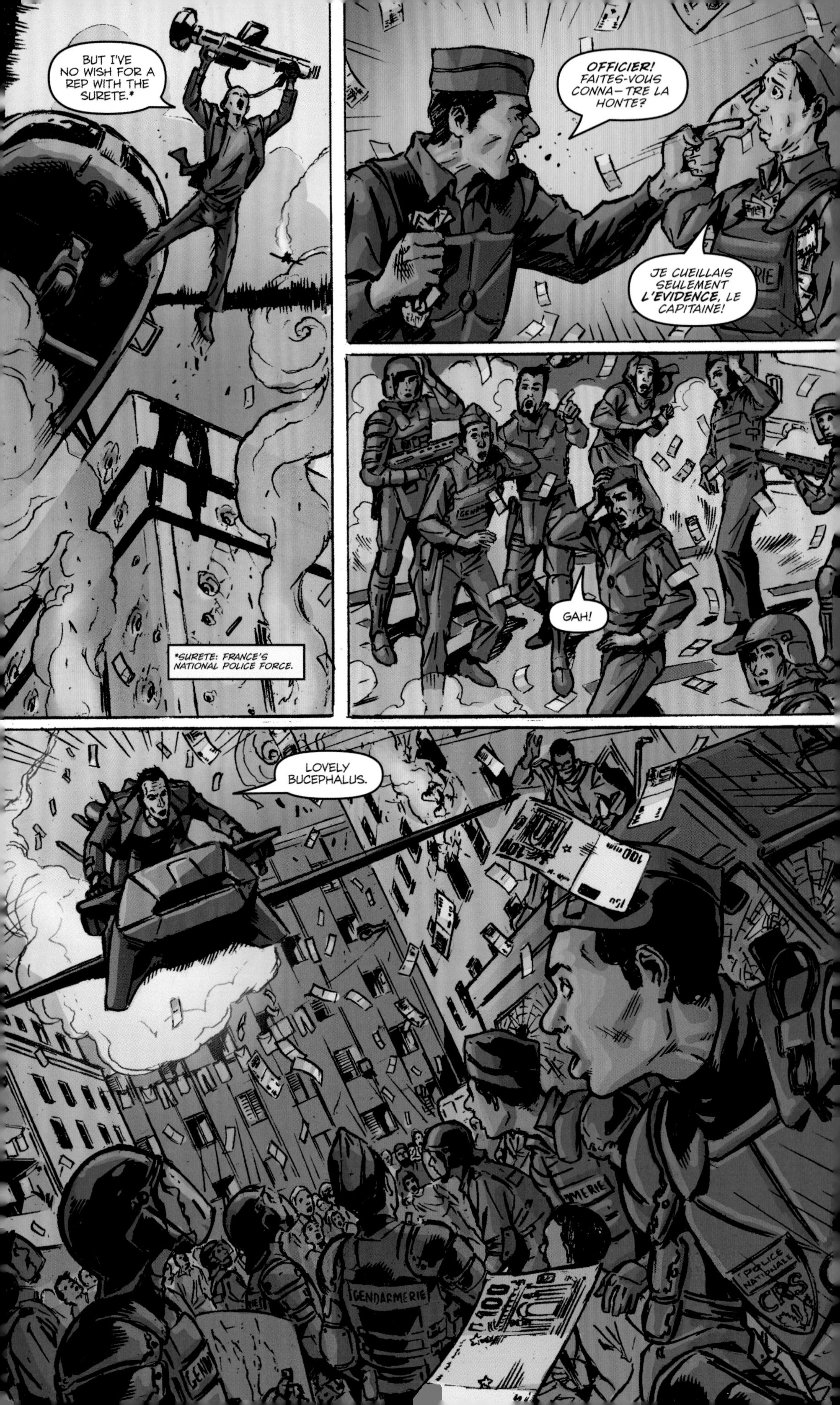
BUT I'VE NO WISH FOR A REP WITH THE SURETE.*
*SURETE: FRANCE'S NATIONAL POLICE FORCE.
OFFICIER! FAITES-VOUS CONNA–TRE LA HONTE?
JE CUEILLAIS SEULEMENT **L'EVIDENCE**, LE CAPITAINE!
GAH!
LOVELY BUCEPHALUS.
GENDARMERIE
POLICE NATIONALE
CRS

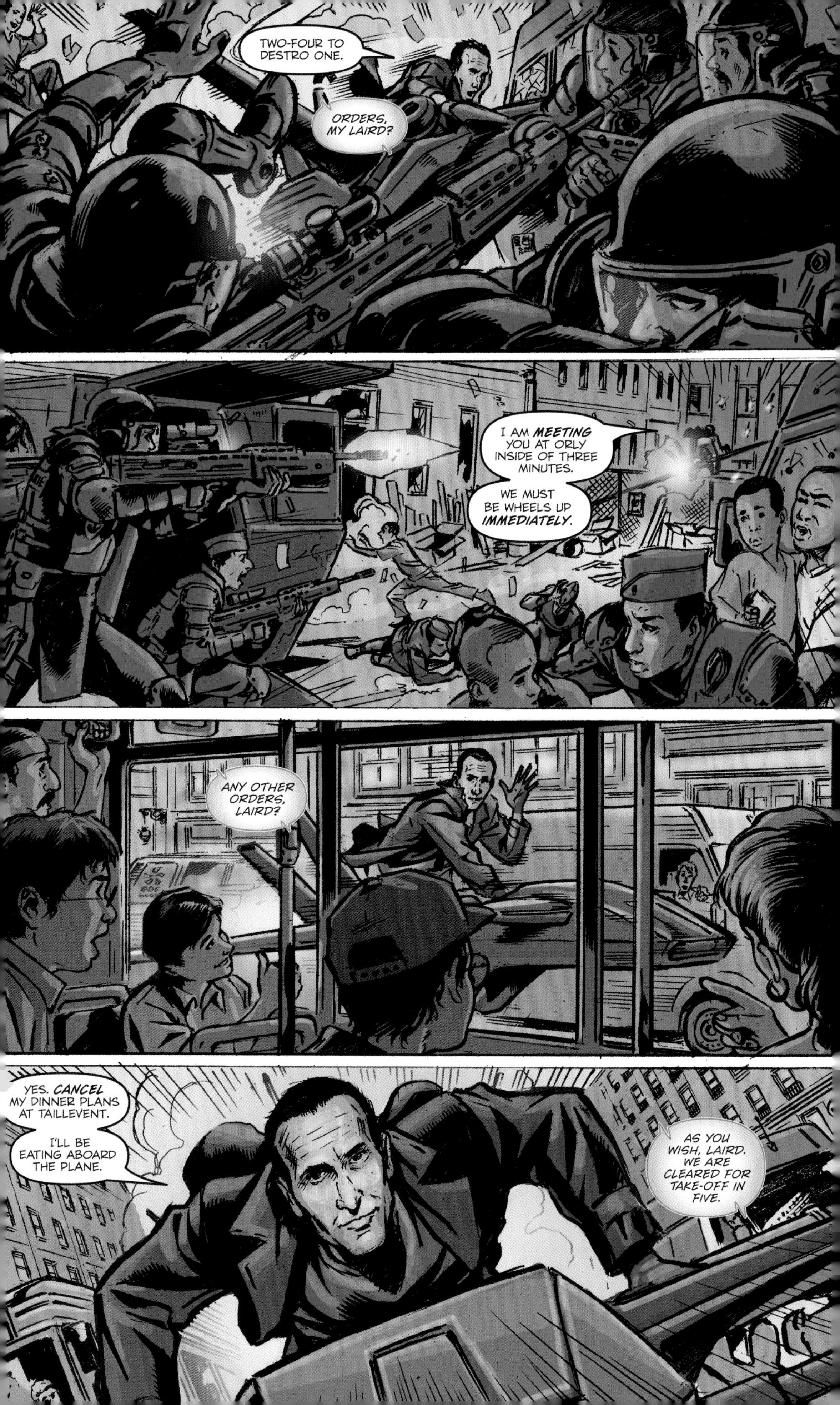
TWO-FOUR TO DESTRO ONE.
ORDERS, MY LAIRD?
I AM MEETING YOU AT ORLY INSIDE OF THREE MINUTES.
WE MUST BE WHEELS UP IMMEDIATELY.
ANY OTHER ORDERS, LAIRD?
YES. CANCEL MY DINNER PLANS AT TAILLEVENT.
I'LL BE EATING ABOARD THE PLANE.
AS YOU WISH, LAIRD. WE ARE CLEARED FOR TAKE-OFF IN FIVE.

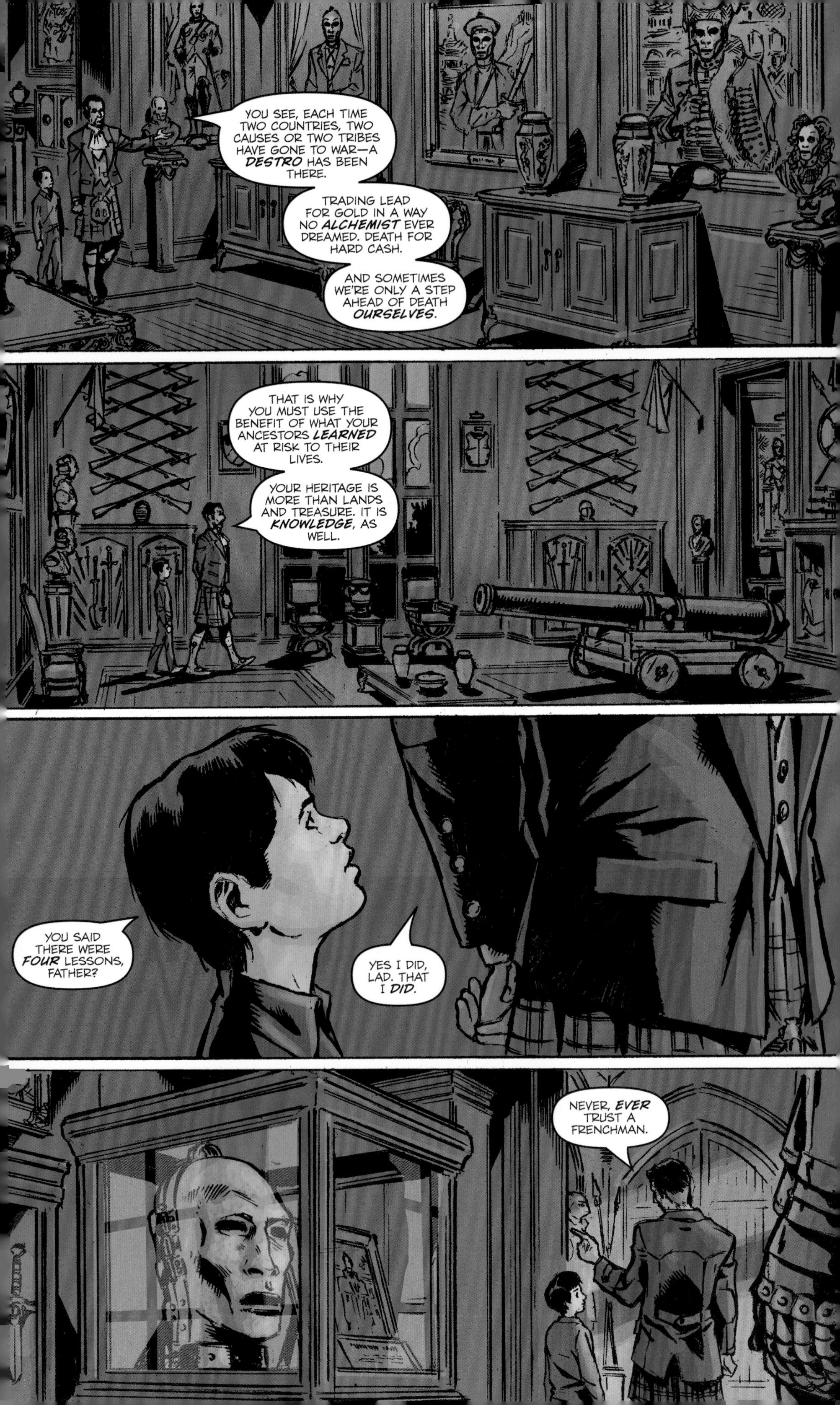
YOU SEE, EACH TIME TWO COUNTRIES, TWO CAUSES OR TWO TRIBES HAVE GONE TO WAR—A *DESTRO* HAS BEEN THERE.
TRADING LEAD FOR GOLD IN A WAY NO *ALCHEMIST* EVER DREAMED. DEATH FOR HARD CASH.
AND SOMETIMES WE'RE ONLY A STEP AHEAD OF DEATH *OURSELVES*.
THAT IS WHY YOU MUST USE THE BENEFIT OF WHAT YOUR ANCESTORS *LEARNED* AT RISK TO THEIR LIVES.
YOUR HERITAGE IS MORE THAN LANDS AND TREASURE. IT IS *KNOWLEDGE*, AS WELL.
YOU SAID THERE WERE *FOUR* LESSONS, FATHER?
YES I DID, LAD. THAT I *DID*.
NEVER, *EVER* TRUST A FRENCHMAN.

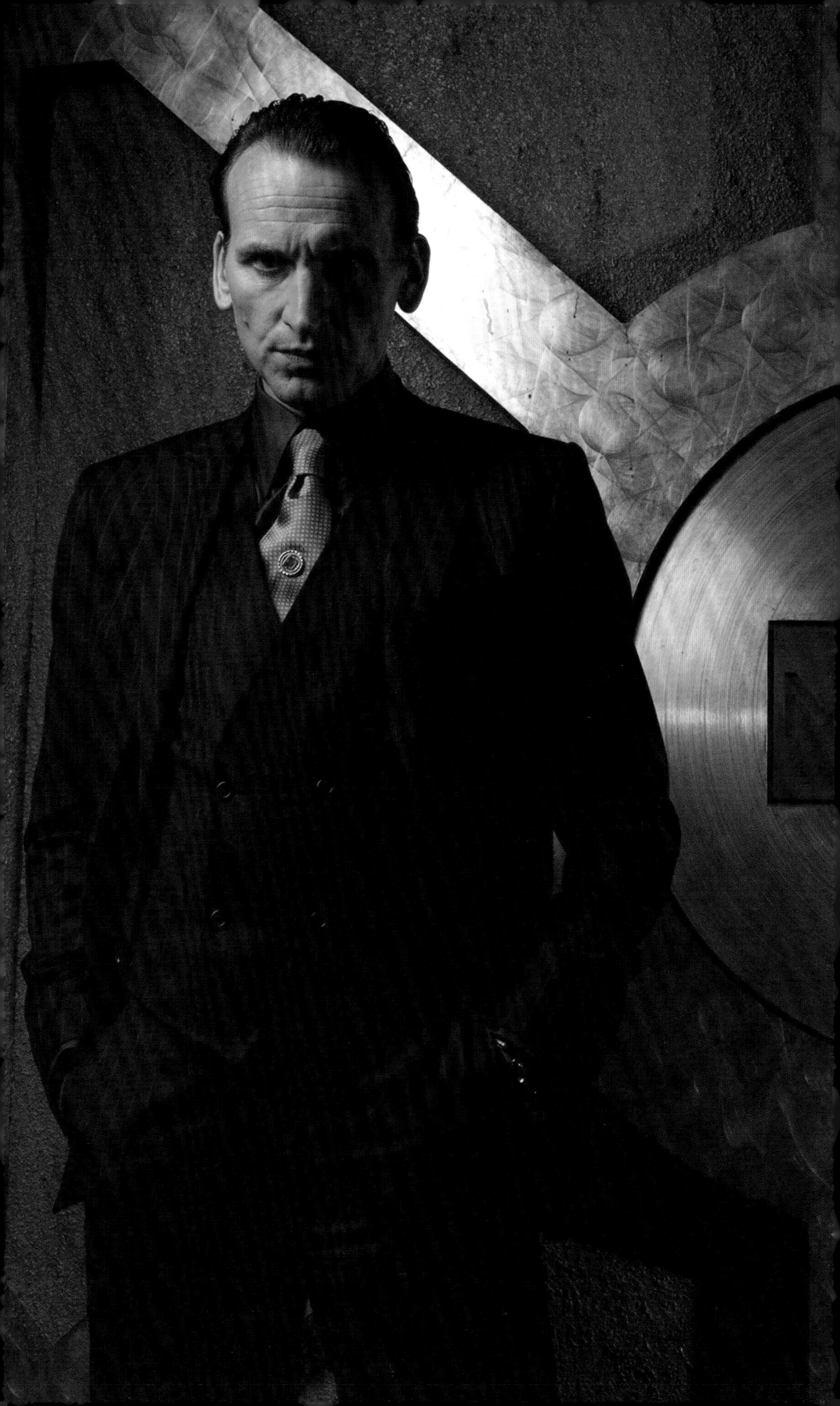

ARTWORK BY
JOE CORRONEY

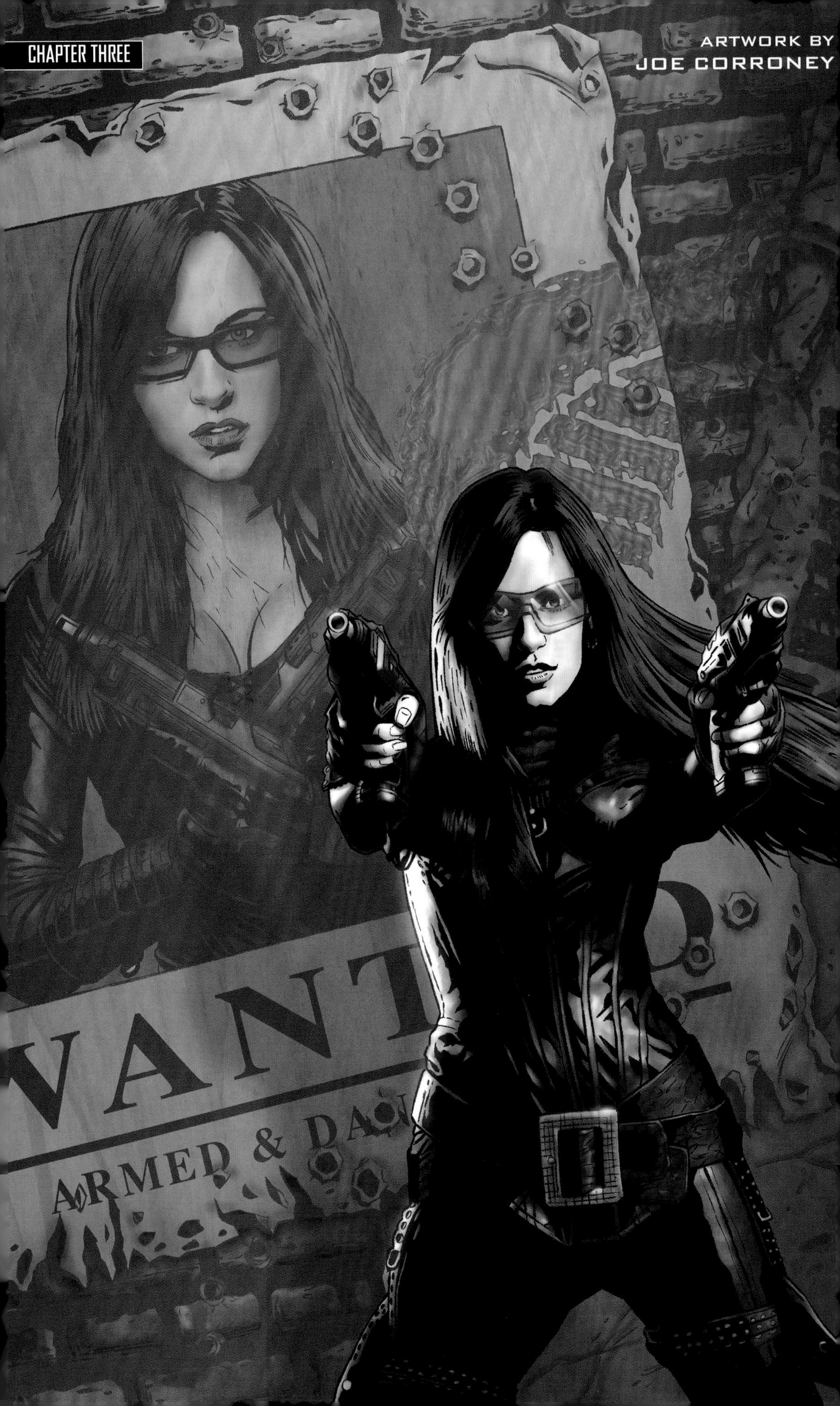
VANT
ARMED & DA

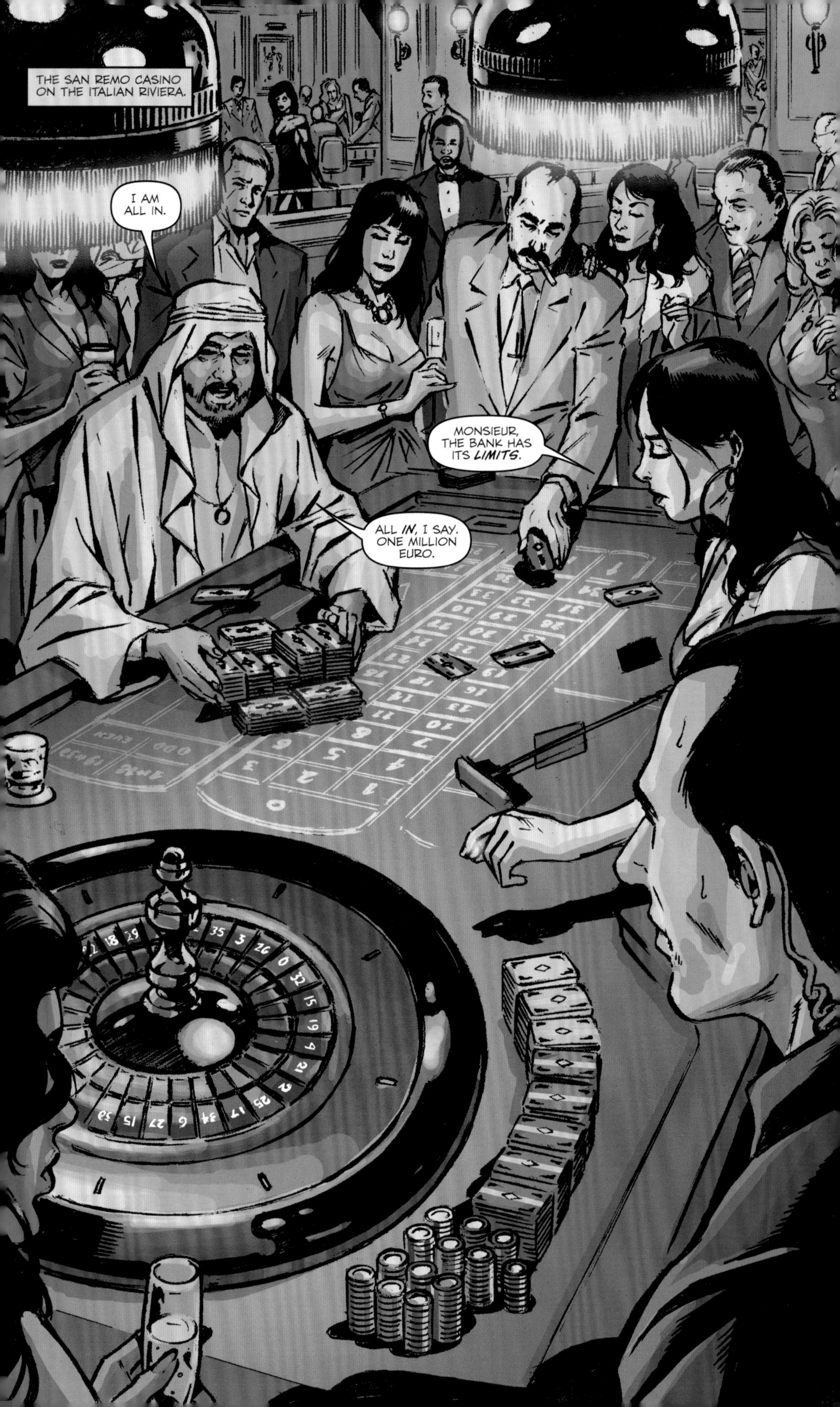

THE SAN REMO CASINO ON THE ITALIAN RIVIERA.
I AM ALL IN.
MONSIEUR, THE BANK HAS ITS LIMITS.
ALL IN, I SAY. ONE MILLION EURO.

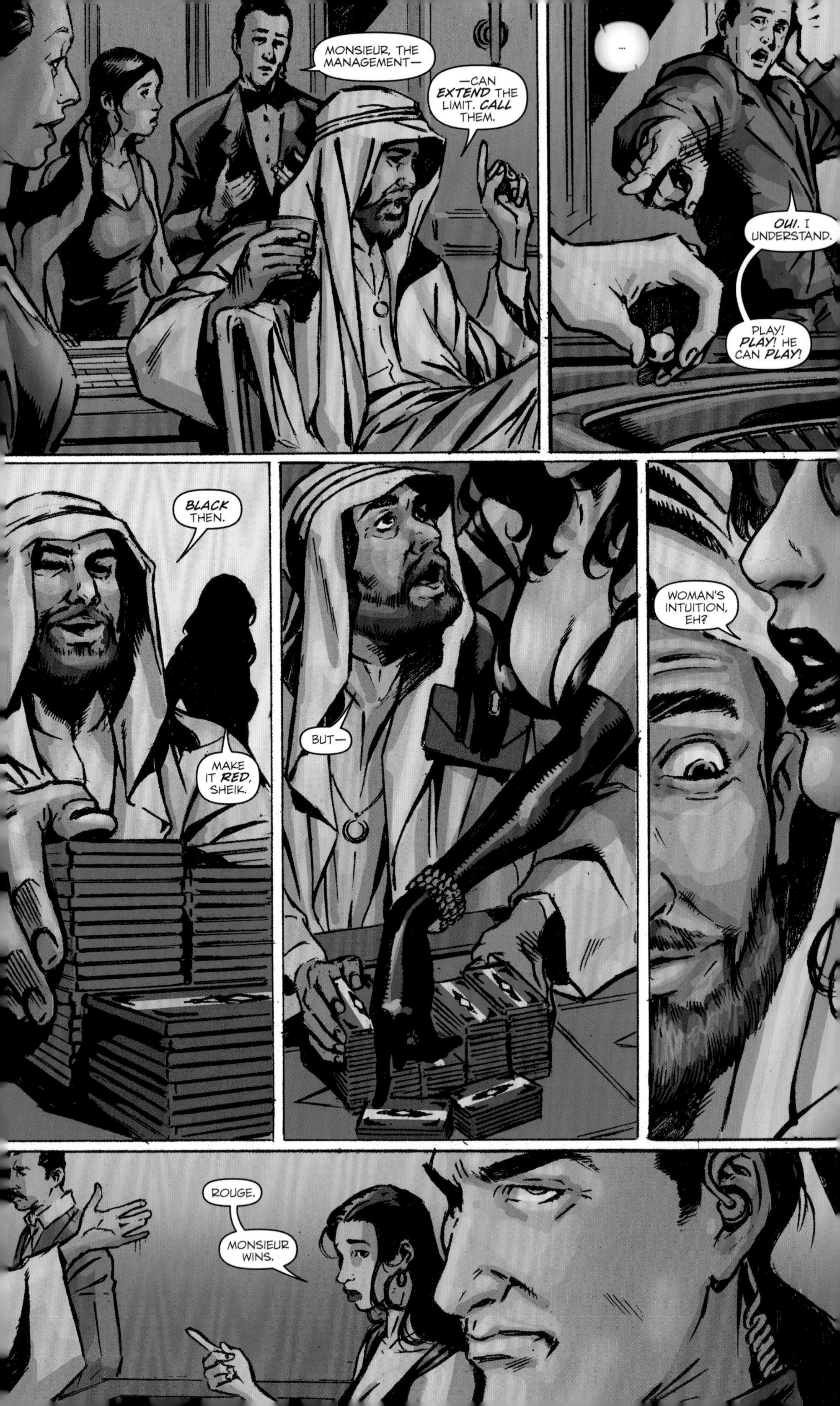
MONSIEUR, THE MANAGEMENT—
—CAN EXTEND THE LIMIT. CALL THEM.
...
OUI. I UNDERSTAND.
PLAY! PLAY! HE CAN PLAY!
BLACK THEN.
MAKE IT RED, SHEIK.
BUT—
WOMAN'S INTUITION, EH?
ROUGE.
MONSIEUR WINS.

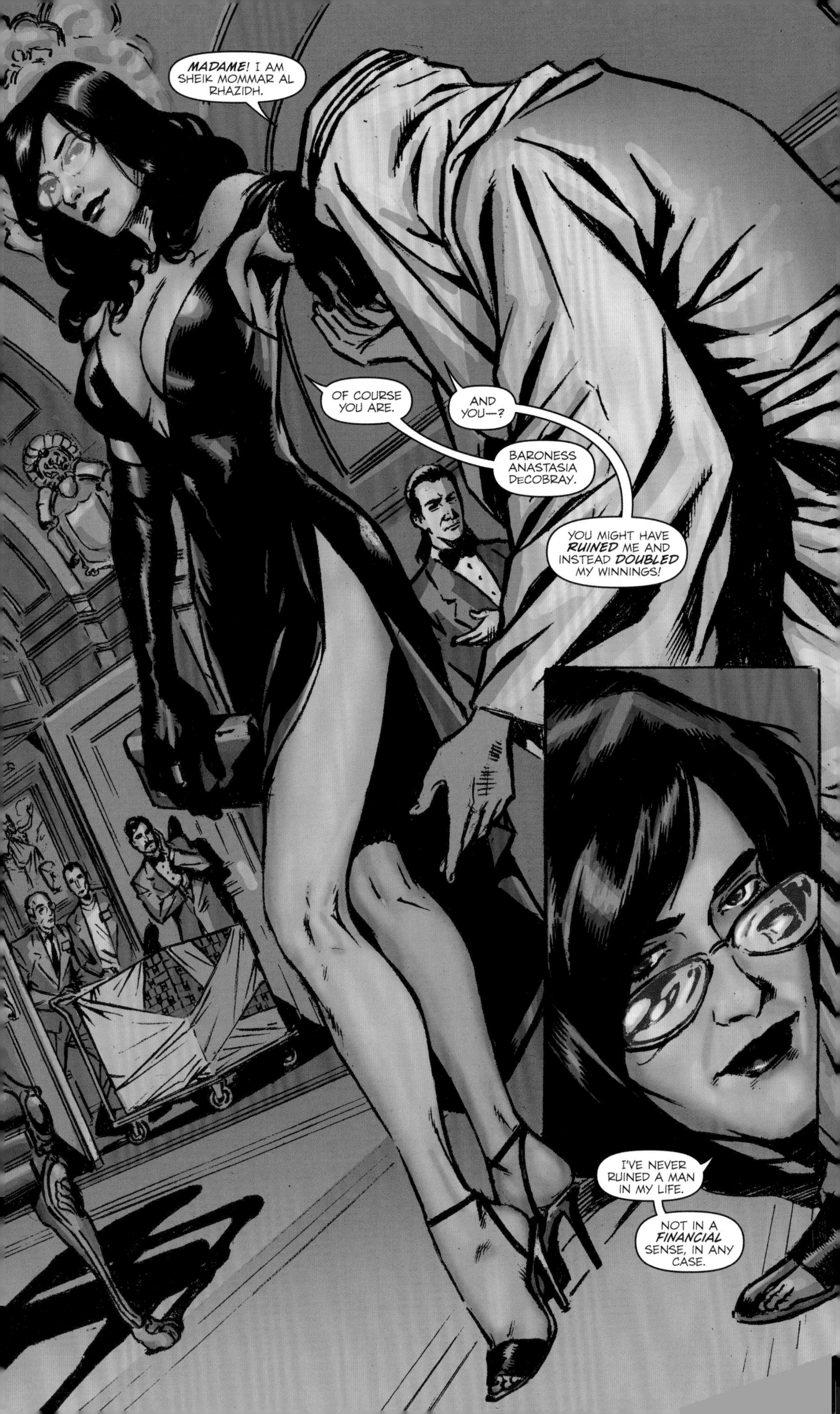

MADAME! I AM SHEIK MOMMAR AL RHAZIDH.
OF COURSE YOU ARE.
AND YOU--?
BARONESS ANASTASIA DeCOBRAY.
YOU MIGHT HAVE RUINED ME AND INSTEAD DOUBLED MY WINNINGS!
I'VE NEVER RUINED A MAN IN MY LIFE.
NOT IN A FINANCIAL SENSE, IN ANY CASE.

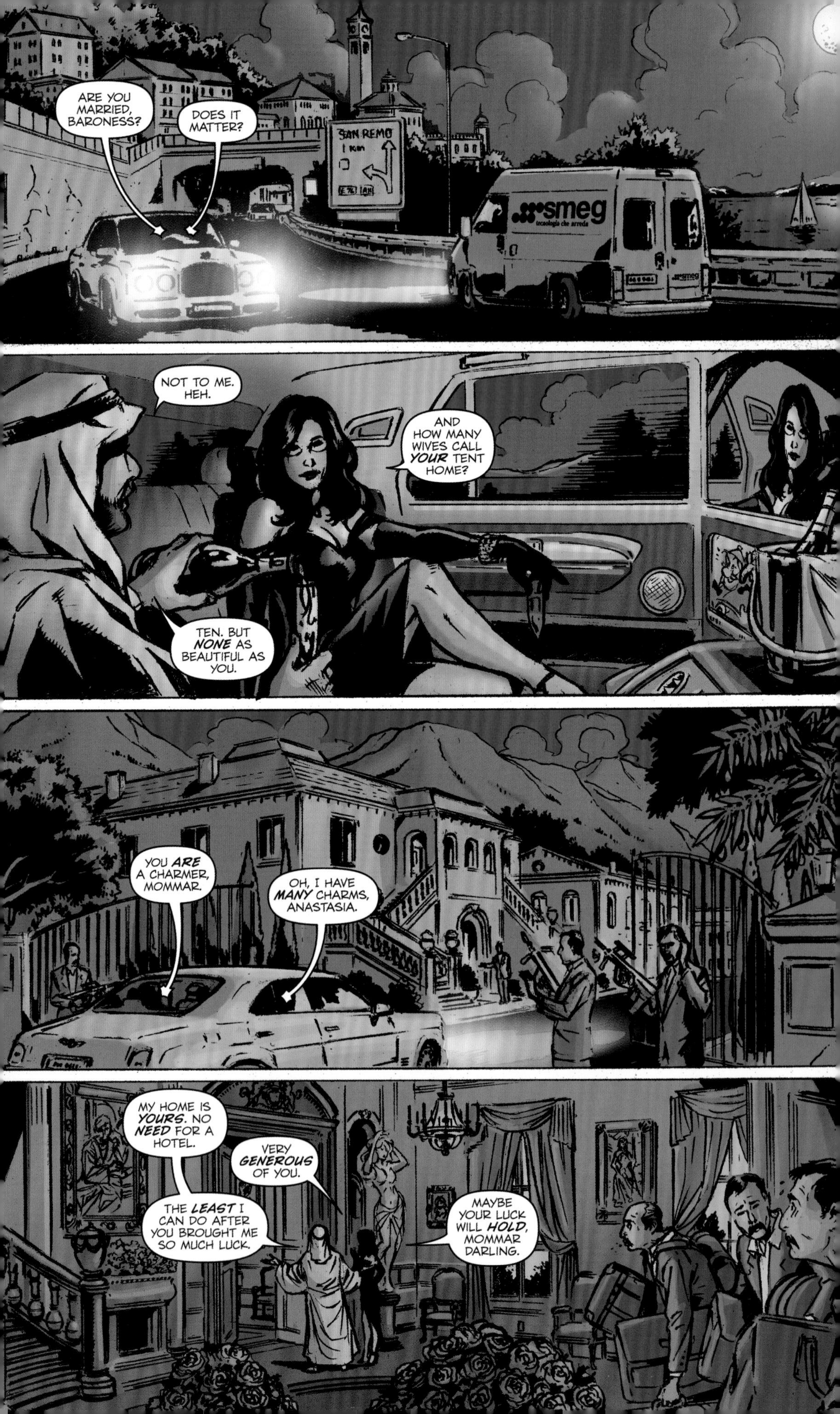
ARE YOU MARRIED, BARONESS?
DOES IT MATTER?
SAN REMO 1 km
smeg tecnologia che arreda
NOT TO ME. HEH.
AND HOW MANY WIVES CALL YOUR TENT HOME?
TEN. BUT NONE AS BEAUTIFUL AS YOU.
YOU ARE A CHARMER, MOMMAR.
OH, I HAVE MANY CHARMS, ANASTASIA.
MY HOME IS YOURS. NO NEED FOR A HOTEL.
VERY GENEROUS OF YOU.
THE LEAST I CAN DO AFTER YOU BROUGHT ME SO MUCH LUCK.
MAYBE YOUR LUCK WILL HOLD, MOMMAR DARLING.

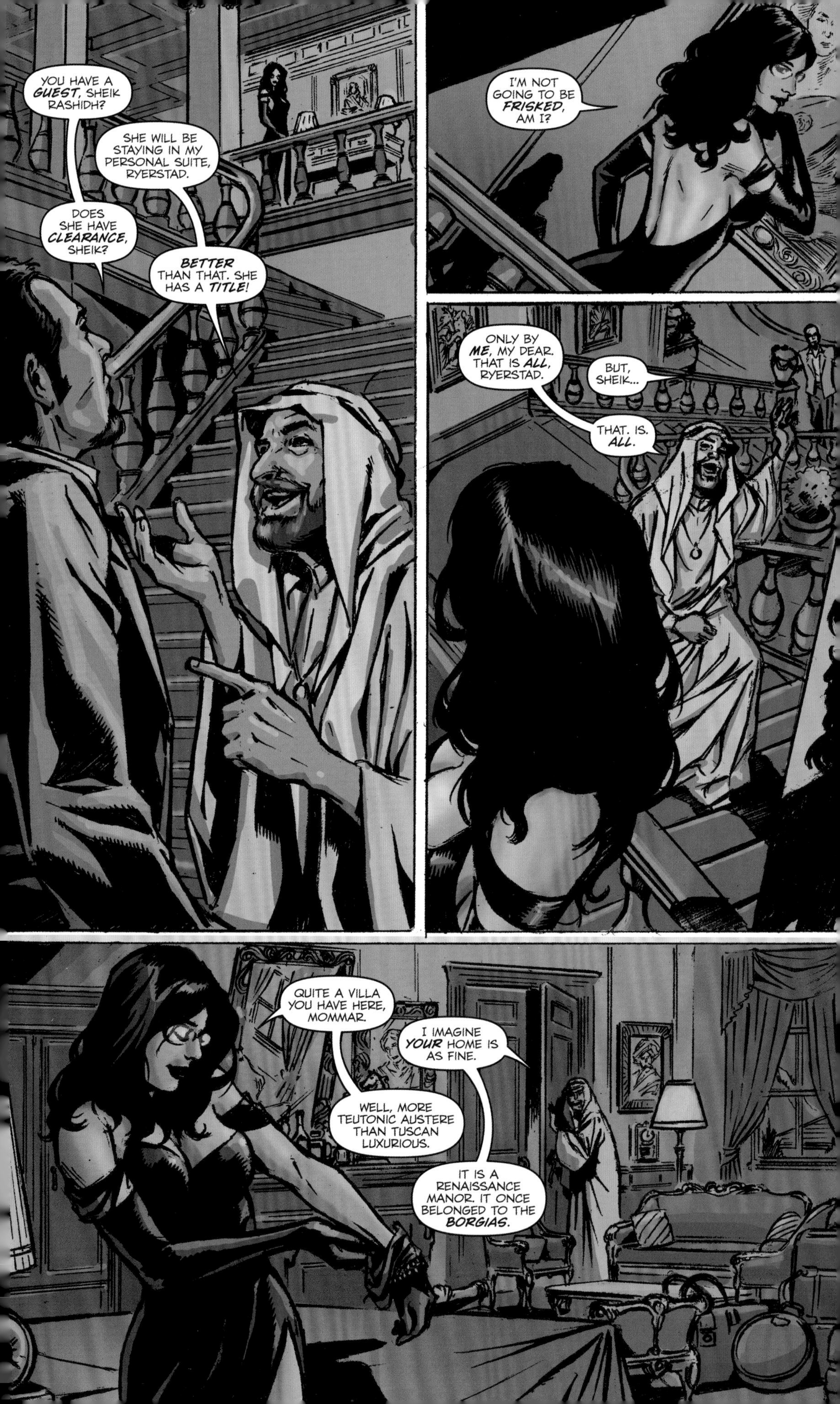

YOU HAVE A GUEST, SHEIK RASHIDH?
SHE WILL BE STAYING IN MY PERSONAL SUITE, RYERSTAD.
DOES SHE HAVE CLEARANCE, SHEIK?
BETTER THAN THAT. SHE HAS A TITLE!
I'M NOT GOING TO BE FRISKED, AM I?
ONLY BY ME, MY DEAR. THAT IS ALL, RYERSTAD.
BUT, SHEIK...
THAT. IS. ALL.
QUITE A VILLA YOU HAVE HERE, MOMMAR.
I IMAGINE YOUR HOME IS AS FINE.
WELL, MORE TEUTONIC AUSTERE THAN TUSCAN LUXURIOUS.
IT IS A RENAISSANCE MANOR. IT ONCE BELONGED TO THE BORGIAS.

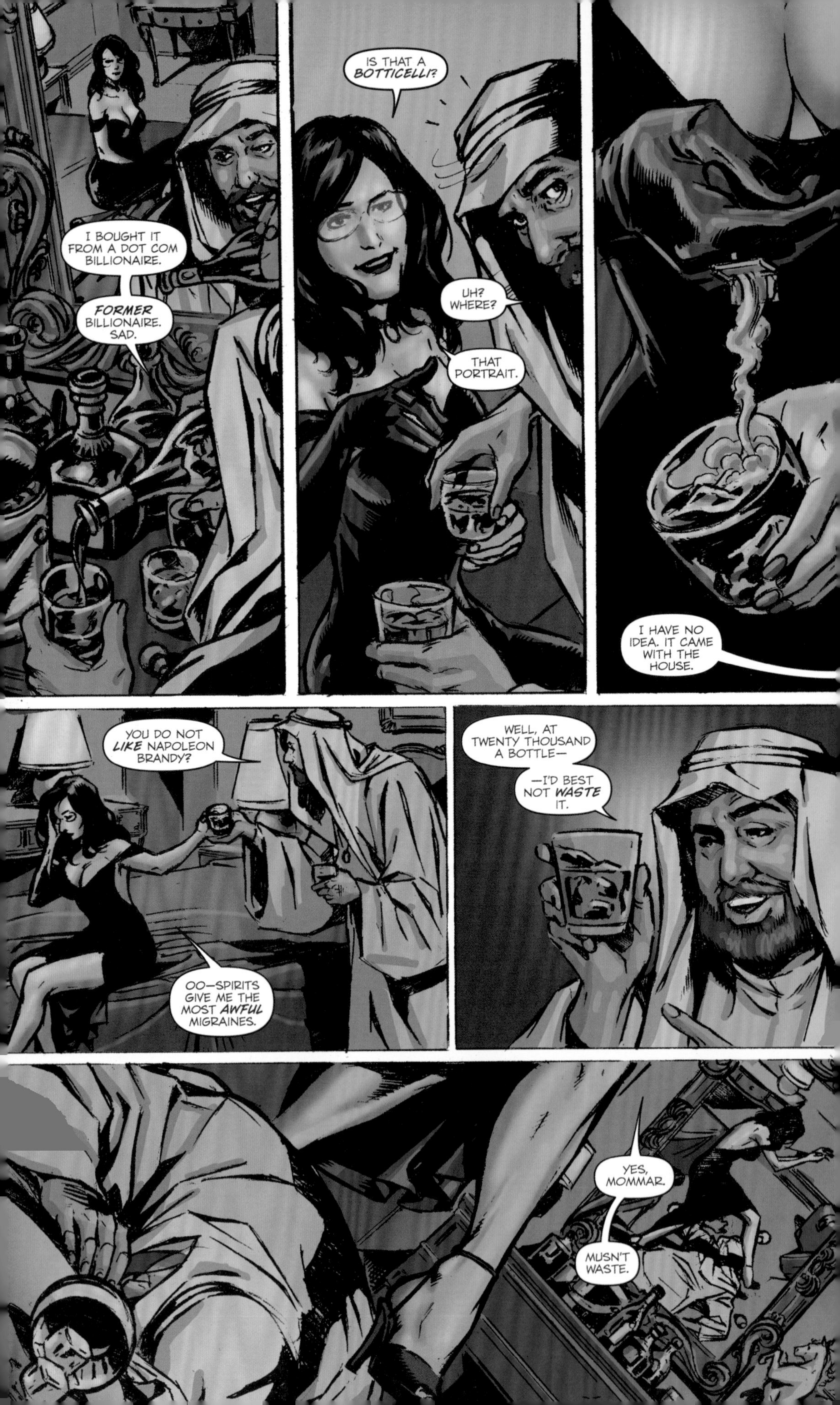
I BOUGHT IT FROM A DOT COM BILLIONAIRE.
FORMER BILLIONAIRE. SAD.
IS THAT A BOTTICELLI?
UH? WHERE?
THAT PORTRAIT.
I HAVE NO IDEA. IT CAME WITH THE HOUSE.
YOU DO NOT LIKE NAPOLEON BRANDY?
OO—SPIRITS GIVE ME THE MOST AWFUL MIGRAINES.
WELL, AT TWENTY THOUSAND A BOTTLE—
—I'D BEST NOT WASTE IT.
YES, MOMMAR.
MUSN'T WASTE.

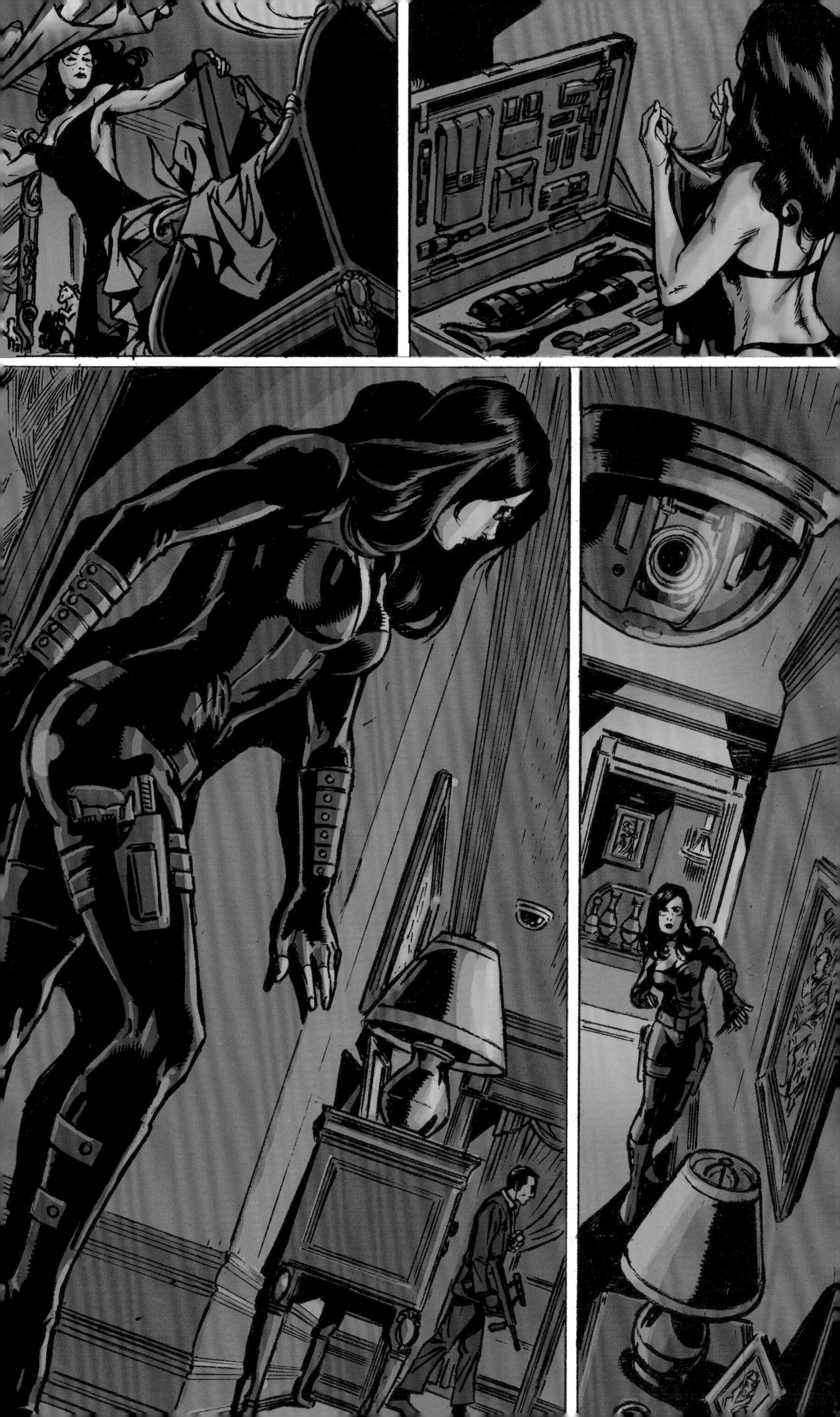

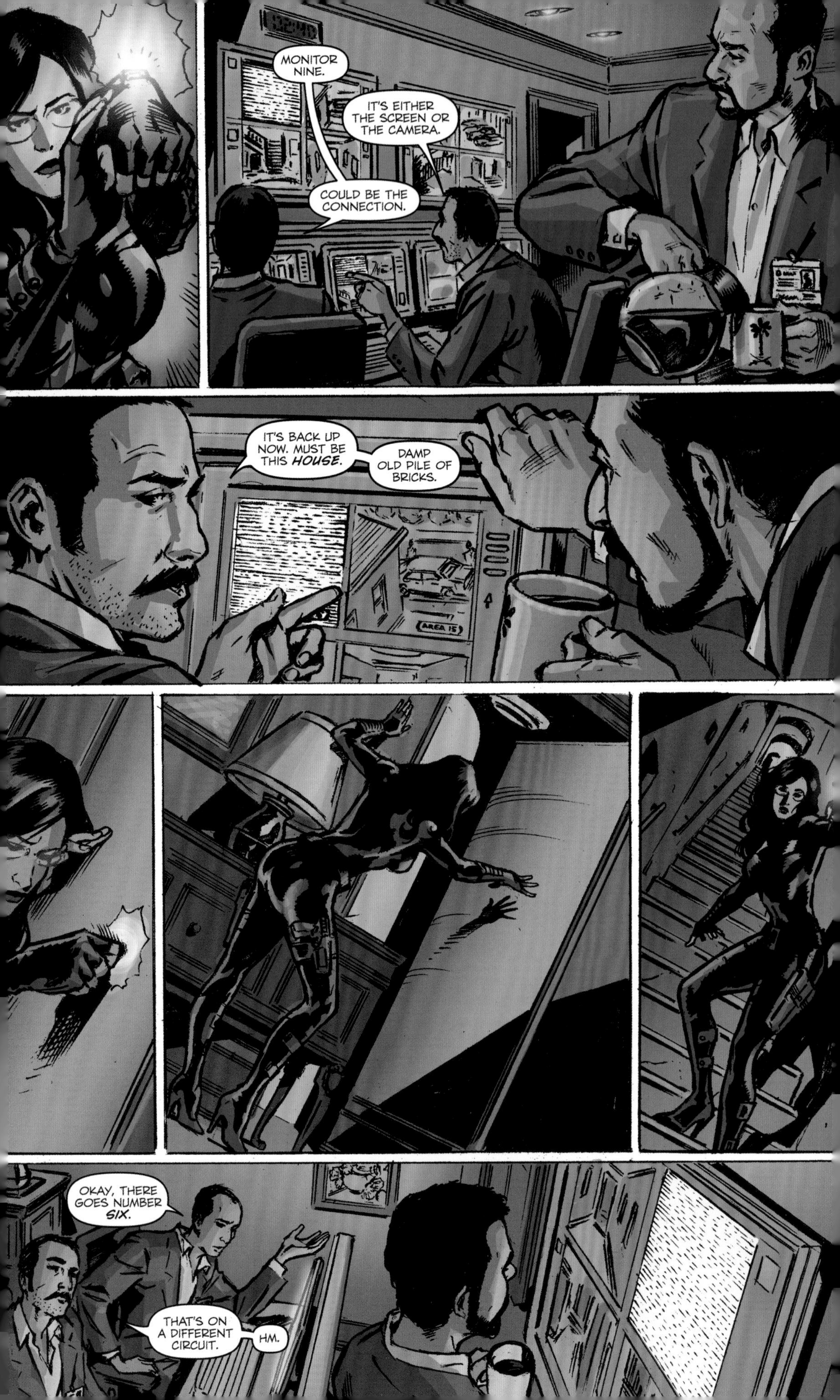
MONITOR NINE.
IT'S EITHER THE SCREEN OR THE CAMERA.
COULD BE THE CONNECTION.
IT'S BACK UP NOW. MUST BE THIS HOUSE.
DAMP OLD PILE OF BRICKS.
AREA 15
OKAY, THERE GOES NUMBER SIX.
THAT'S ON A DIFFERENT CIRCUIT.
HM.

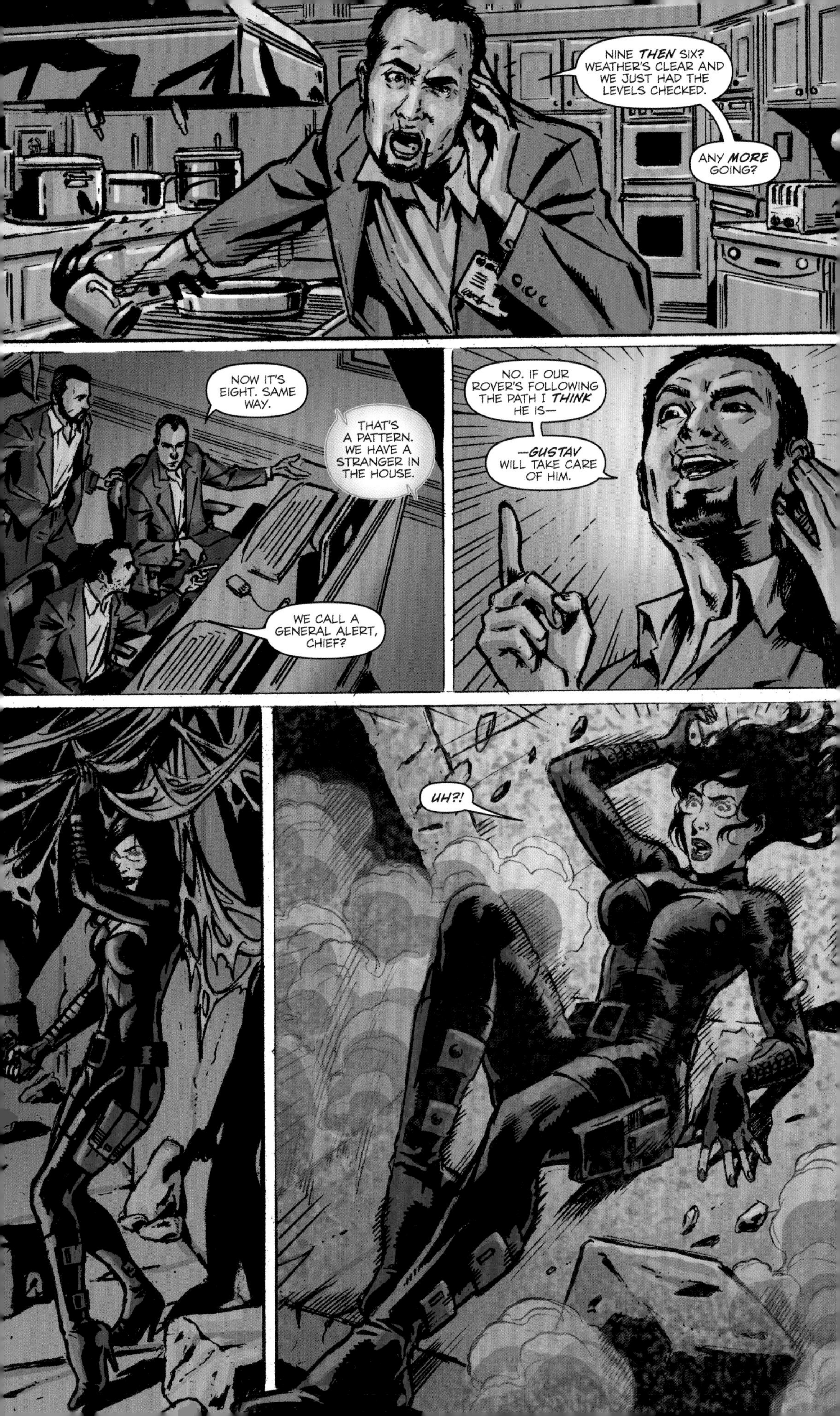
NINE THEN SIX? WEATHER'S CLEAR AND WE JUST HAD THE LEVELS CHECKED.
ANY MORE GOING?
NOW IT'S EIGHT. SAME WAY.
THAT'S A PATTERN. WE HAVE A STRANGER IN THE HOUSE.
WE CALL A GENERAL ALERT, CHIEF?
NO. IF OUR ROVER'S FOLLOWING THE PATH I THINK HE IS—
—GUSTAV WILL TAKE CARE OF HIM.
UH?!

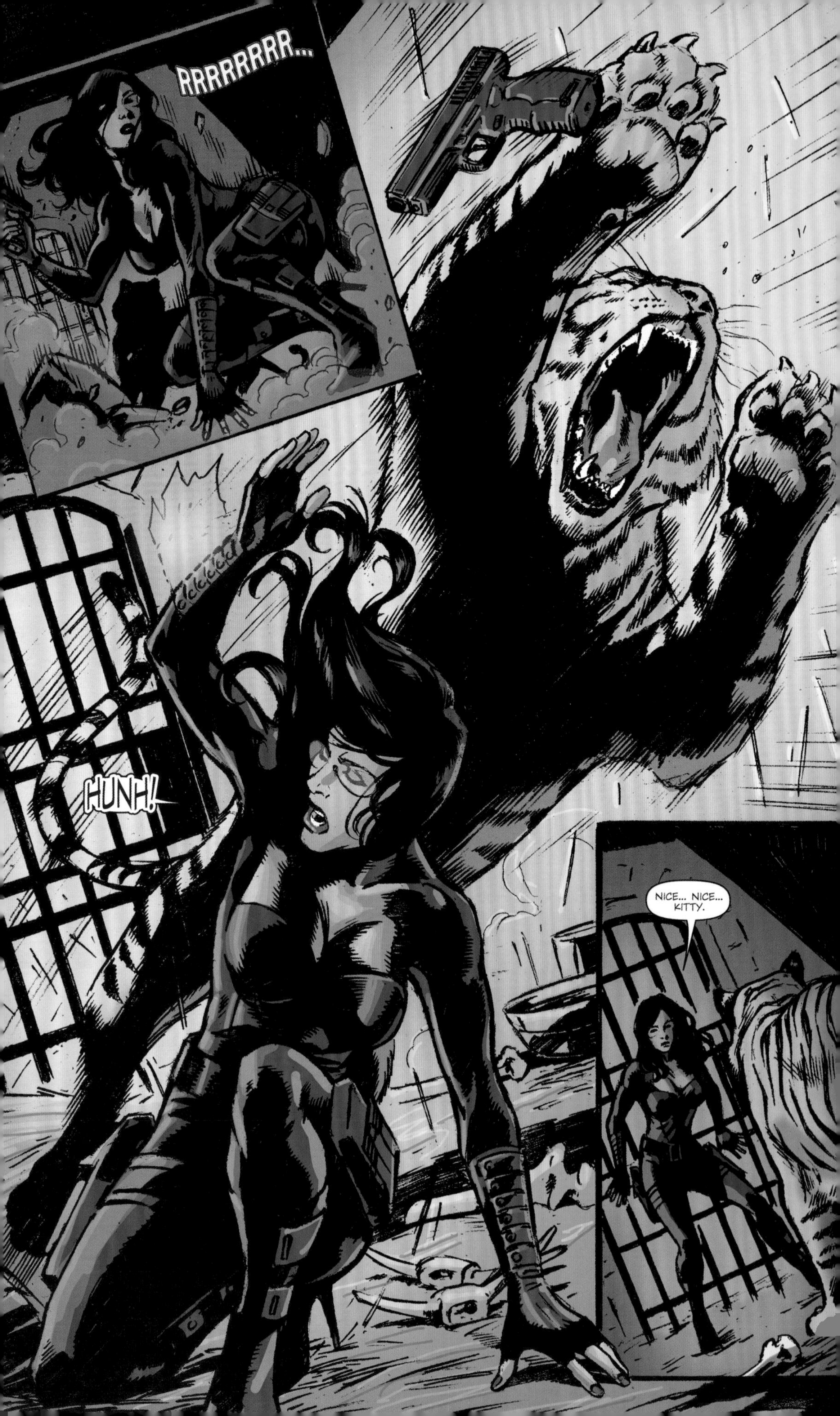
RRRRRRRR...
HUNH!
NICE... NICE... KITTY.

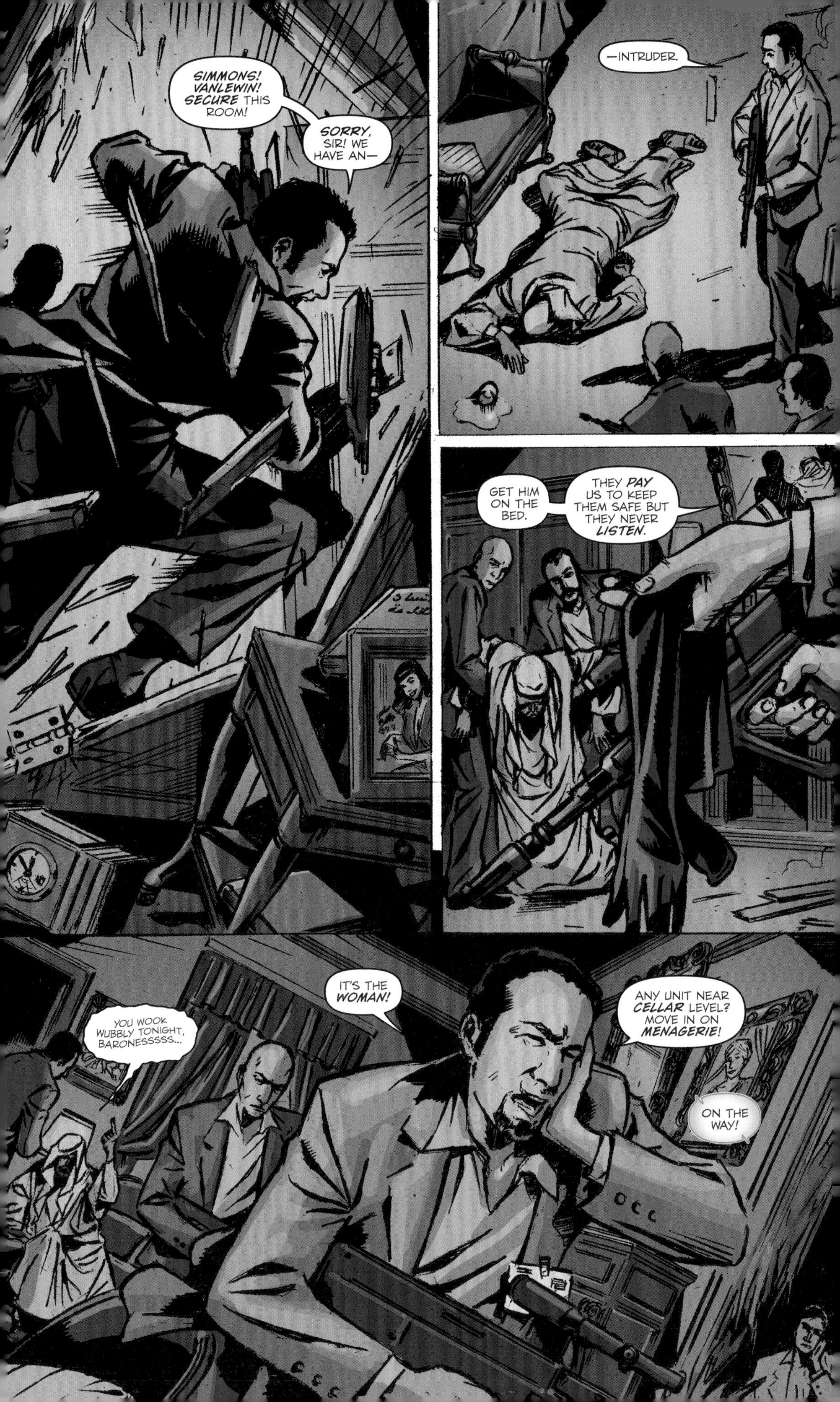
SIMMONS! VANLEWIN! SECURE THIS ROOM!
SORRY, SIR! WE HAVE AN—
—INTRUDER.
GET HIM ON THE BED.
THEY PAY US TO KEEP THEM SAFE BUT THEY NEVER LISTEN.
YOU WOOK WUBBLY TONIGHT, BARONESSSSS...
IT'S THE WOMAN!
ANY UNIT NEAR CELLAR LEVEL? MOVE IN ON MENAGERIE!
ON THE WAY!

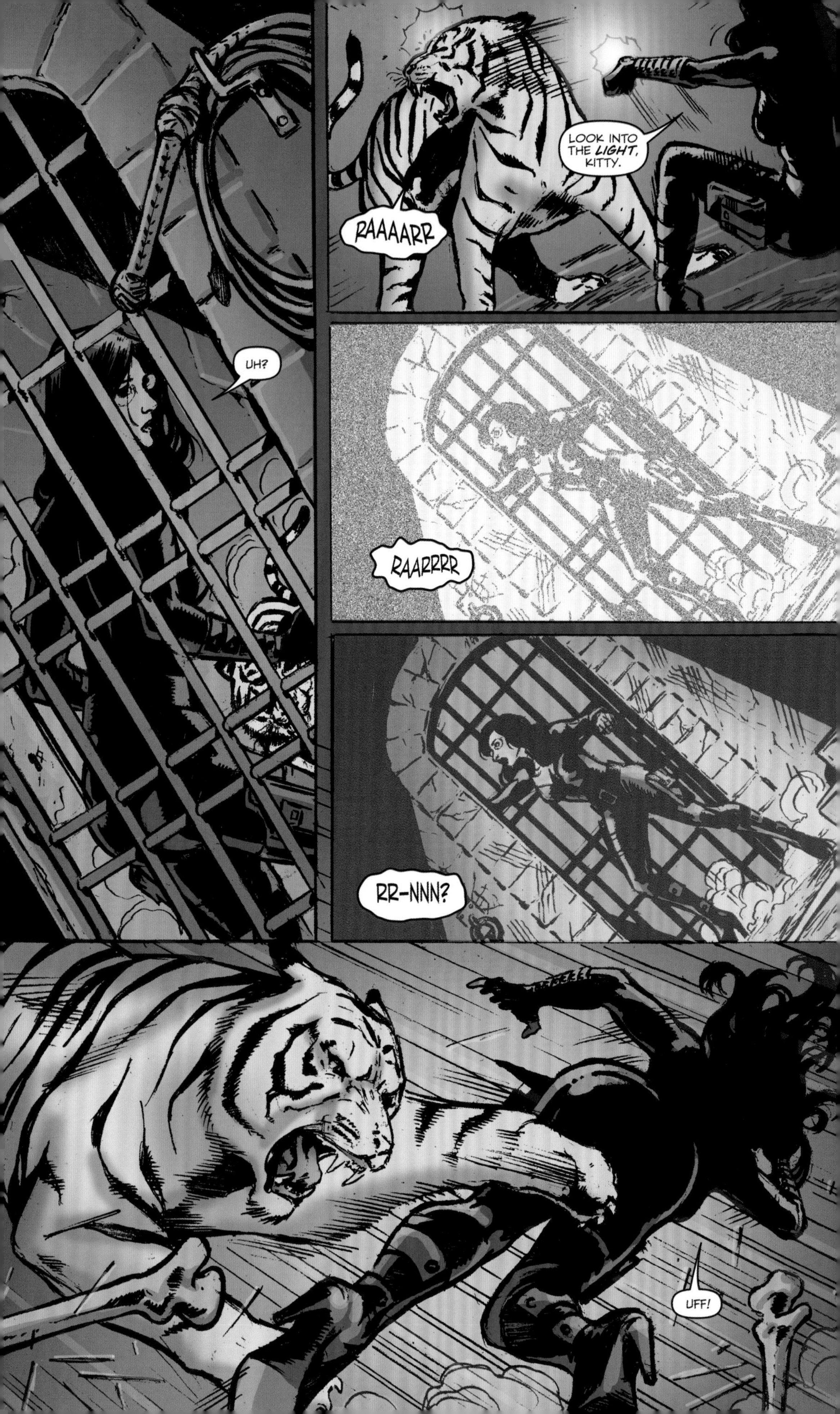

LOOK INTO THE LIGHT, KITTY.
RAAAARR
UH?
RAARRRR
RR-NNN?
UFF!

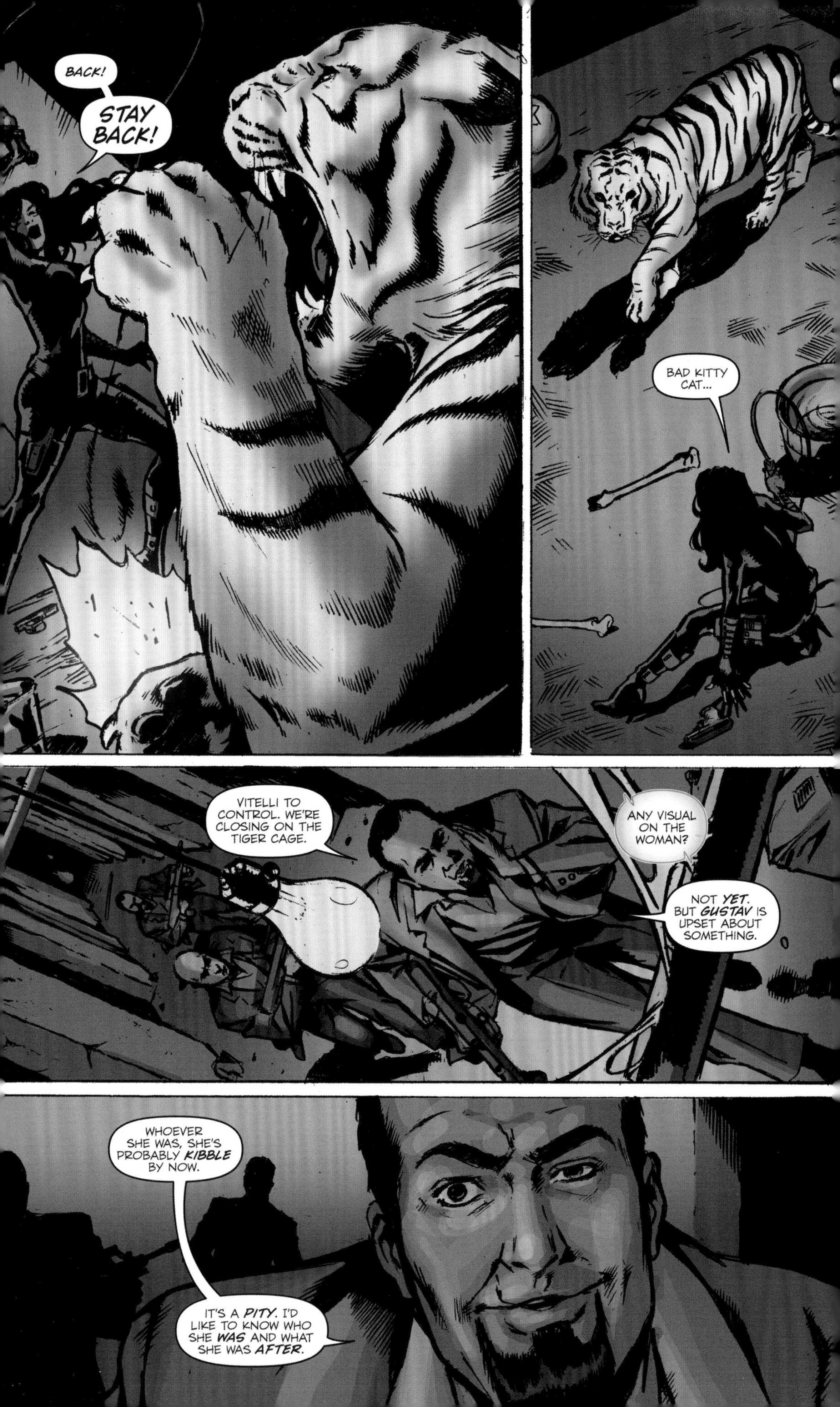
BACK!
STAY BACK!
BAD KITTY CAT...
VITELLI TO CONTROL. WE'RE CLOSING ON THE TIGER CAGE.
ANY VISUAL ON THE WOMAN?
NOT YET. BUT GUSTAV IS UPSET ABOUT SOMETHING.
WHOEVER SHE WAS, SHE'S PROBABLY KIBBLE BY NOW.
IT'S A PITY. I'D LIKE TO KNOW WHO SHE WAS AND WHAT SHE WAS AFTER.

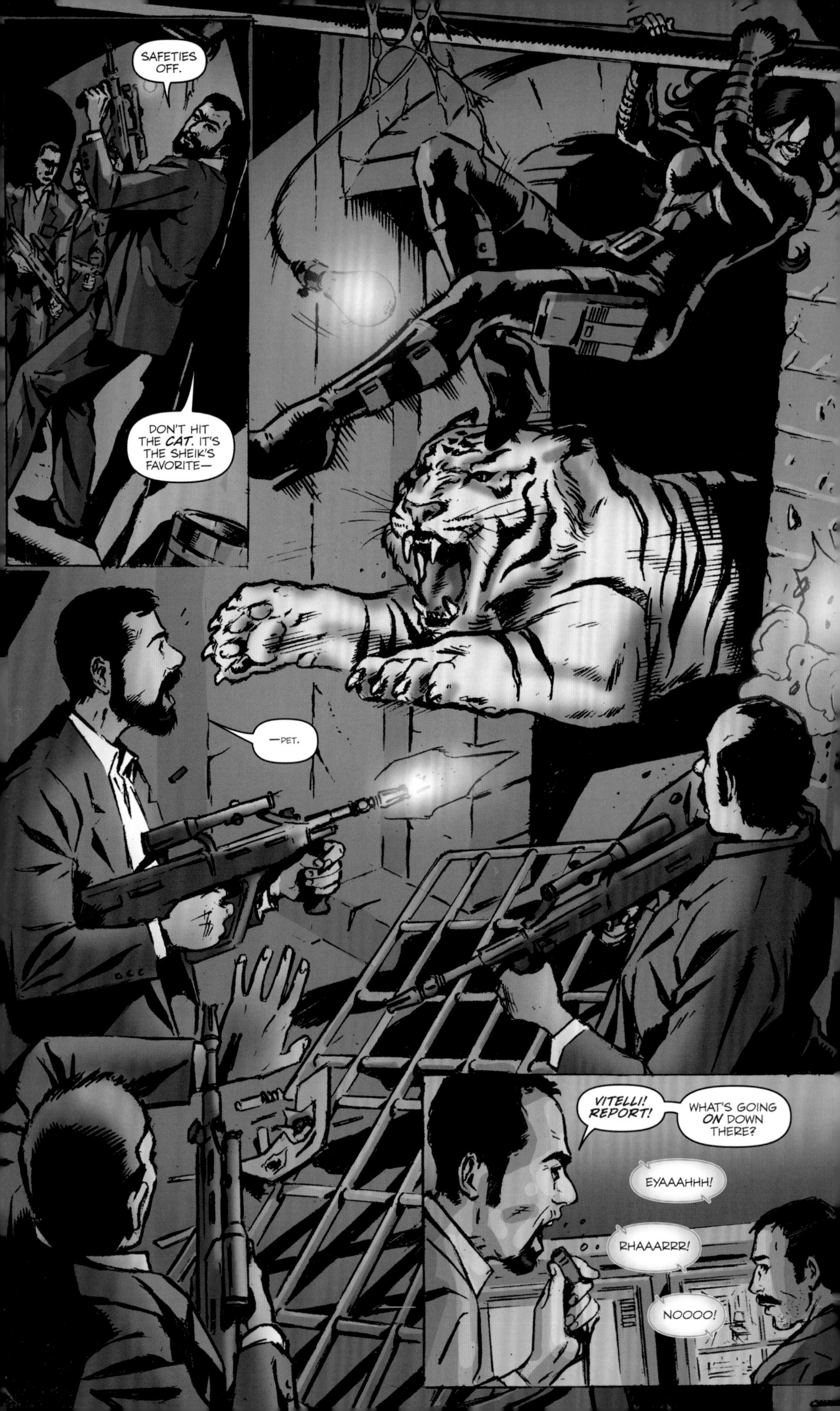
SAFETIES OFF.
DON'T HIT THE CAT. IT'S THE SHEIK'S FAVORITE—
—PET.
VITELLI! REPORT!
WHAT'S GOING ON DOWN THERE?
EYAAAHHH!
RHAAARRR!
NOOOO!

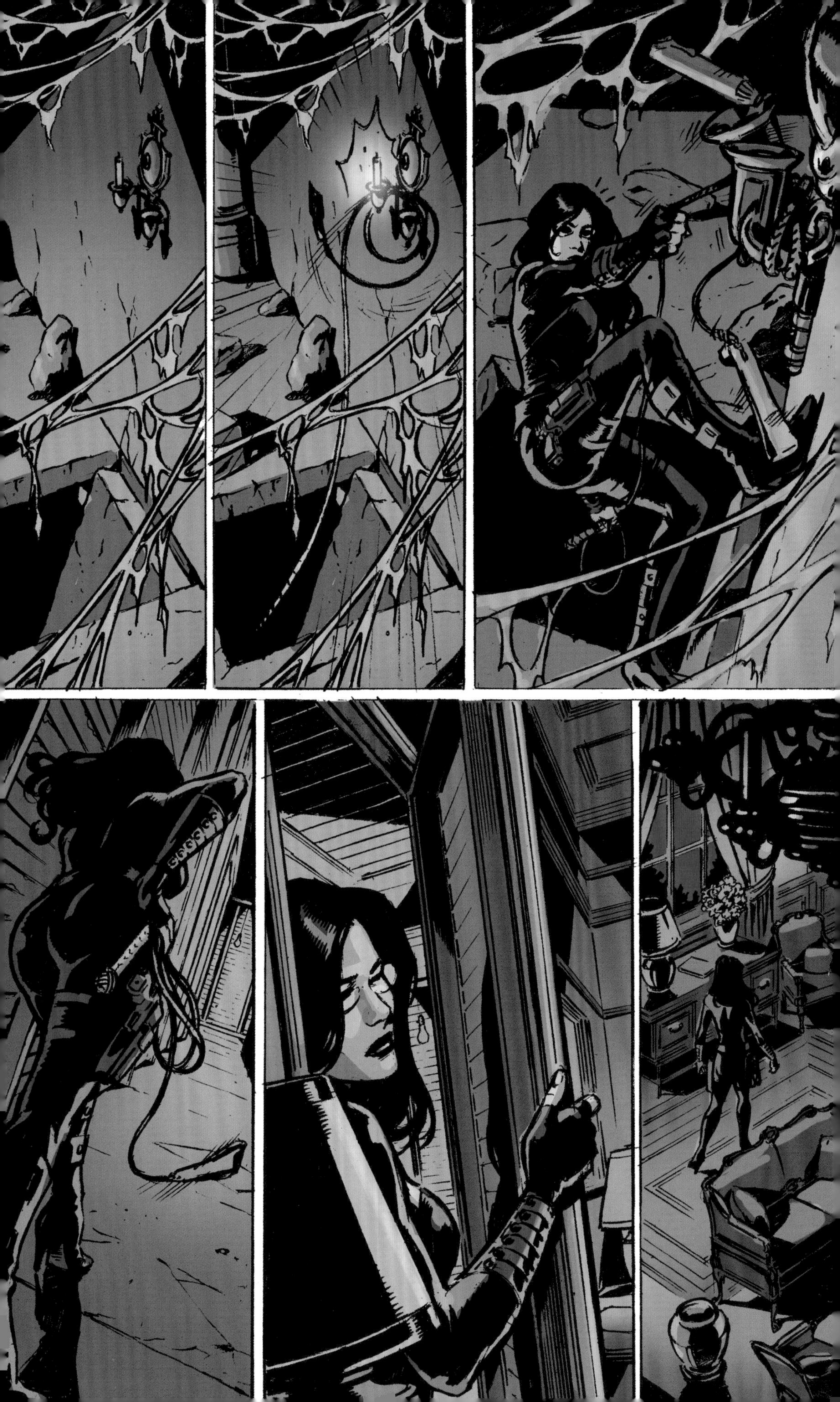

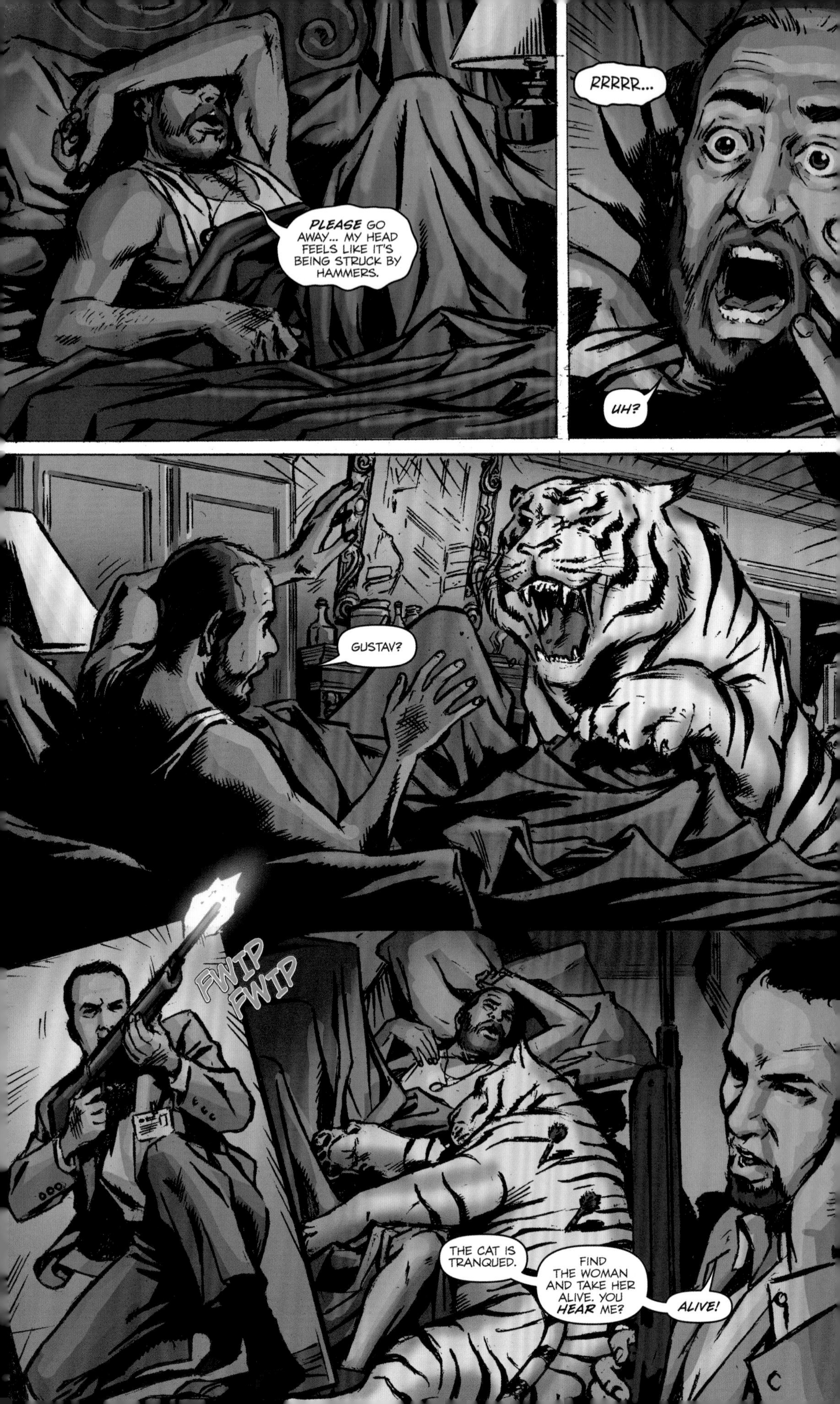
PLEASE GO AWAY... MY HEAD FEELS LIKE IT'S BEING STRUCK BY HAMMERS.
RRRRR...
UH?
GUSTAV?
FWIP FWIP
THE CAT IS TRANQUED.
FIND THE WOMAN AND TAKE HER ALIVE. YOU HEAR ME?
ALIVE!

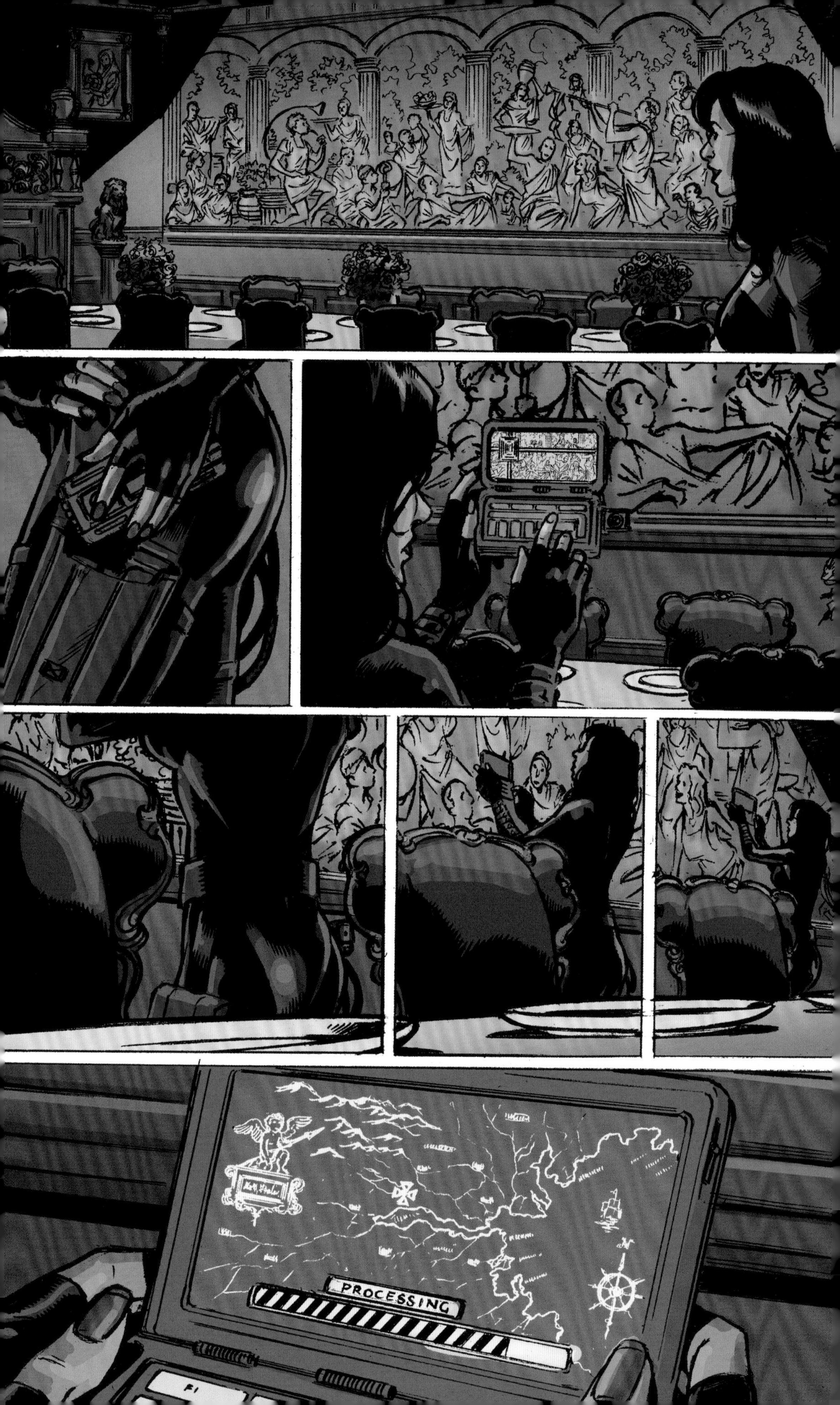
PROCESSING
F1

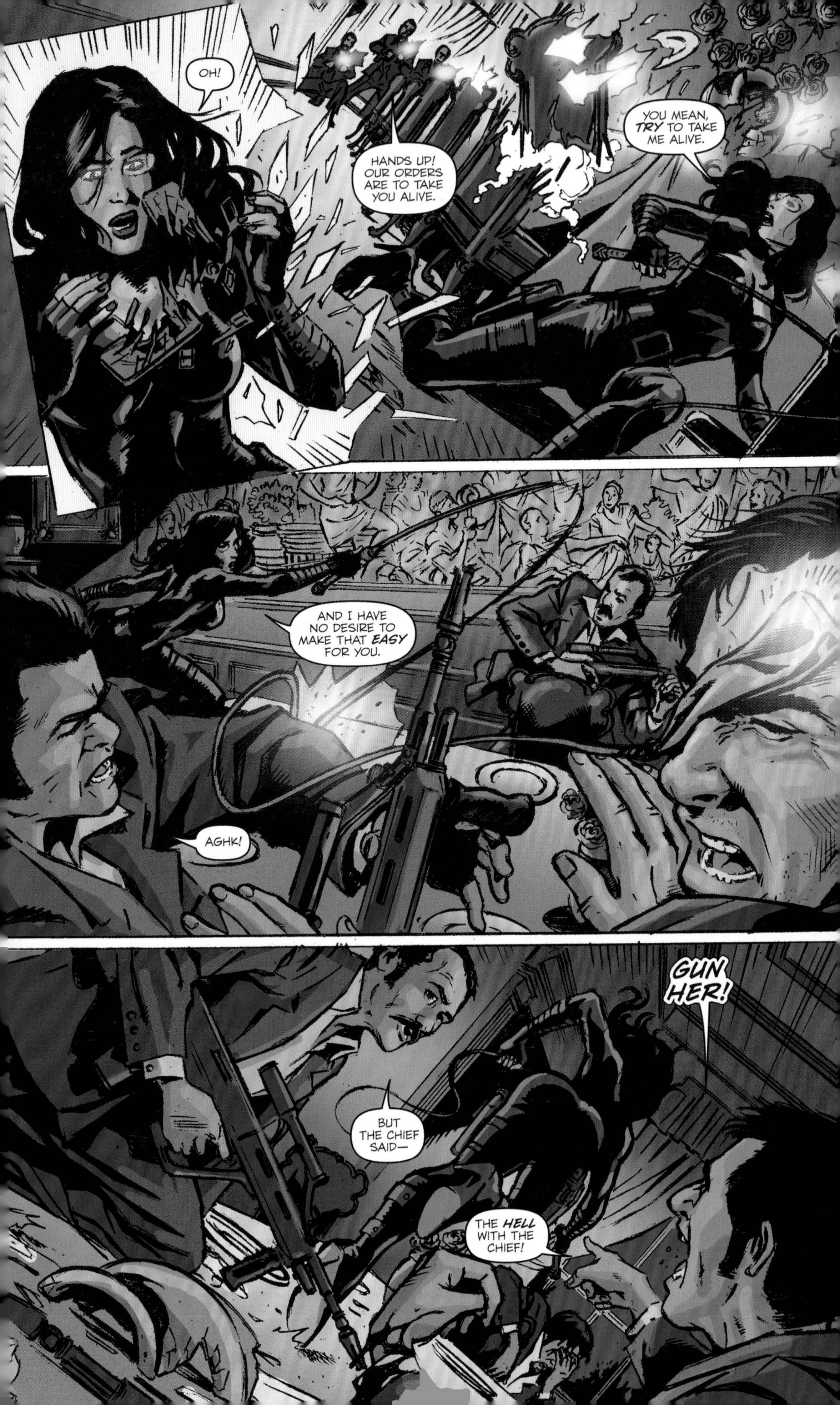
OH!
HANDS UP! OUR ORDERS ARE TO TAKE YOU ALIVE.
YOU MEAN, TRY TO TAKE ME ALIVE.
AND I HAVE NO DESIRE TO MAKE THAT EASY FOR YOU.
AGHK!
GUN HER!
BUT THE CHIEF SAID—
THE HELL WITH THE CHIEF!

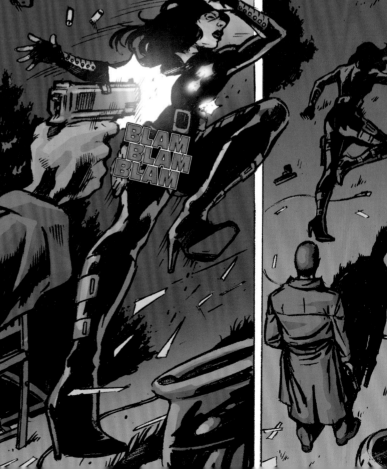

BLAM
BLAM
BLAM

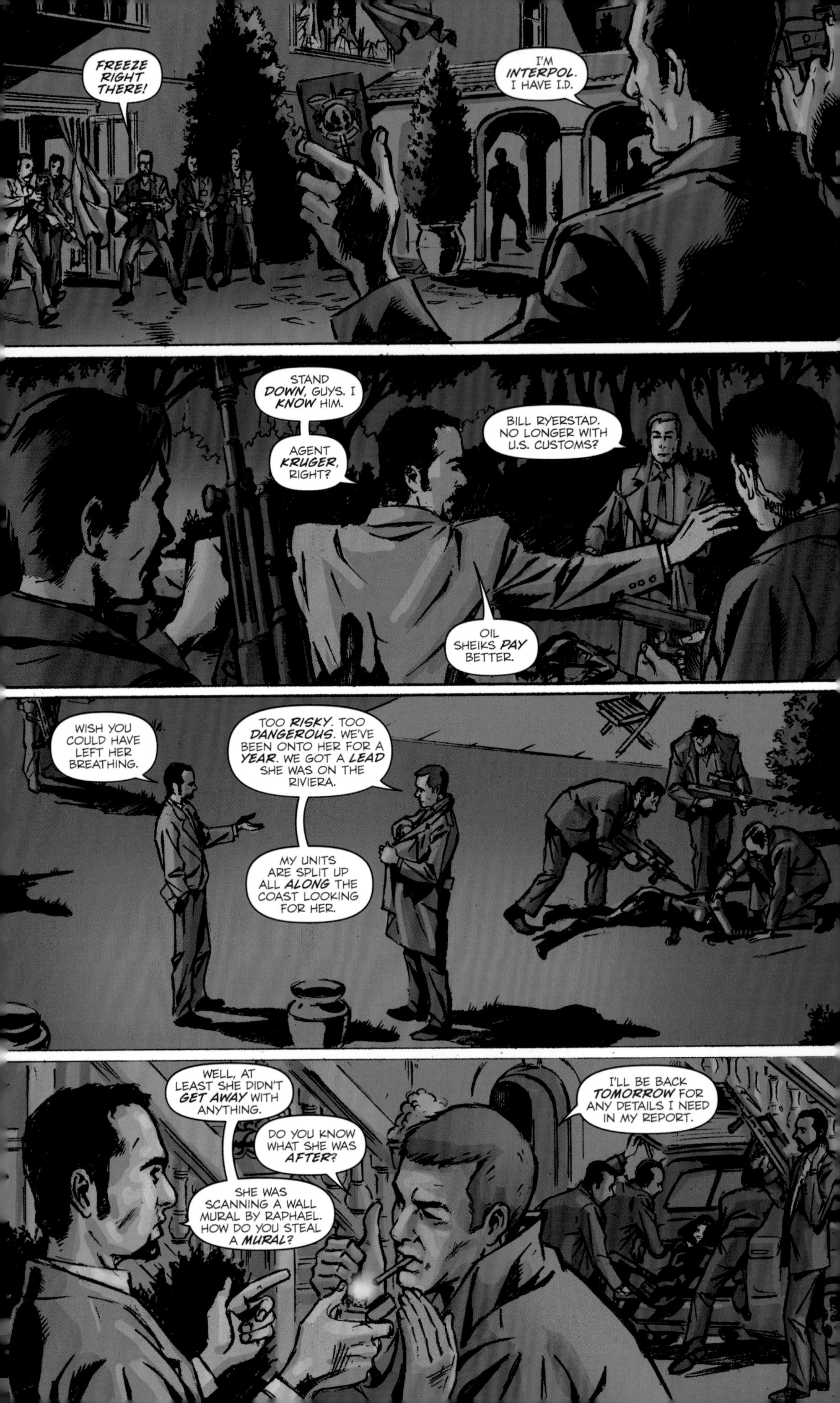

FREEZE RIGHT THERE!
I'M INTERPOL. I HAVE I.D.
STAND DOWN, GUYS. I KNOW HIM.
AGENT KRUGER, RIGHT?
BILL RYERSTAD. NO LONGER WITH U.S. CUSTOMS?
OIL SHEIKS PAY BETTER.
WISH YOU COULD HAVE LEFT HER BREATHING.
TOO RISKY. TOO DANGEROUS. WE'VE BEEN ONTO HER FOR A YEAR. WE GOT A LEAD SHE WAS ON THE RIVIERA.
MY UNITS ARE SPLIT UP ALL ALONG THE COAST LOOKING FOR HER.
WELL, AT LEAST SHE DIDN'T GET AWAY WITH ANYTHING.
DO YOU KNOW WHAT SHE WAS AFTER?
SHE WAS SCANNING A WALL MURAL BY RAPHAEL. HOW DO YOU STEAL A MURAL?
I'LL BE BACK TOMORROW FOR ANY DETAILS I NEED IN MY REPORT.

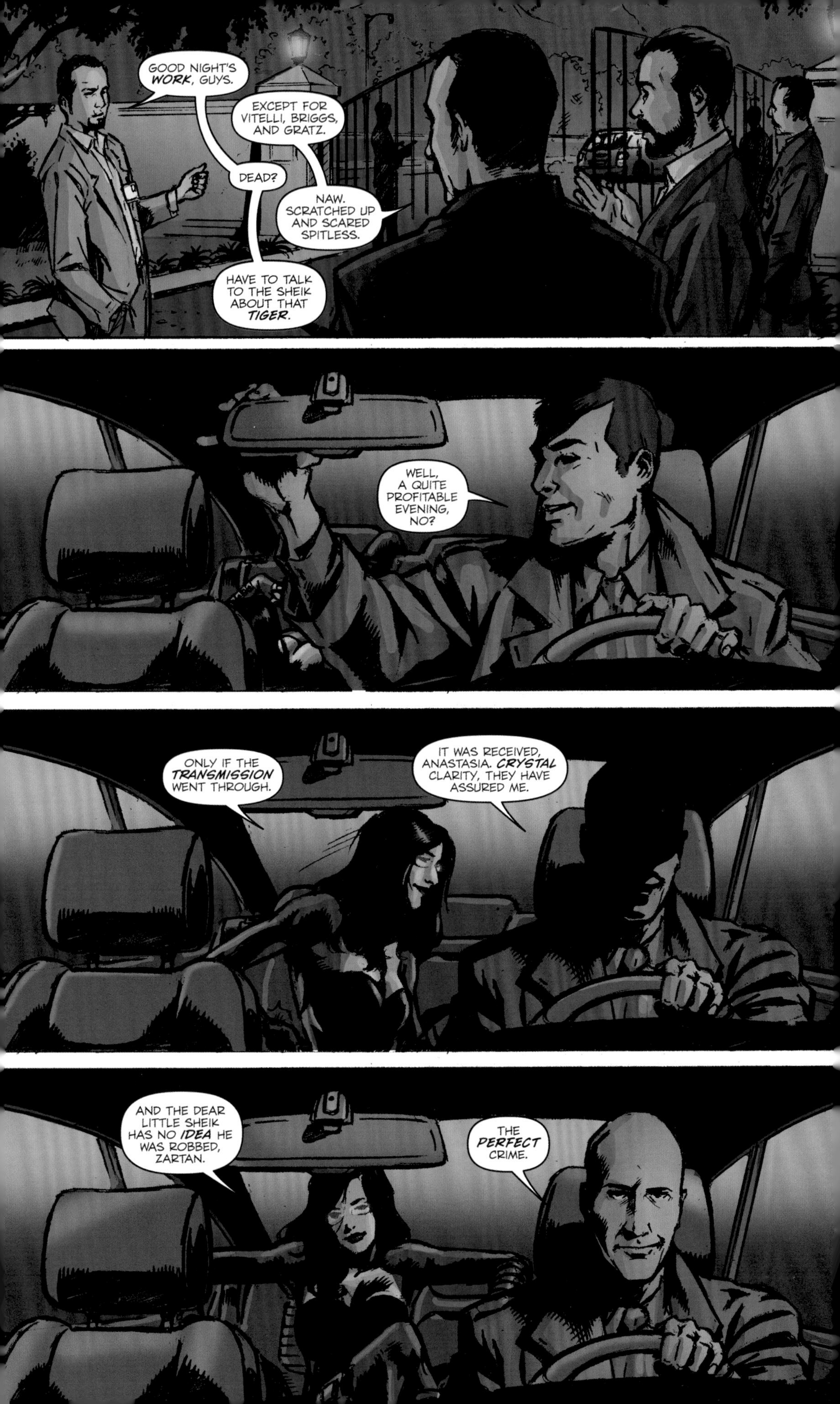
GOOD NIGHT'S *WORK*, GUYS.
EXCEPT FOR VITELLI, BRIGGS, AND GRATZ.
DEAD?
NAW. SCRATCHED UP AND SCARED SPITLESS.
HAVE TO TALK TO THE SHEIK ABOUT THAT *TIGER*.
WELL, A QUITE PROFITABLE EVENING, NO?
ONLY IF THE *TRANSMISSION* WENT THROUGH.
IT WAS RECEIVED, ANASTASIA. *CRYSTAL* CLARITY, THEY HAVE ASSURED ME.
AND THE DEAR LITTLE SHEIK HAS NO *IDEA* HE WAS ROBBED, ZARTAN.
THE *PERFECT* CRIME.

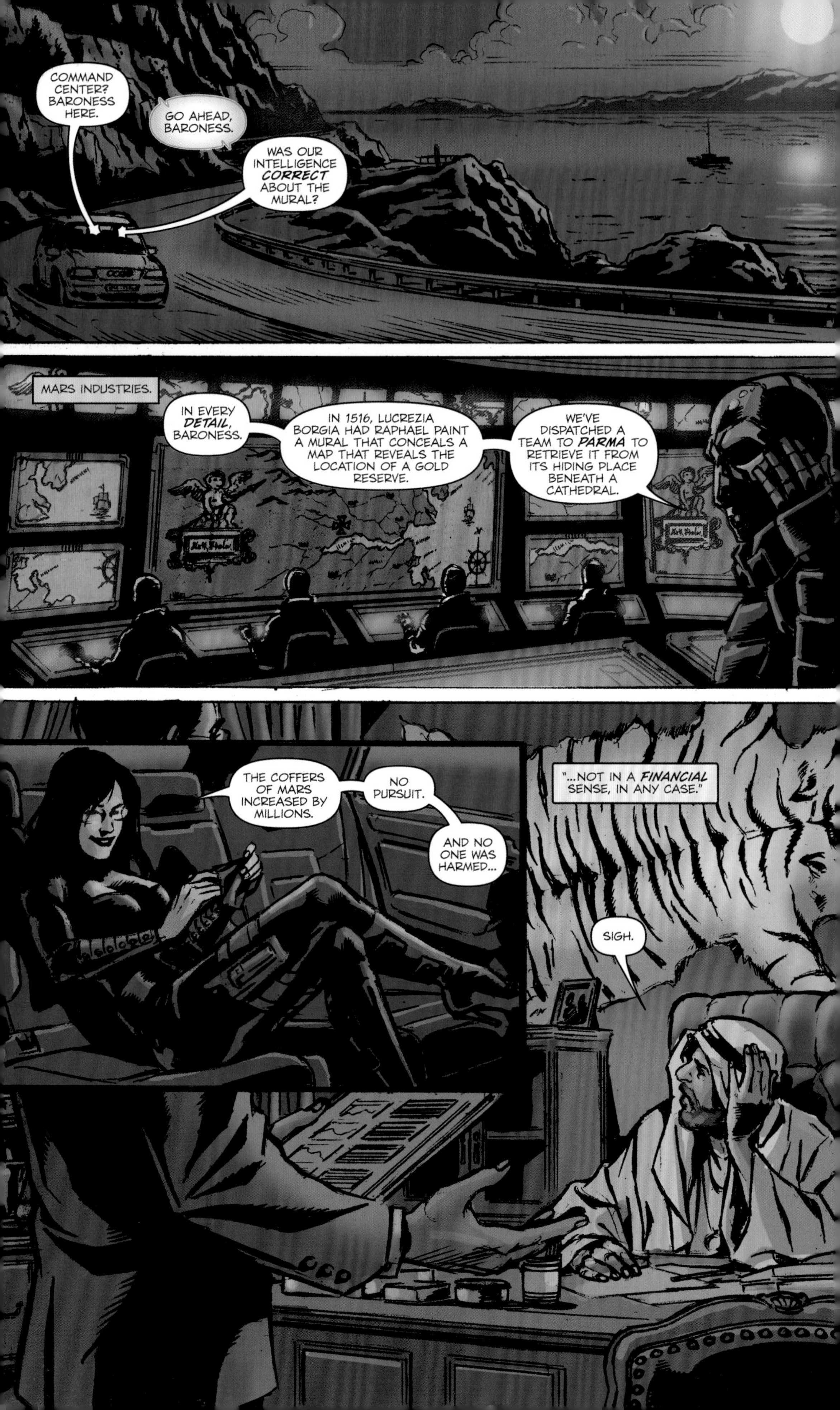
COMMAND CENTER? BARONESS HERE.
GO AHEAD, BARONESS.
WAS OUR INTELLIGENCE CORRECT ABOUT THE MURAL?
MARS INDUSTRIES.
IN EVERY DETAIL, BARONESS.
IN 1516, LUCREZIA BORGIA HAD RAPHAEL PAINT A MURAL THAT CONCEALS A MAP THAT REVEALS THE LOCATION OF A GOLD RESERVE.
WE'VE DISPATCHED A TEAM TO PARMA TO RETRIEVE IT FROM ITS HIDING PLACE BENEATH A CATHEDRAL.
THE COFFERS OF MARS INCREASED BY MILLIONS.
NO PURSUIT.
AND NO ONE WAS HARMED...
"...NOT IN A FINANCIAL SENSE, IN ANY CASE."
SIGH.

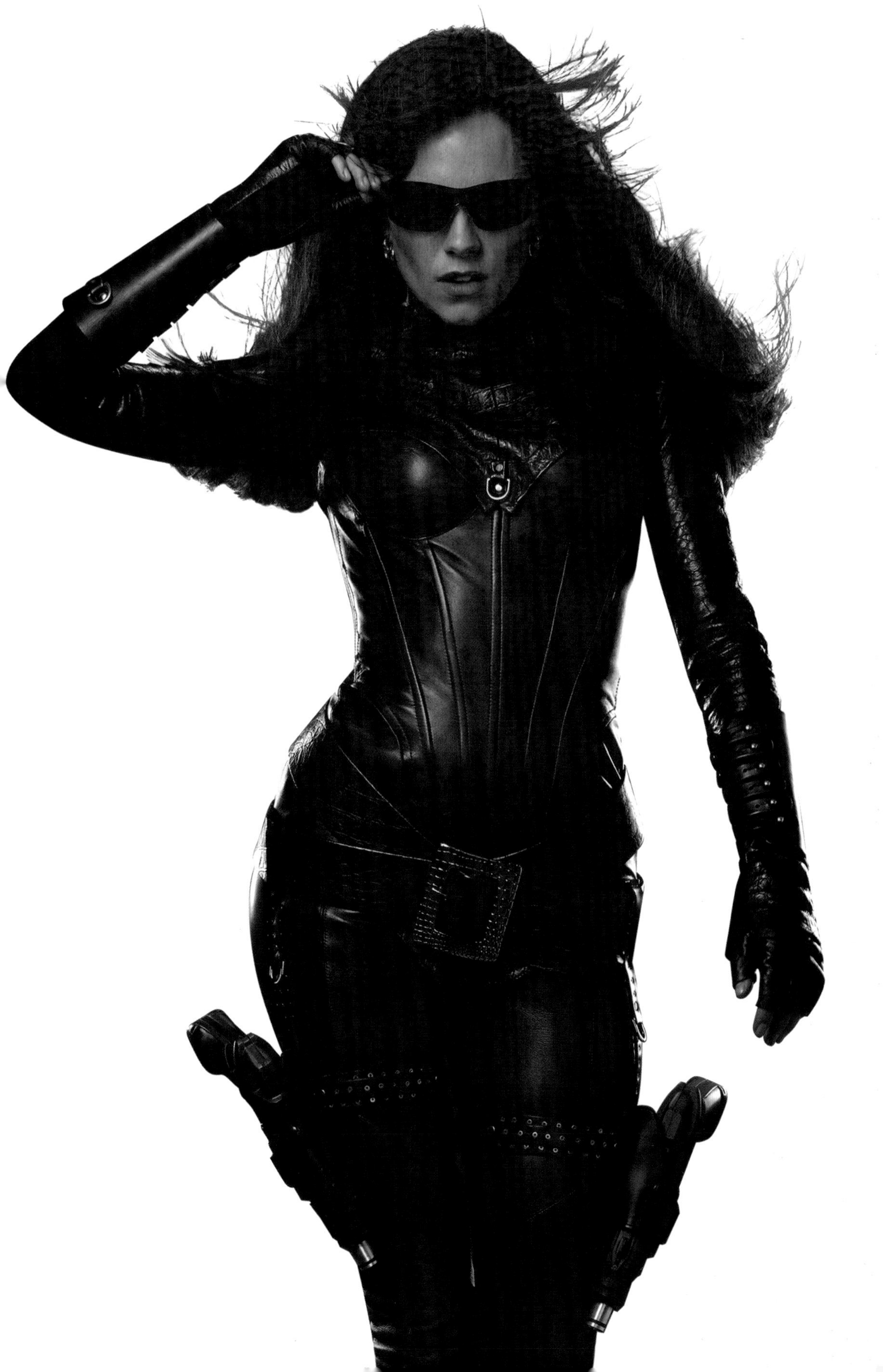

CHAPTER FOUR

ARTWORK B
JOE CORRONEY

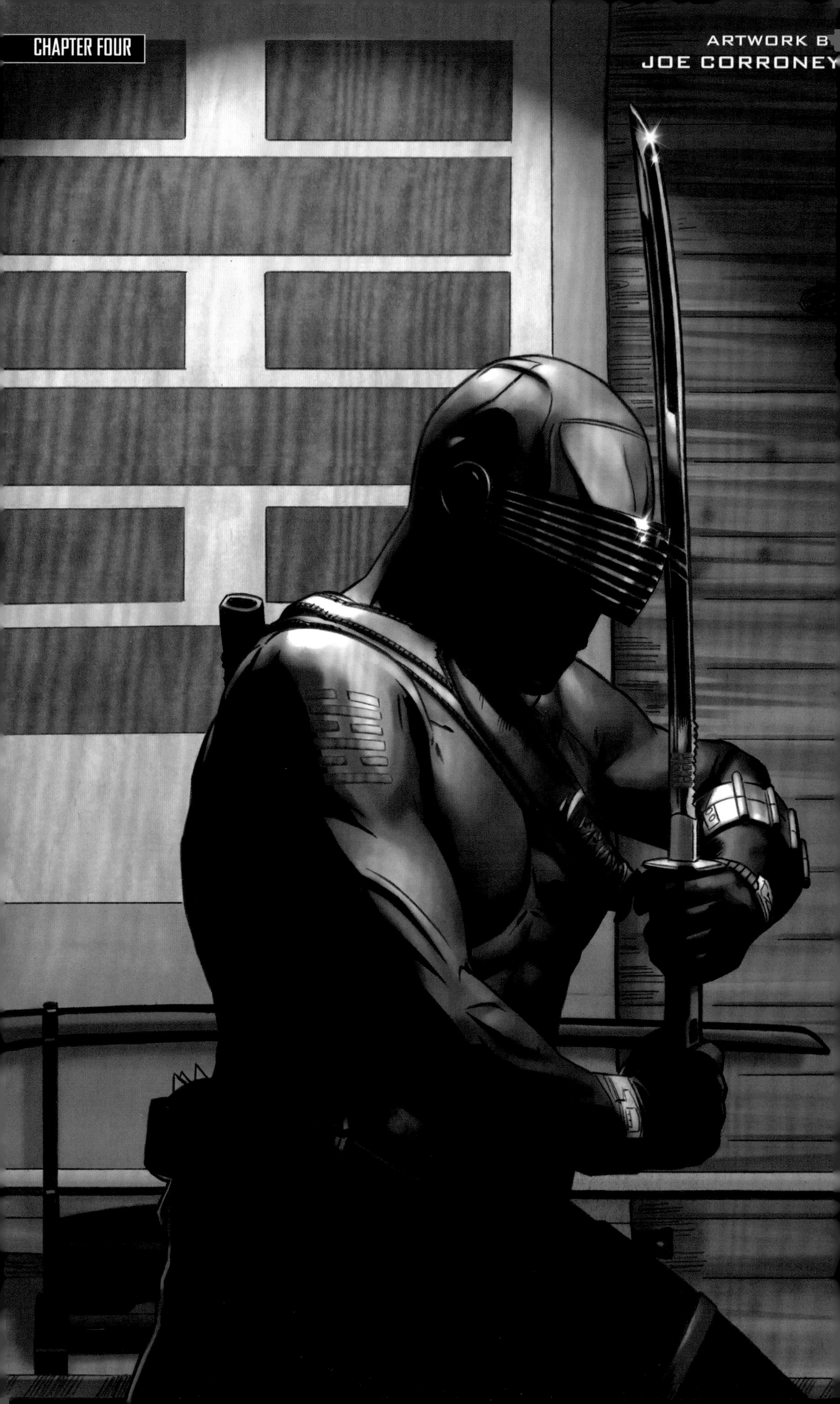

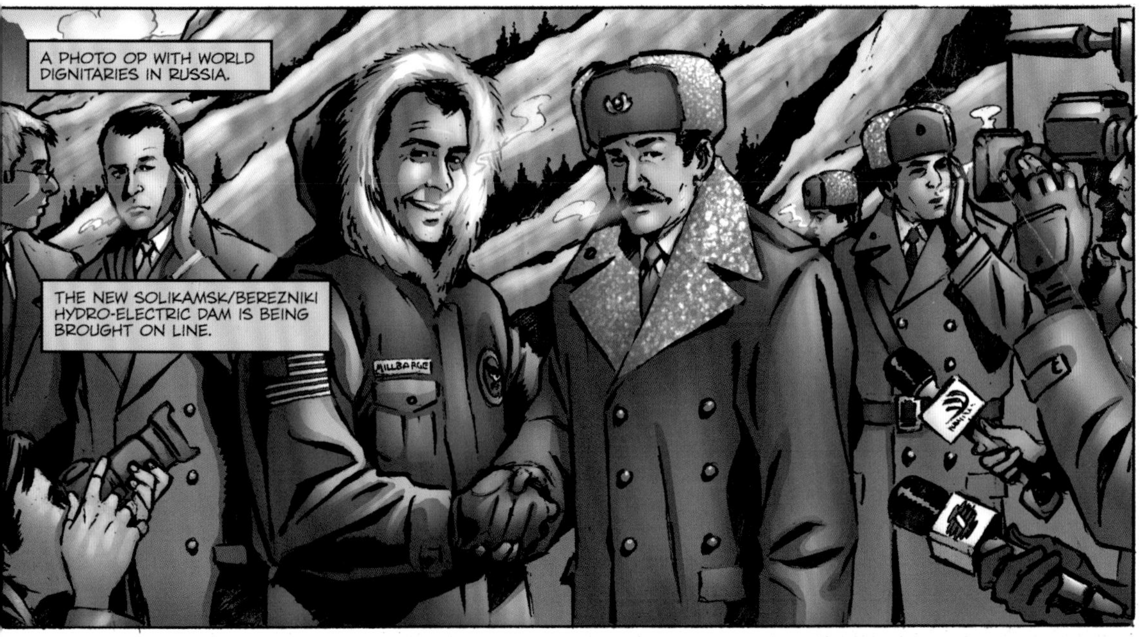
A PHOTO OP WITH WORLD DIGNITARIES IN RUSSIA.
THE NEW SOLIKAMSK/BEREZNIKI HYDRO-ELECTRIC DAM IS BEING BROUGHT ON LINE.

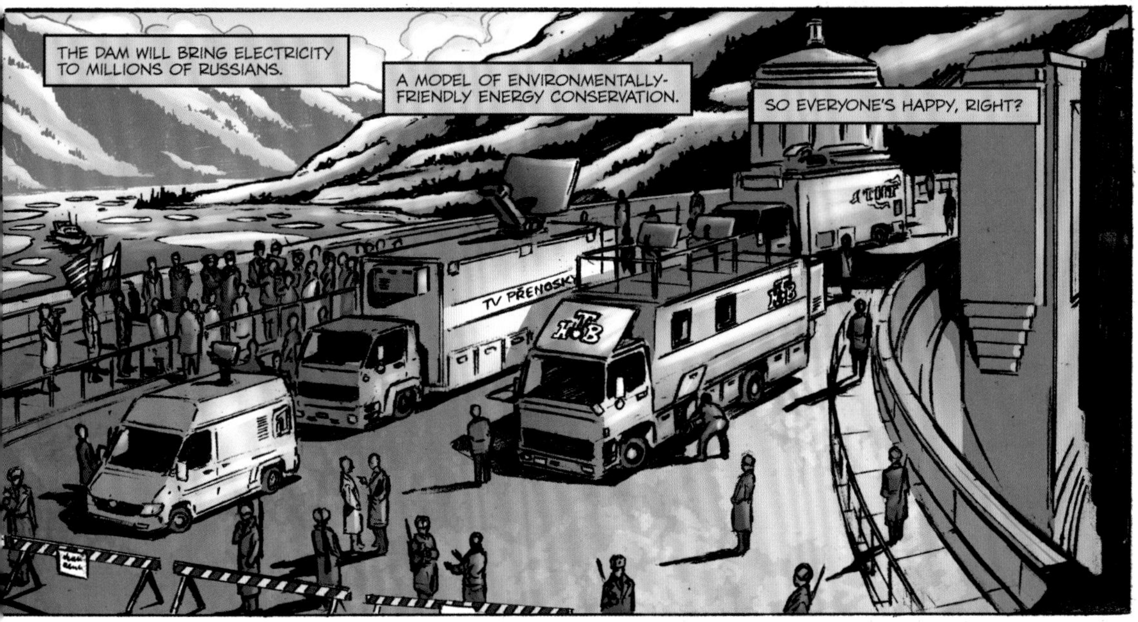
THE DAM WILL BRING ELECTRICITY TO MILLIONS OF RUSSIANS.
A MODEL OF ENVIRONMENTALLY-FRIENDLY ENERGY CONSERVATION.
SO EVERYONE'S HAPPY, RIGHT?
TV PŘENOSKY

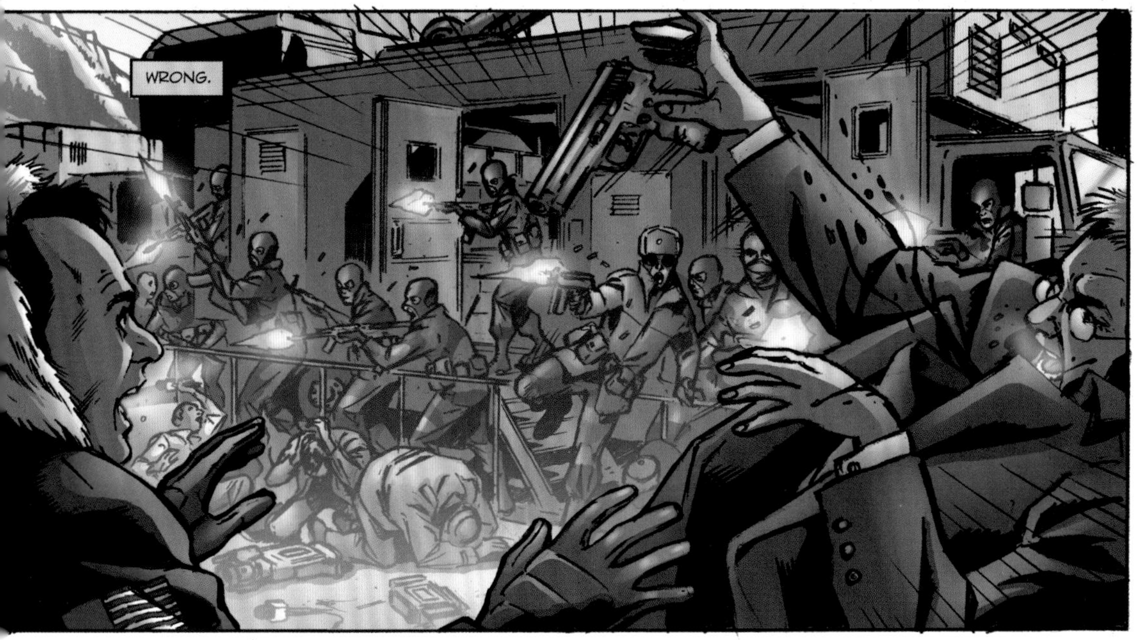
WRONG.

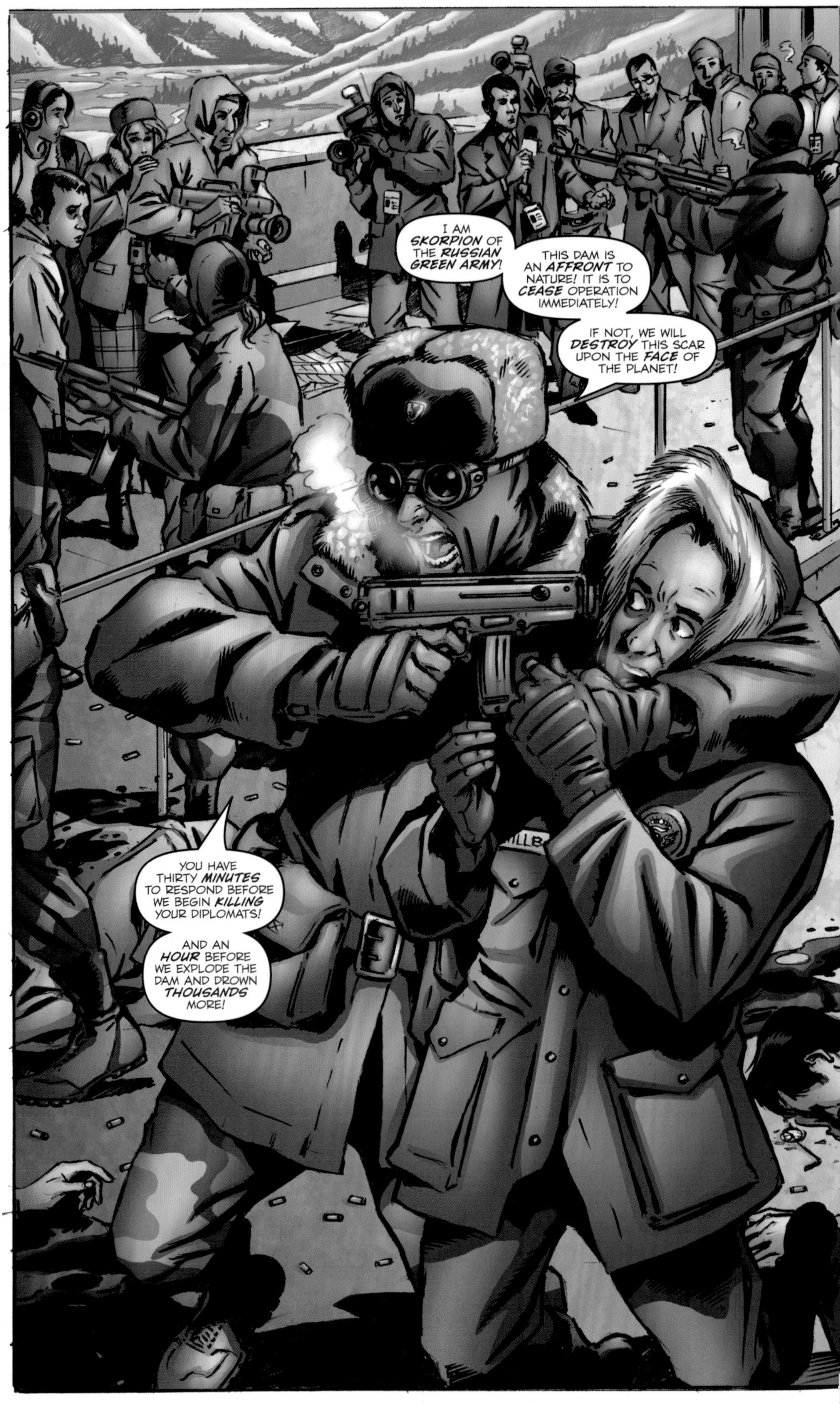

I AM SKORPION OF THE RUSSIAN GREEN ARMY!
THIS DAM IS AN AFFRONT TO NATURE! IT IS TO CEASE OPERATION IMMEDIATELY!
IF NOT, WE WILL DESTROY THIS SCAR UPON THE FACE OF THE PLANET!
YOU HAVE THIRTY MINUTES TO RESPOND BEFORE WE BEGIN KILLING YOUR DIPLOMATS!
AND AN HOUR BEFORE WE EXPLODE THE DAM AND DROWN THOUSANDS MORE!

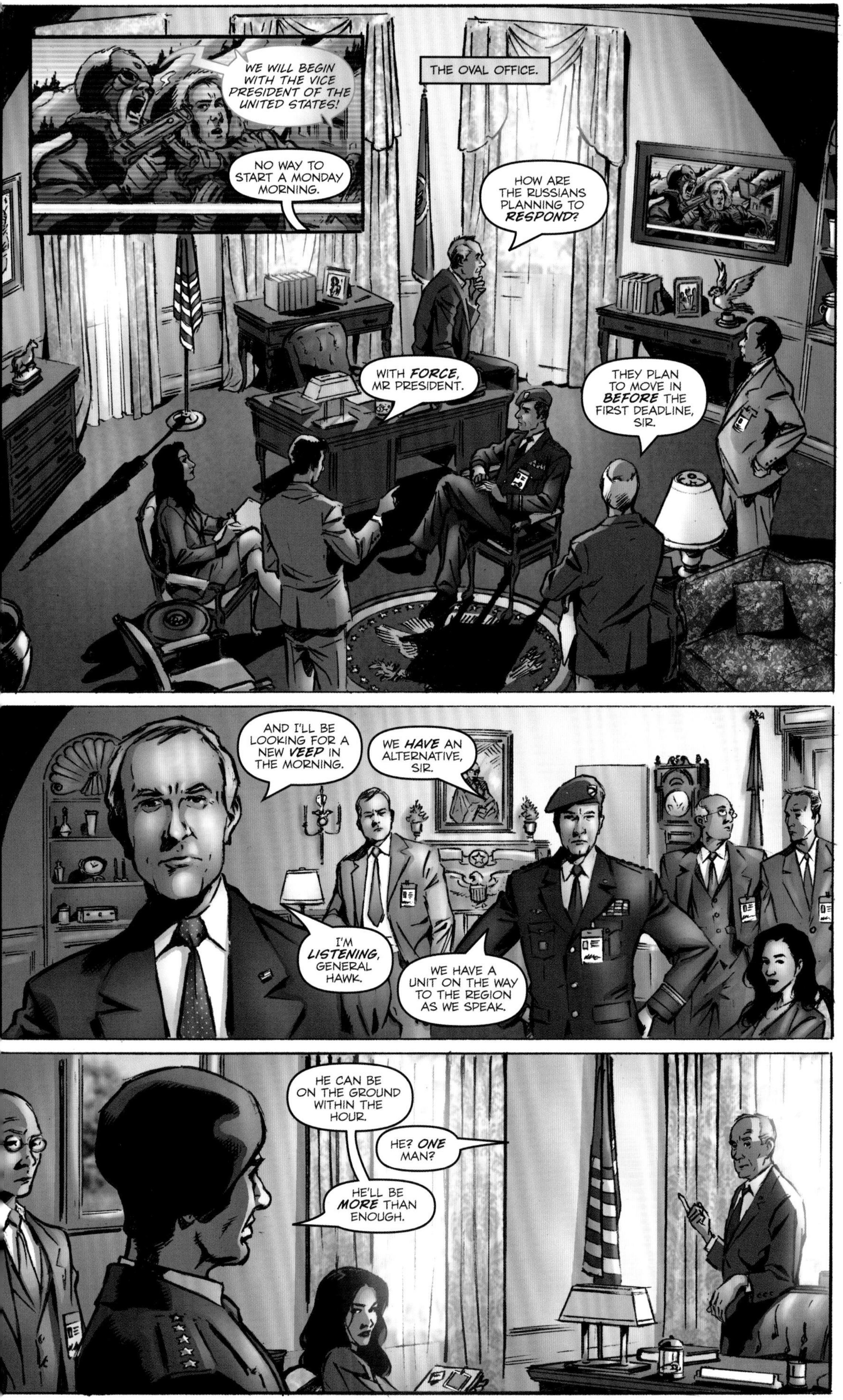
WE WILL BEGIN WITH THE VICE PRESIDENT OF THE UNITED STATES!
NO WAY TO START A MONDAY MORNING.
THE OVAL OFFICE.
HOW ARE THE RUSSIANS PLANNING TO RESPOND?
WITH FORCE, MR PRESIDENT.
THEY PLAN TO MOVE IN BEFORE THE FIRST DEADLINE, SIR.
AND I'LL BE LOOKING FOR A NEW VEEP IN THE MORNING.
WE HAVE AN ALTERNATIVE, SIR.
I'M LISTENING, GENERAL HAWK.
WE HAVE A UNIT ON THE WAY TO THE REGION AS WE SPEAK.
HE CAN BE ON THE GROUND WITHIN THE HOUR.
HE? ONE MAN?
HE'LL BE MORE THAN ENOUGH.

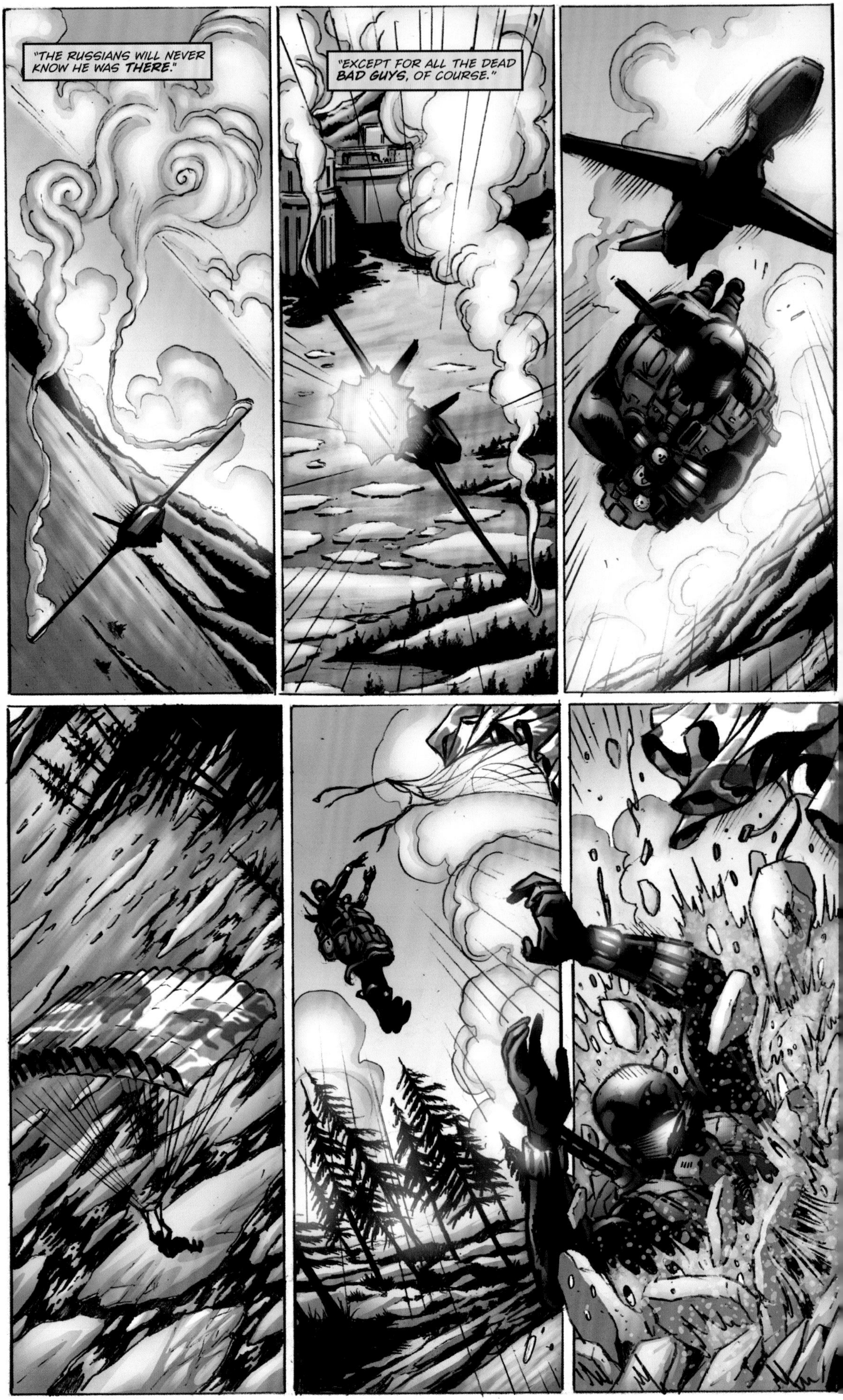
"THE RUSSIANS WILL NEVER KNOW HE WAS THERE."
"EXCEPT FOR ALL THE DEAD BAD GUYS, OF COURSE."

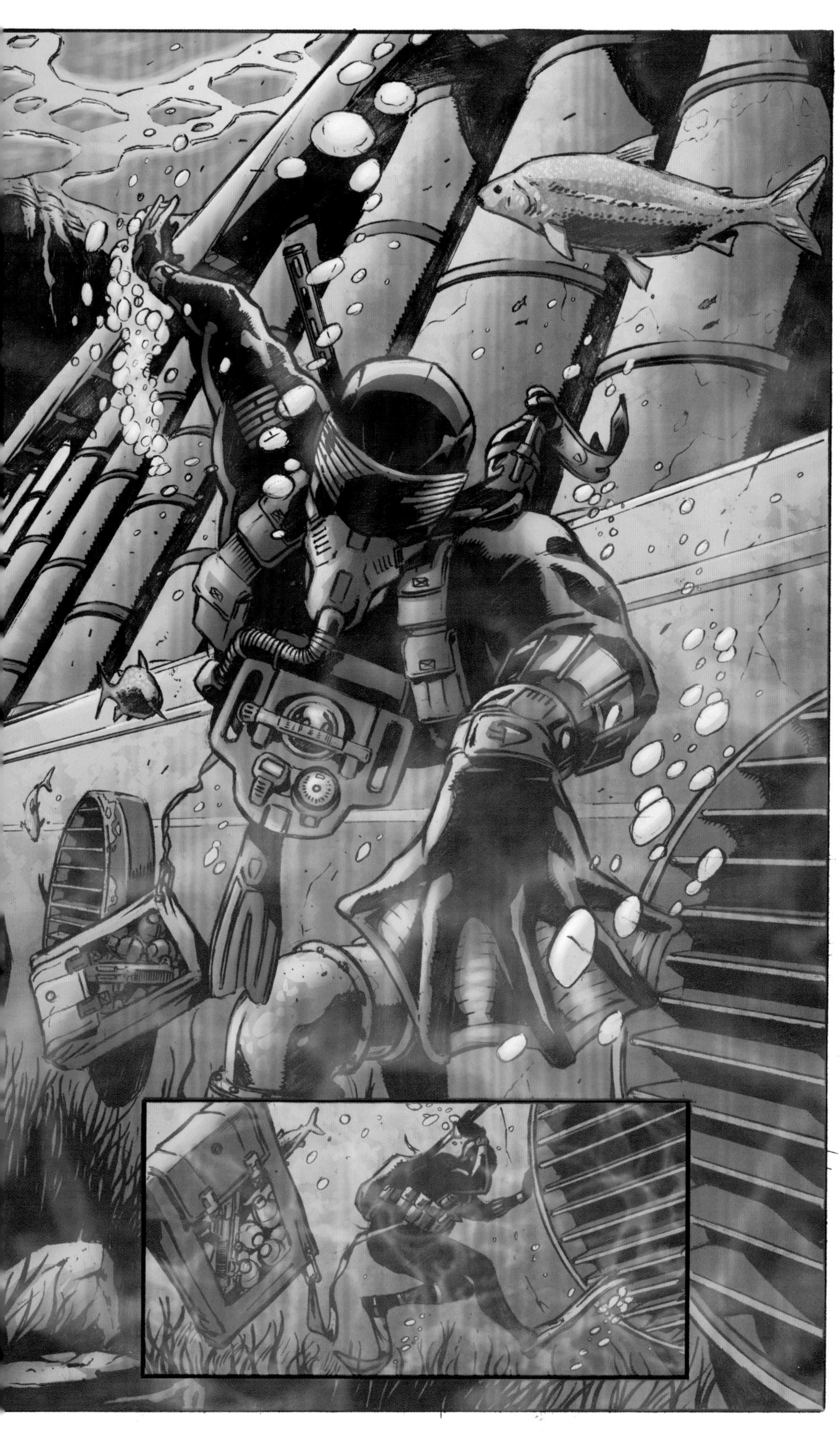

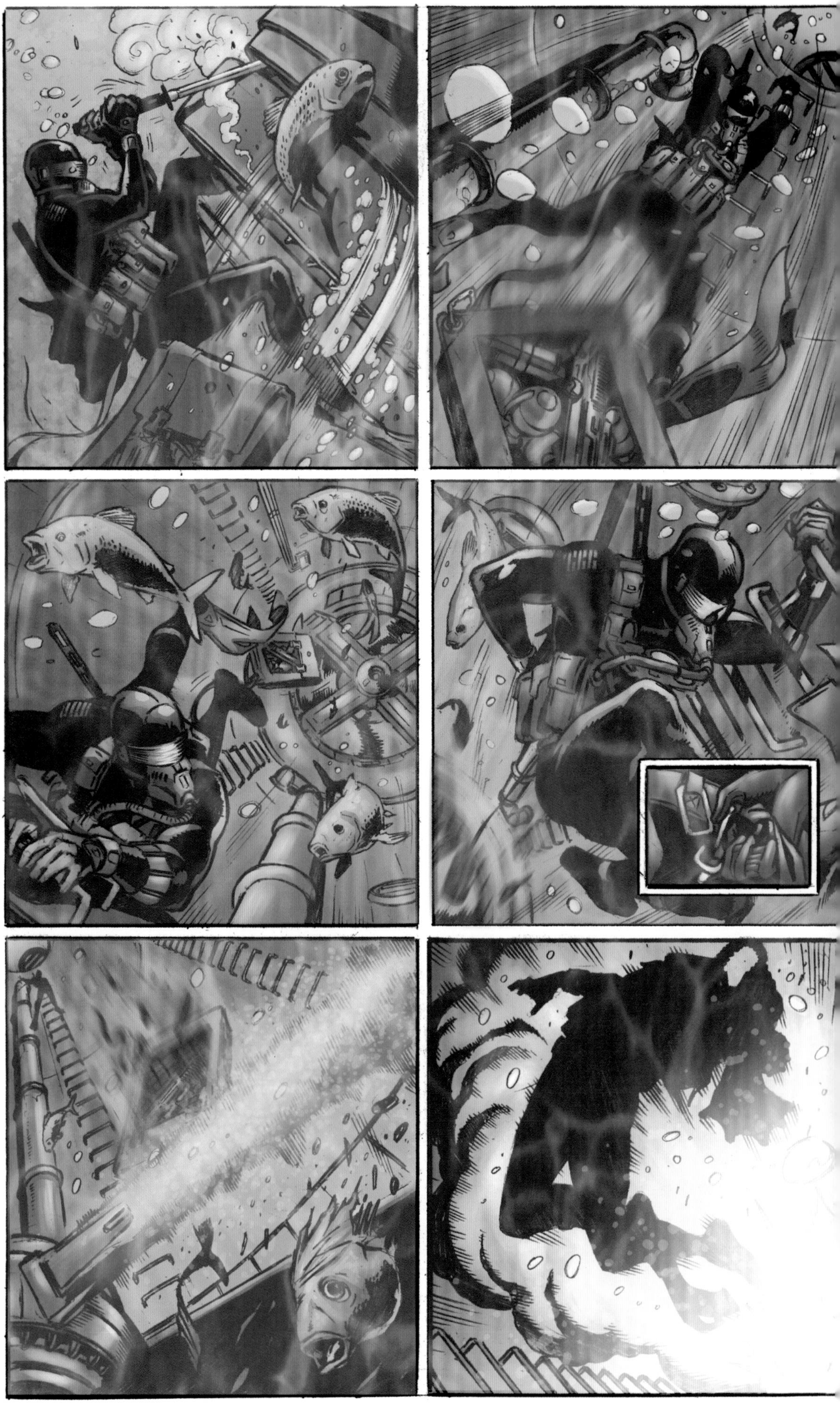

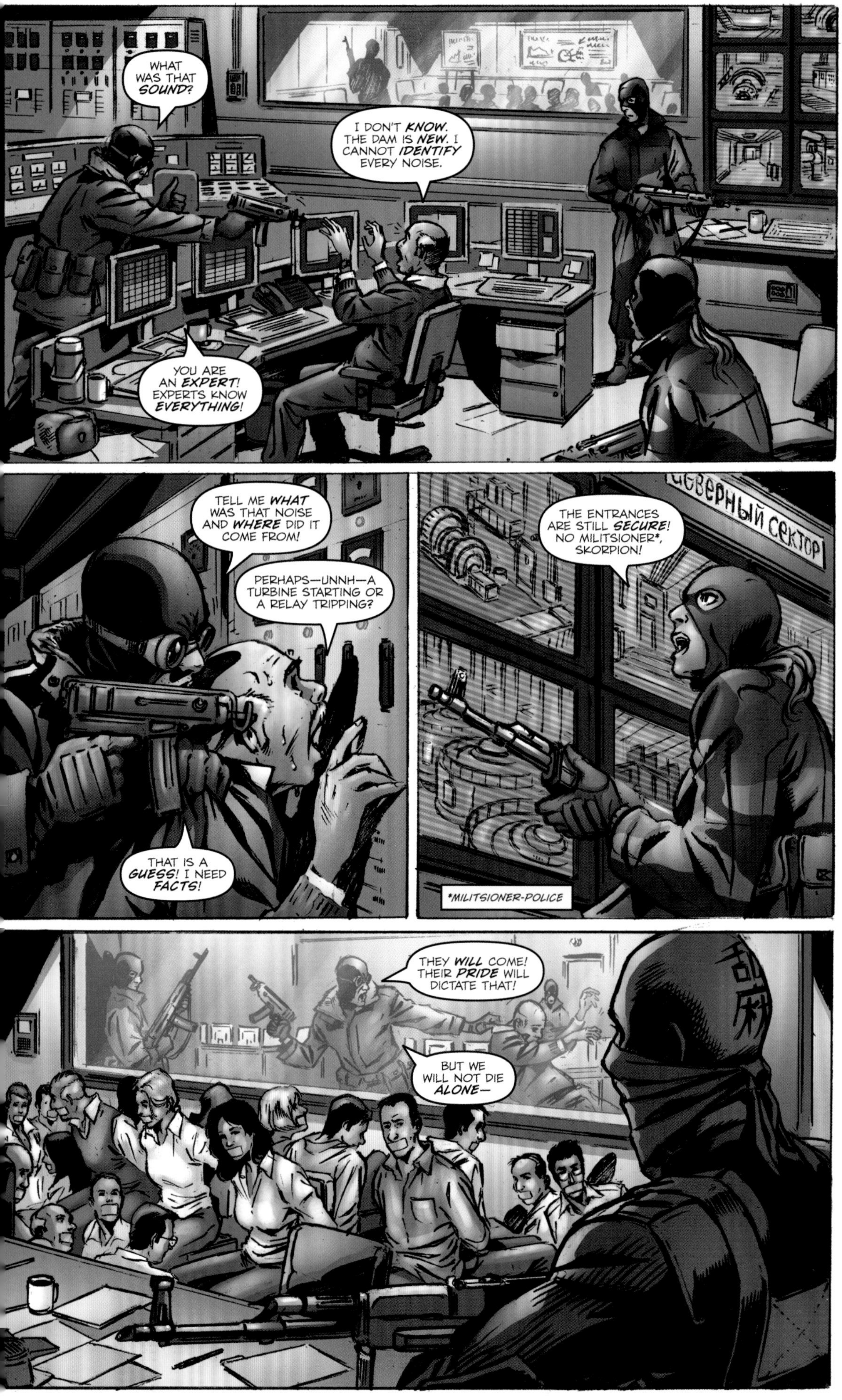

WHAT WAS THAT ***SOUND?***
I DON'T ***KNOW***. THE DAM IS ***NEW***. I CANNOT ***IDENTIFY*** EVERY NOISE.
YOU ARE AN ***EXPERT***! EXPERTS KNOW ***EVERYTHING***!
TELL ME ***WHAT*** WAS THAT NOISE AND ***WHERE*** DID IT COME FROM!
PERHAPS—UNNH—A TURBINE STARTING OR A RELAY TRIPPING?
THAT IS A ***GUESS***! I NEED ***FACTS***!
СЕВЕРНЫЙ СЕКТОР
THE ENTRANCES ARE STILL ***SECURE***! NO MILITSIONER*, SKORPION!
*MILITSIONER-POLICE
THEY ***WILL*** COME! THEIR ***PRIDE*** WILL DICTATE THAT!
BUT WE WILL NOT DIE ***ALONE***—

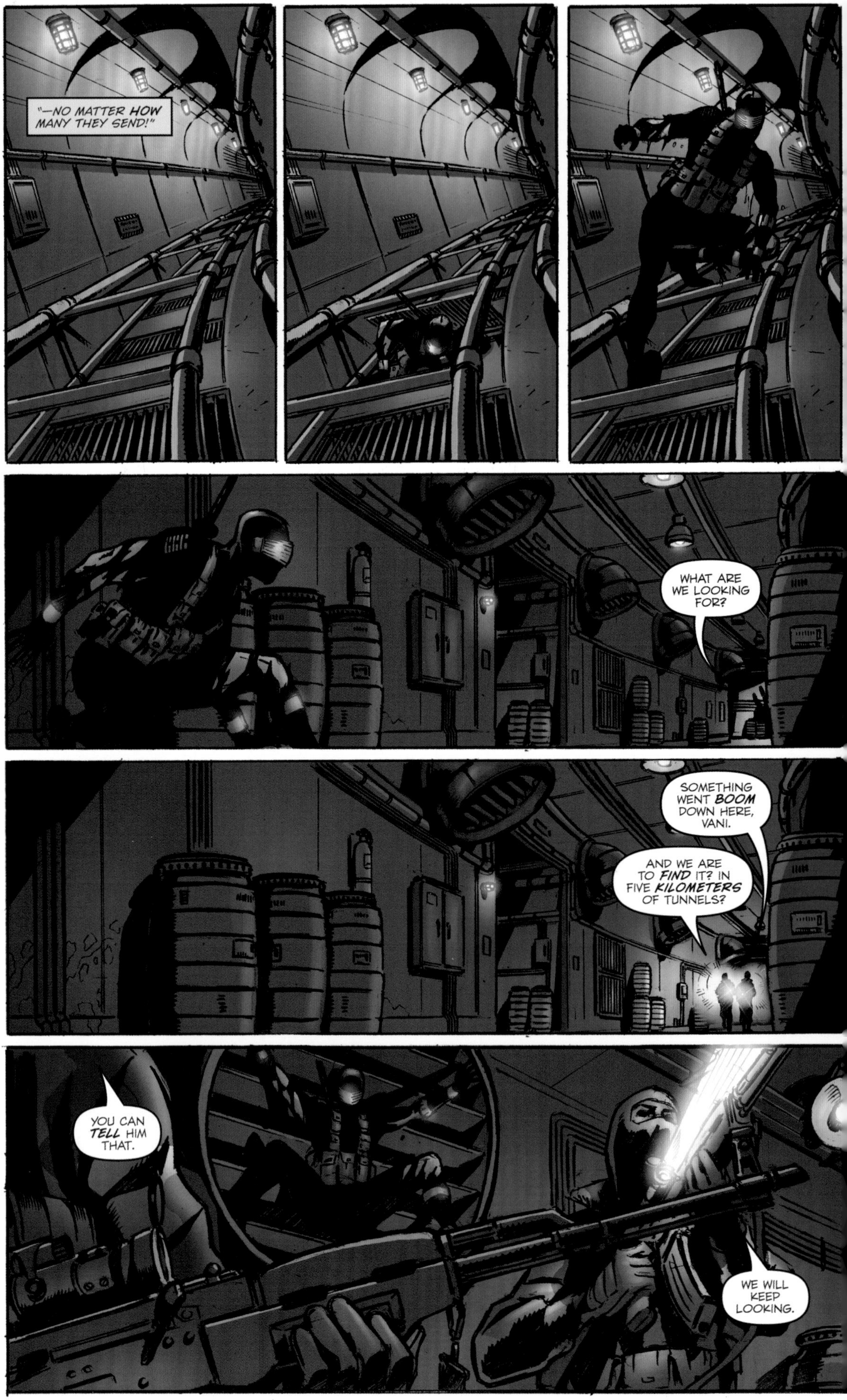

"—NO MATTER HOW MANY THEY SEND!"
WHAT ARE WE LOOKING FOR?
SOMETHING WENT BOOM DOWN HERE, VANI.
AND WE ARE TO FIND IT? IN FIVE KILOMETERS OF TUNNELS?
YOU CAN TELL HIM THAT.
WE WILL KEEP LOOKING.

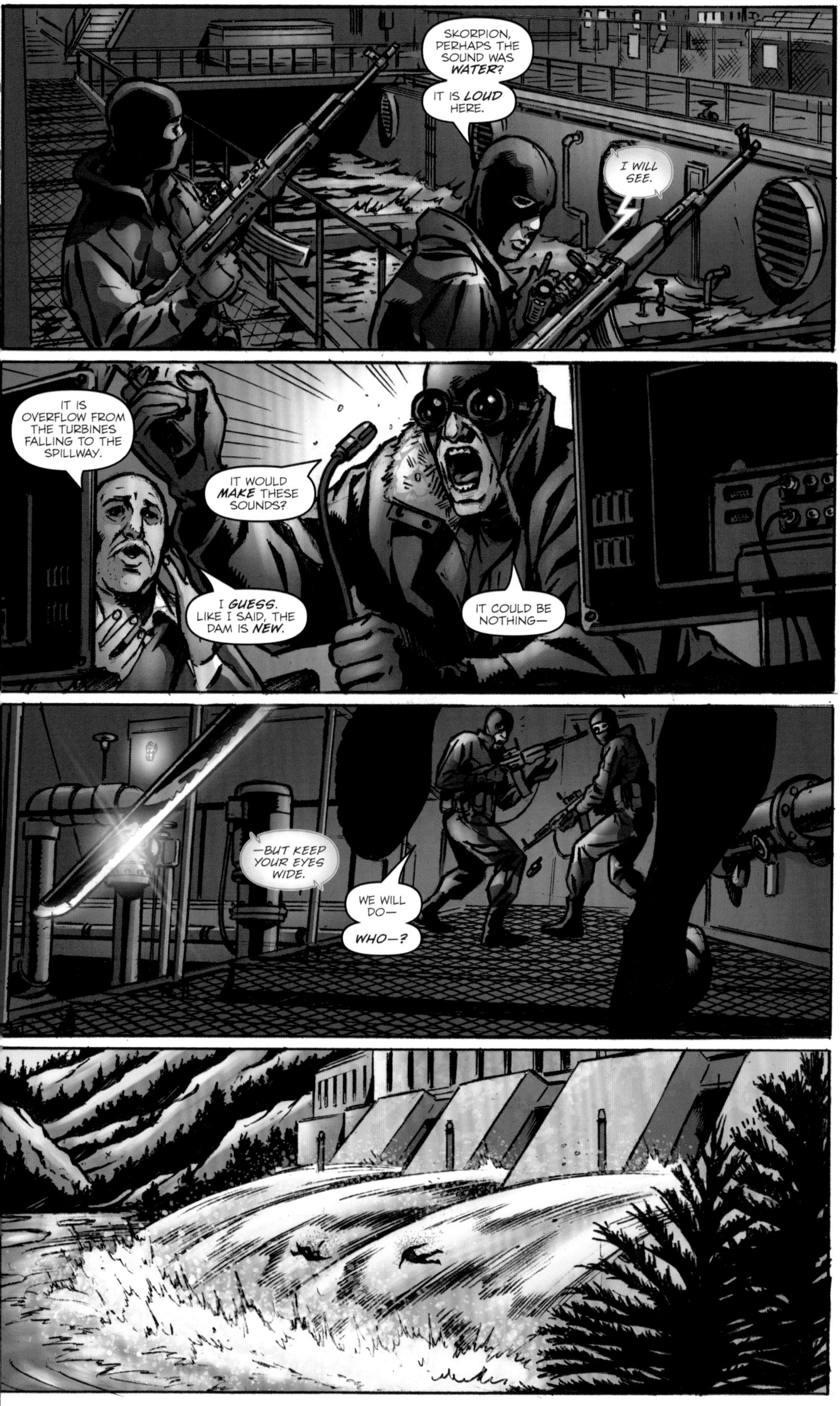

SKORPION, PERHAPS THE SOUND WAS WATER?
IT IS LOUD HERE.
I WILL SEE.
IT IS OVERFLOW FROM THE TURBINES FALLING TO THE SPILLWAY.
IT WOULD MAKE THESE SOUNDS?
I GUESS. LIKE I SAID, THE DAM IS NEW.
IT COULD BE NOTHING—
—BUT KEEP YOUR EYES WIDE.
WE WILL DO—
WHO—?

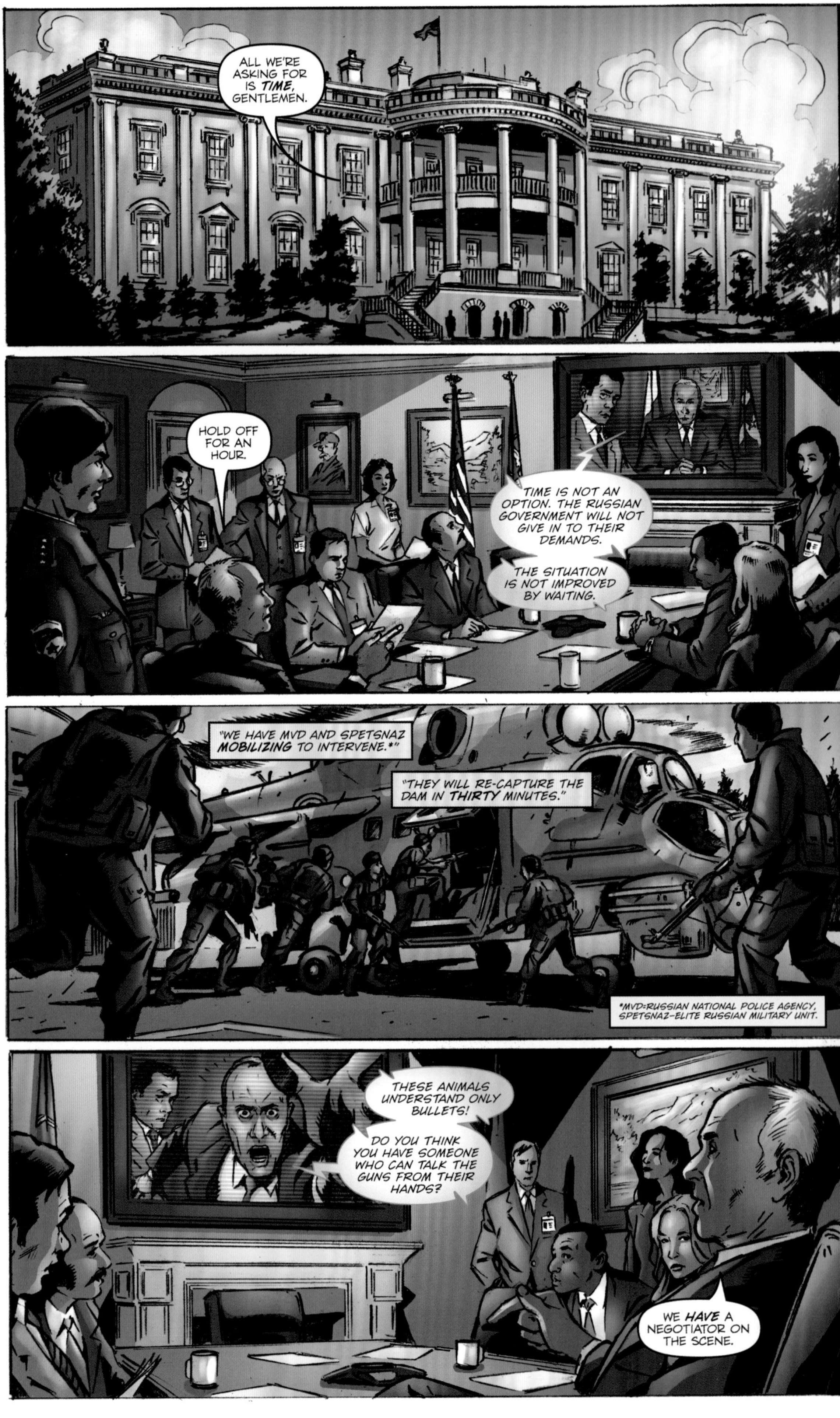

ALL WE'RE ASKING FOR IS *TIME*, GENTLEMEN.
HOLD OFF FOR AN HOUR.
TIME IS NOT AN OPTION. THE RUSSIAN GOVERNMENT WILL NOT GIVE IN TO THEIR DEMANDS.
THE SITUATION IS NOT IMPROVED BY WAITING.
"WE HAVE MVD AND SPETSNAZ *MOBILIZING* TO INTERVENE.*"
"THEY WILL RE-CAPTURE THE DAM IN *THIRTY* MINUTES."
*MVD=RUSSIAN NATIONAL POLICE AGENCY, SPETSNAZ=ELITE RUSSIAN MILITARY UNIT.
THESE ANIMALS UNDERSTAND ONLY BULLETS!
DO YOU THINK YOU HAVE SOMEONE WHO CAN TALK THE GUNS FROM THEIR HANDS?
WE *HAVE* A NEGOTIATOR ON THE SCENE.

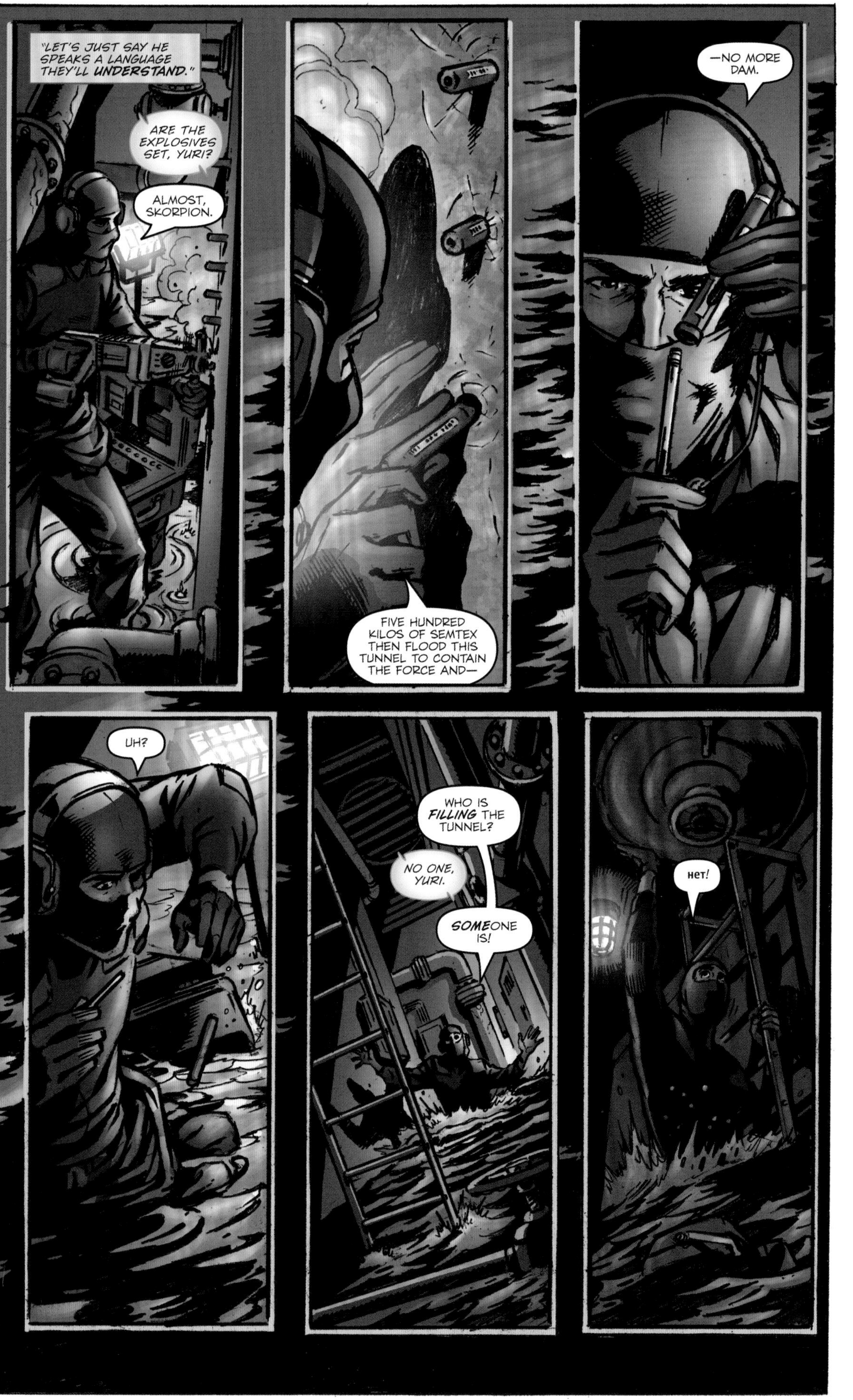

"LET'S JUST SAY HE SPEAKS A LANGUAGE THEY'LL **UNDERSTAND**."
ARE THE EXPLOSIVES SET, YURI?
ALMOST, SKORPION.
FIVE HUNDRED KILOS OF SEMTEX THEN FLOOD THIS TUNNEL TO CONTAIN THE FORCE AND—
—NO MORE DAM.
UH?
WHO IS *FILLING* THE TUNNEL?
NO ONE, YURI.
***SOME*ONE IS!**
НЕТ!

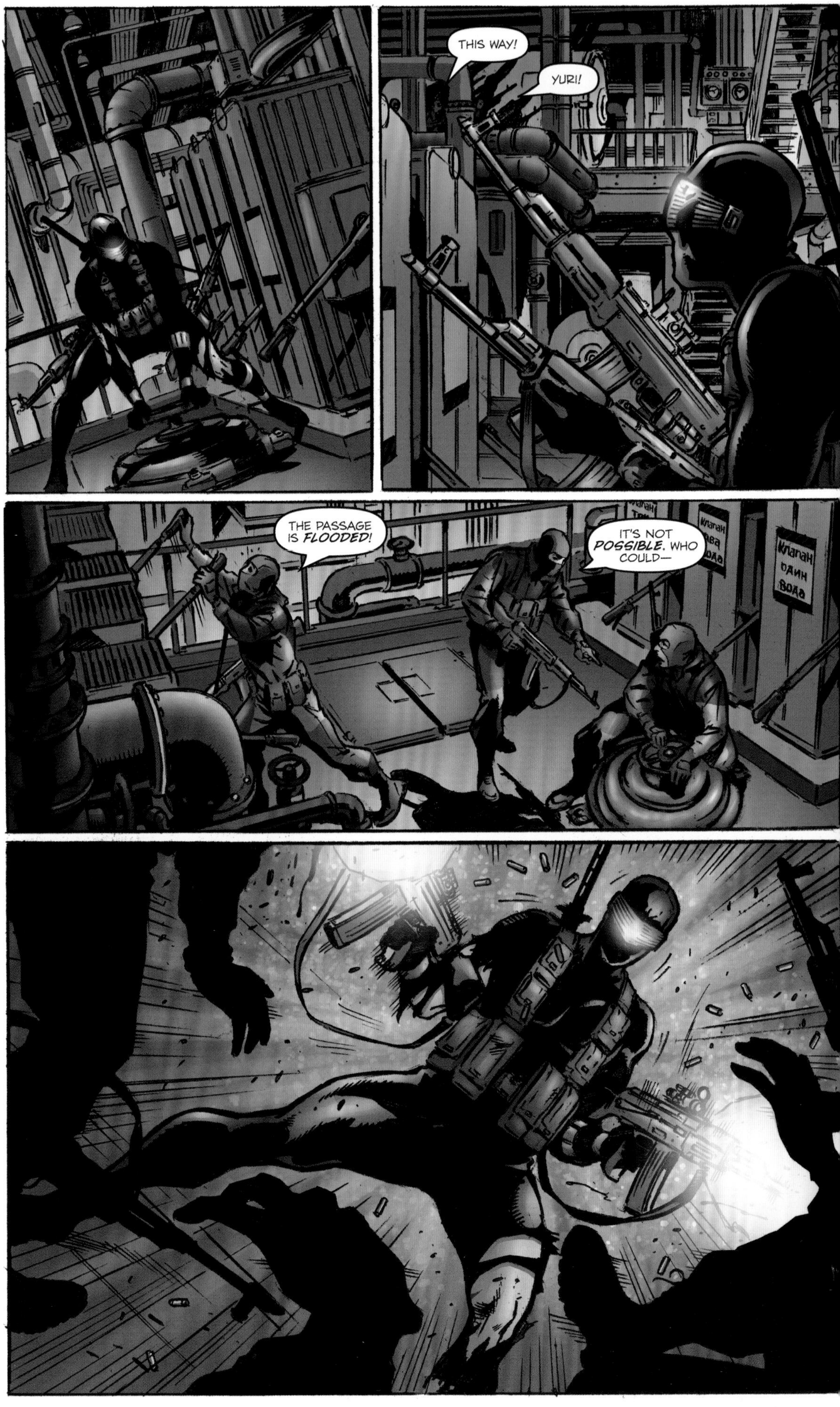
THIS WAY!
YURI!
THE PASSAGE IS *FLOODED*!
IT'S NOT ***POSSIBLE.*** WHO COULD—
Клапан один вода

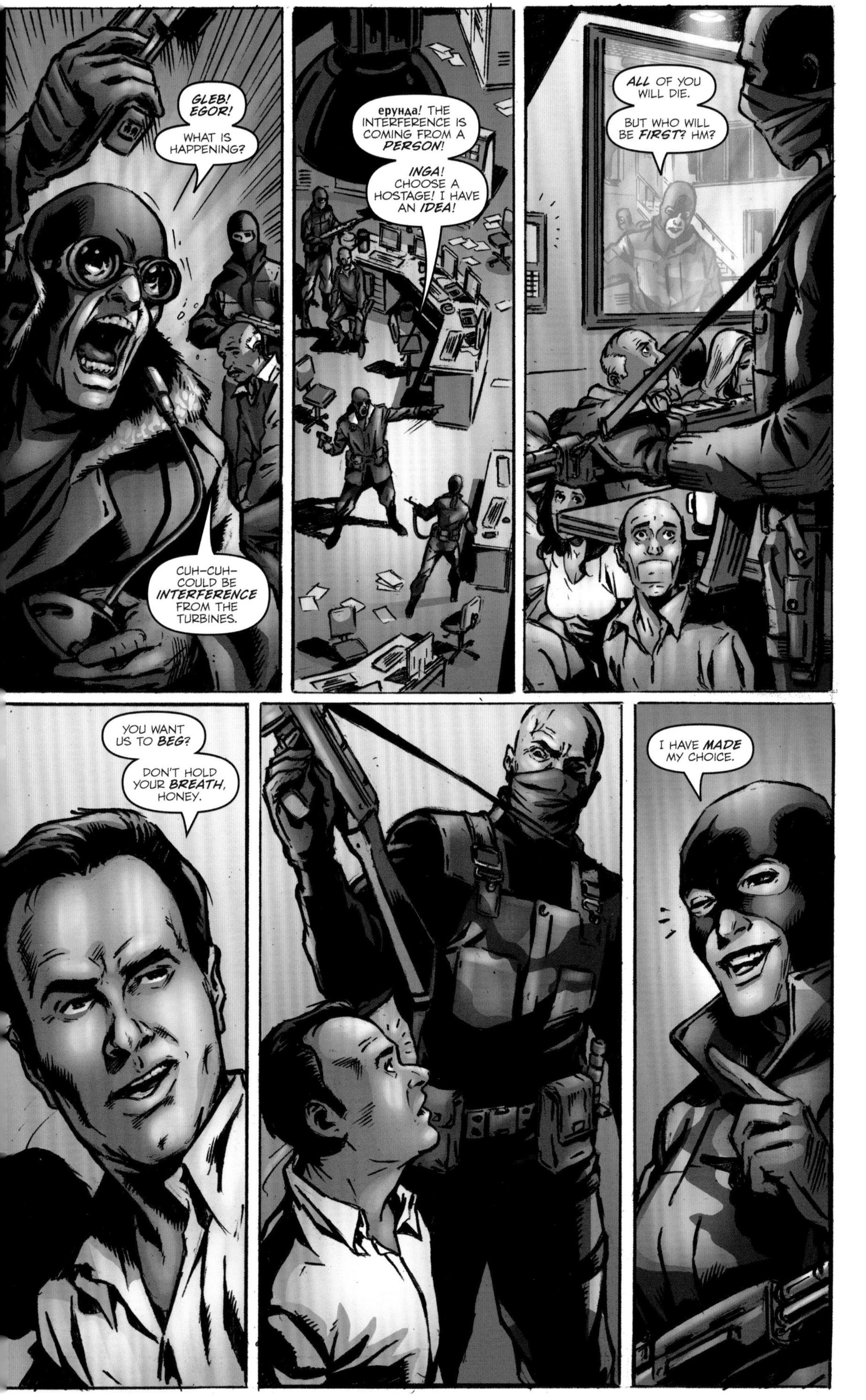
GLEB! EGOR!
WHAT IS HAPPENING?
CUH-CUH-COULD BE INTERFERENCE FROM THE TURBINES.
ерунда! THE INTERFERENCE IS COMING FROM A PERSON!
INGA! CHOOSE A HOSTAGE! I HAVE AN IDEA!
ALL OF YOU WILL DIE.
BUT WHO WILL BE FIRST? HM?
YOU WANT US TO BEG?
DON'T HOLD YOUR BREATH, HONEY.
I HAVE MADE MY CHOICE.

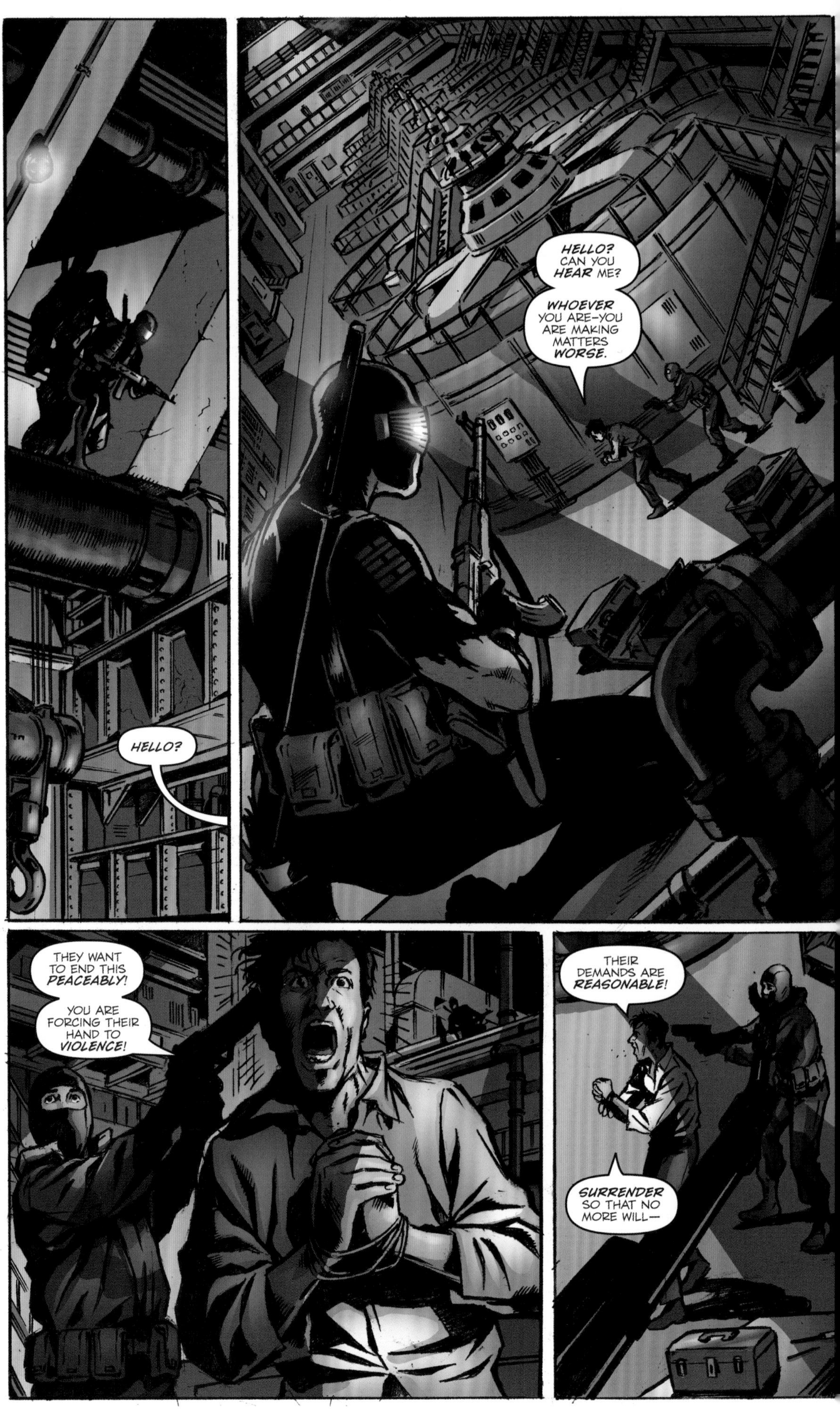
HELLO?
HELLO? CAN YOU HEAR ME?
WHOEVER YOU ARE--YOU ARE MAKING MATTERS WORSE.
THEY WANT TO END THIS PEACEABLY!
YOU ARE FORCING THEIR HAND TO VIOLENCE!
THEIR DEMANDS ARE REASONABLE!
SURRENDER SO THAT NO MORE WILL—

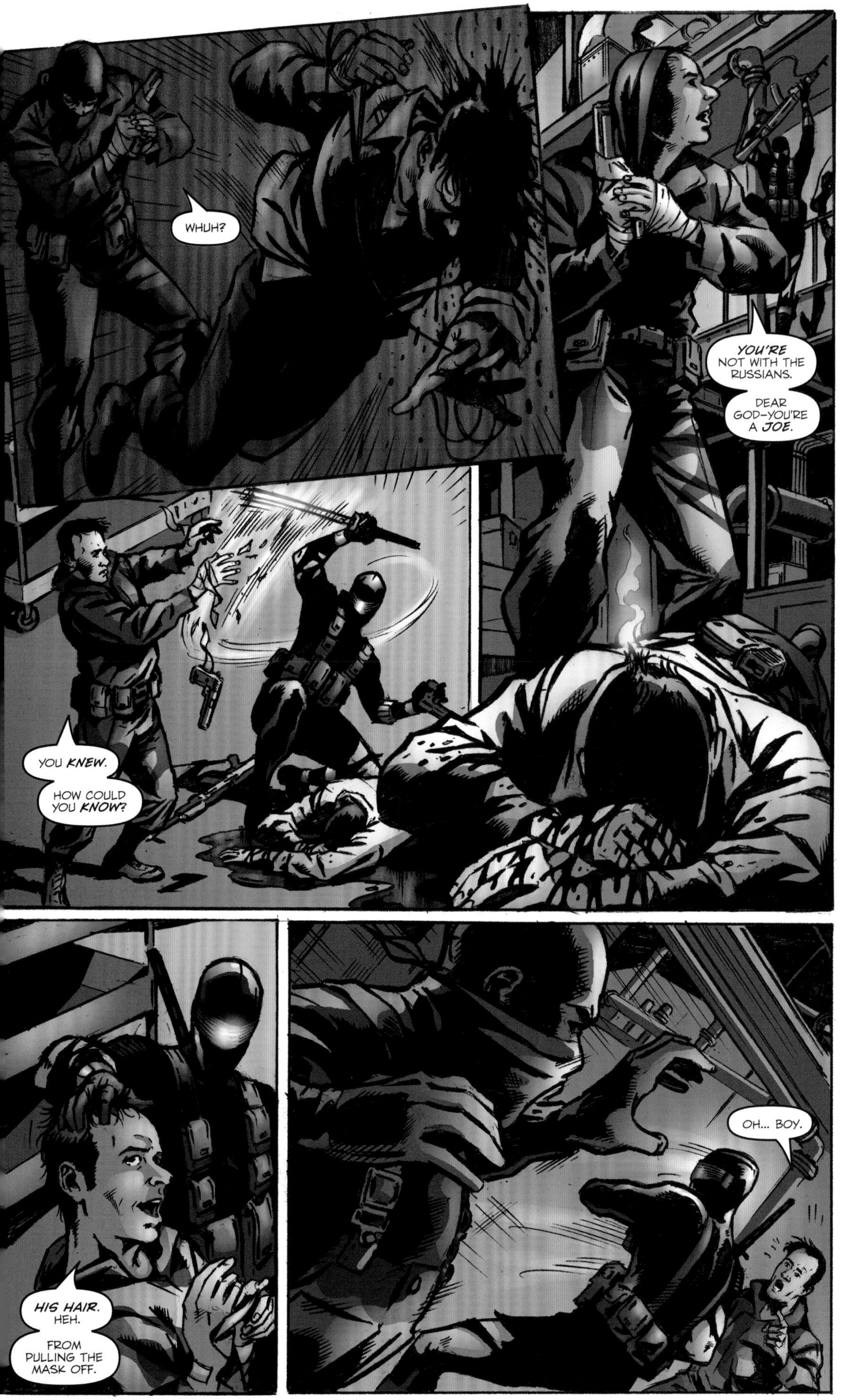
WHUH?
YOU'RE NOT WITH THE RUSSIANS.
DEAR GOD--YOU'RE A *JOE*.
YOU *KNEW*.
HOW COULD YOU *KNOW*?
HIS HAIR. HEH.
FROM PULLING THE MASK OFF.
OH... BOY.

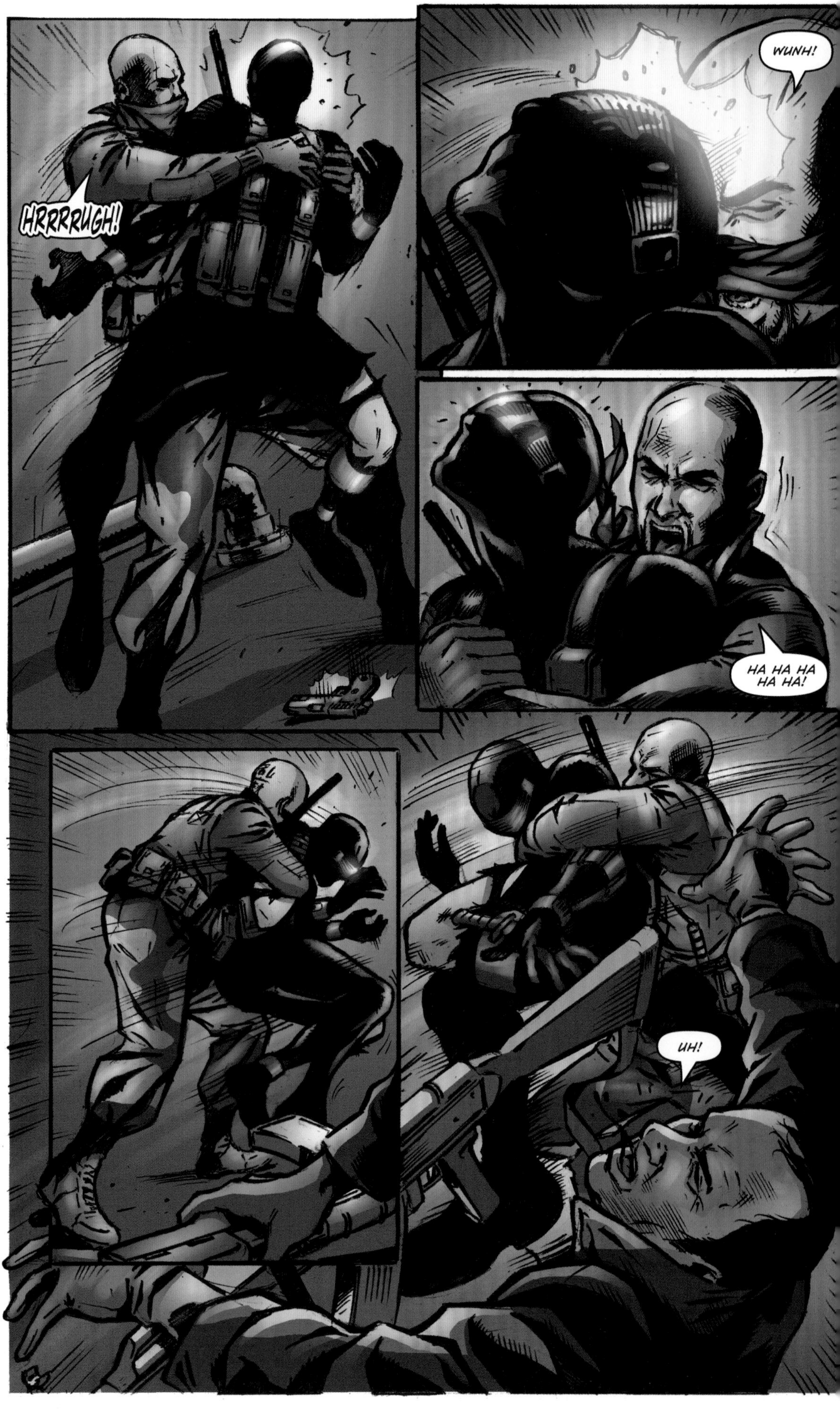
HRRRRUGH!
WUNH!
HA HA HA
HA HA!
UH!

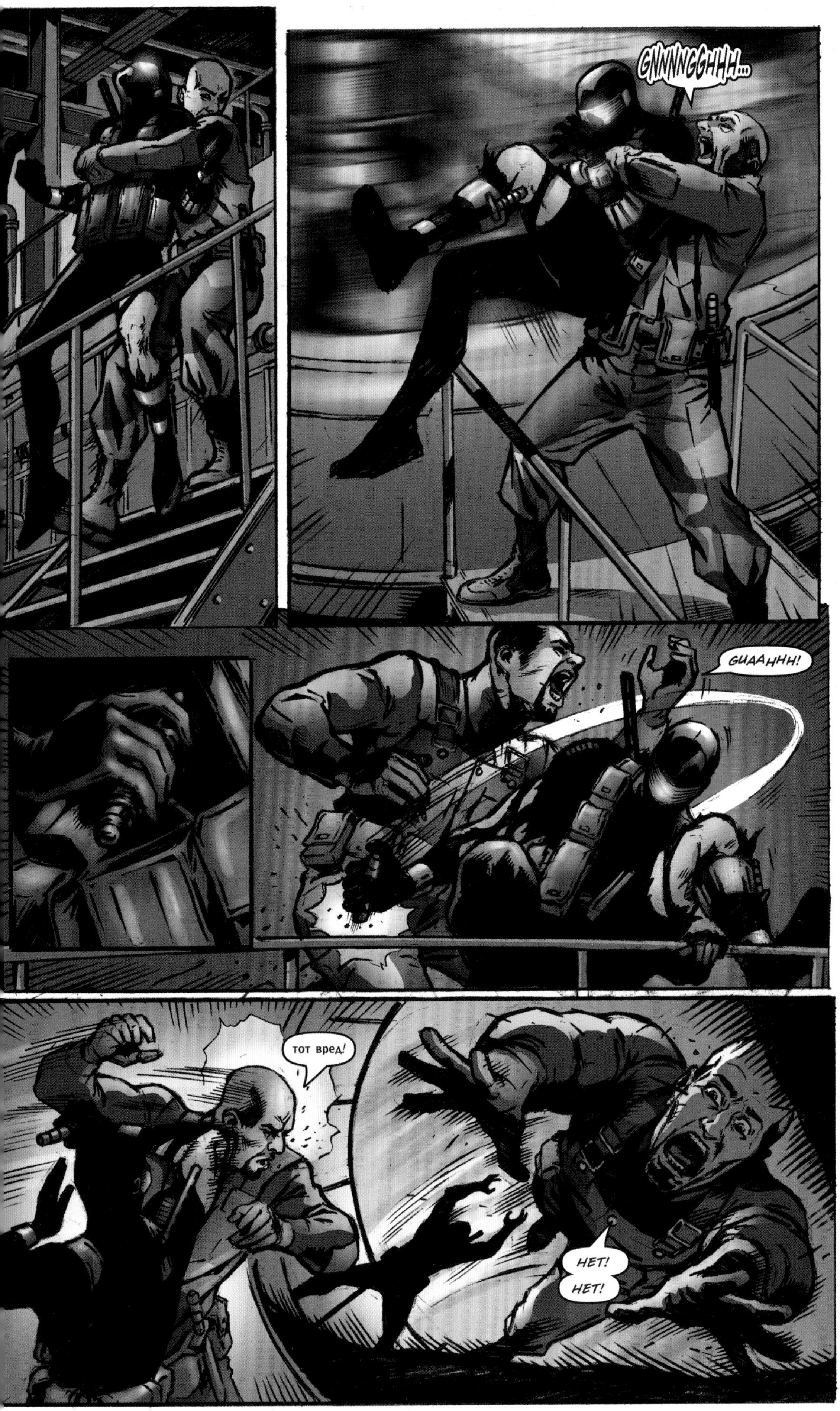
GNNNNGGHHH...
GUAAHHH!
тот вред!
НЕТ!
НЕТ!

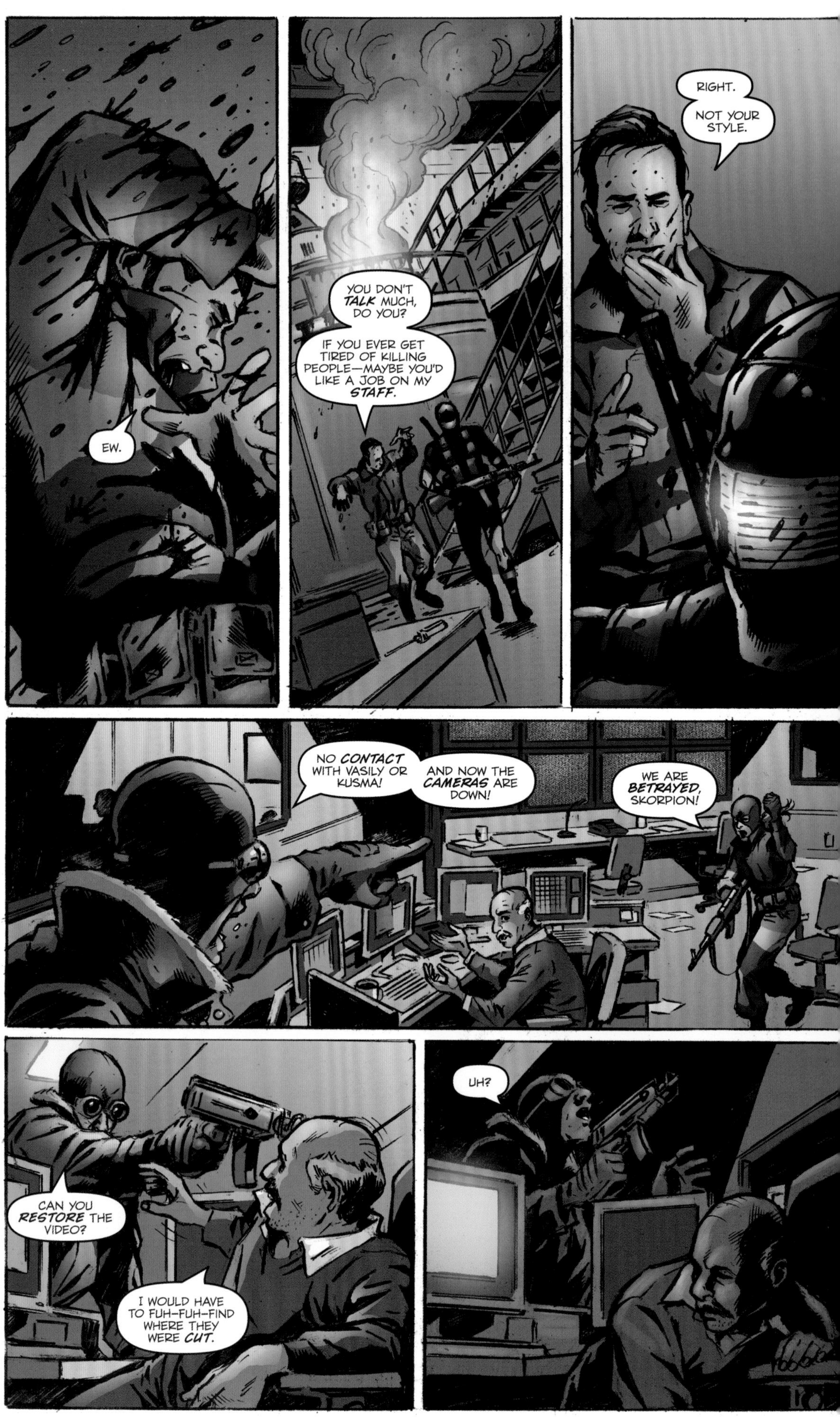
EW.
YOU DON'T *TALK* MUCH, DO YOU?
IF YOU EVER GET TIRED OF KILLING PEOPLE—MAYBE YOU'D LIKE A JOB ON MY *STAFF*.
RIGHT.
NOT YOUR STYLE.
NO *CONTACT* WITH VASILY OR KUSMA!
AND NOW THE *CAMERAS* ARE DOWN!
WE ARE *BETRAYED*, SKORPION!
CAN YOU *RESTORE* THE VIDEO?
I WOULD HAVE TO FUH-FUH-FIND WHERE THEY WERE *CUT*.
UH?

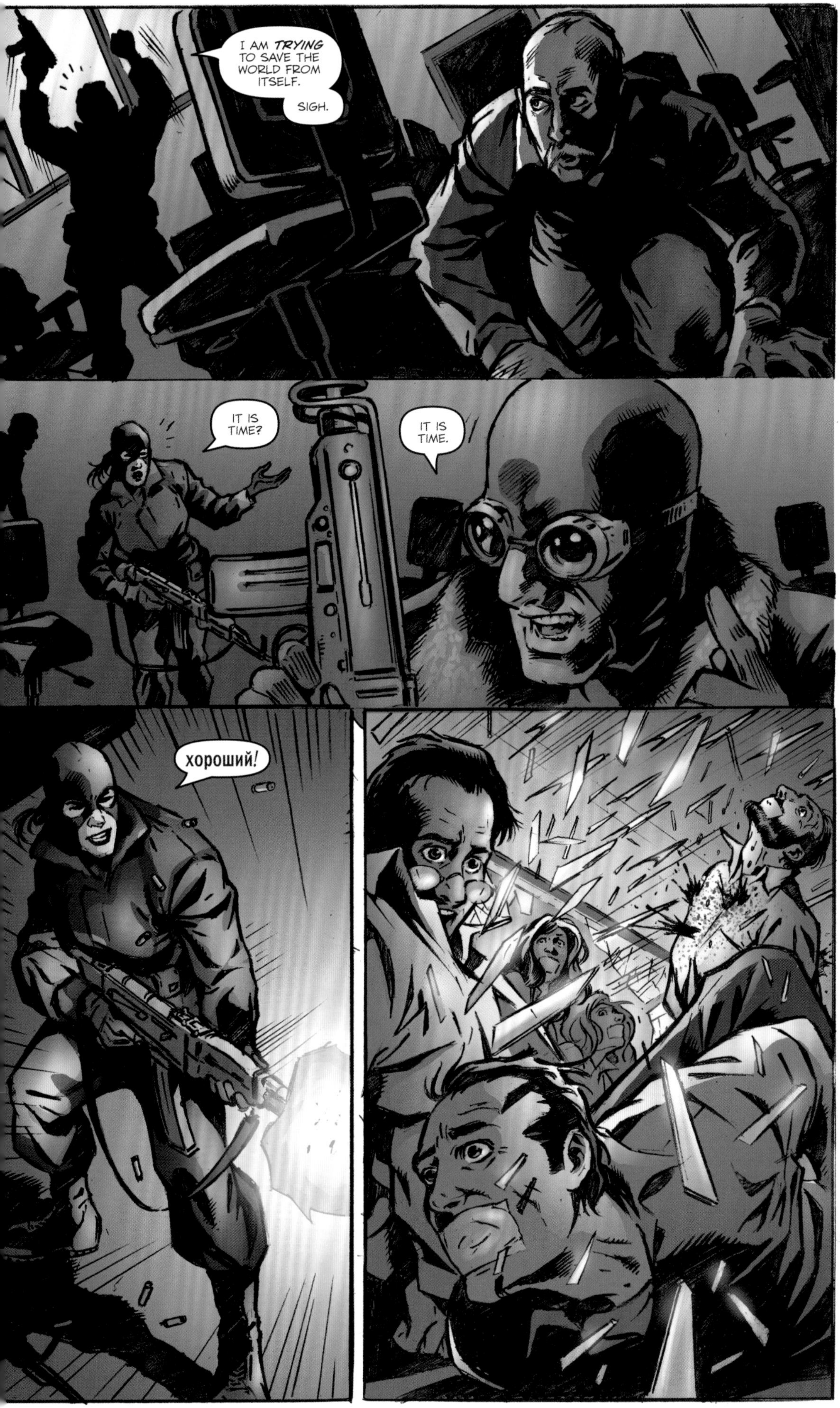

I AM *TRYING* TO SAVE THE WORLD FROM ITSELF.
SIGH.
IT IS TIME?
IT IS TIME.
хороший!

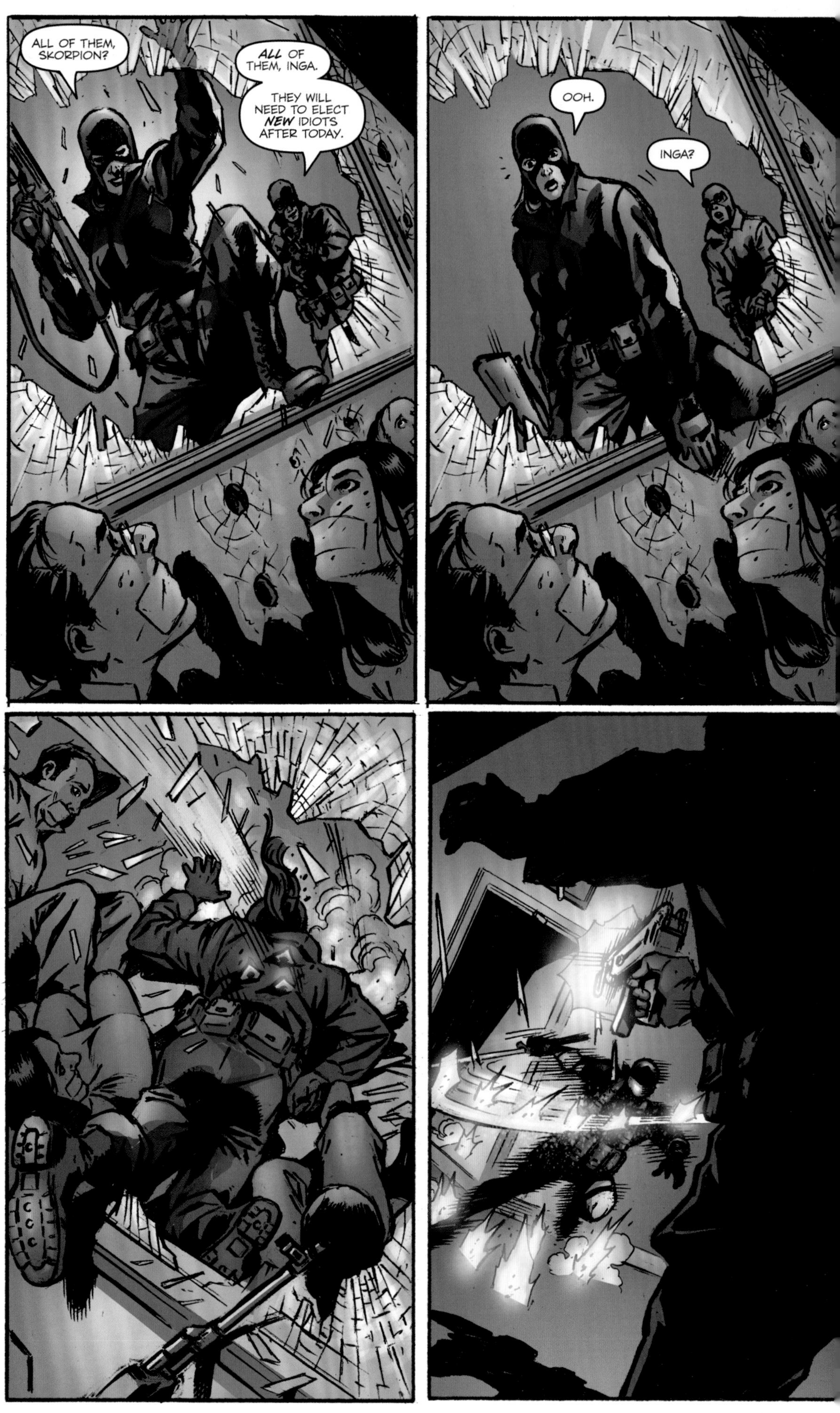
ALL OF THEM, SKORPION?
ALL OF THEM, INGA.
THEY WILL NEED TO ELECT NEW IDIOTS AFTER TODAY.
OOH.
INGA?

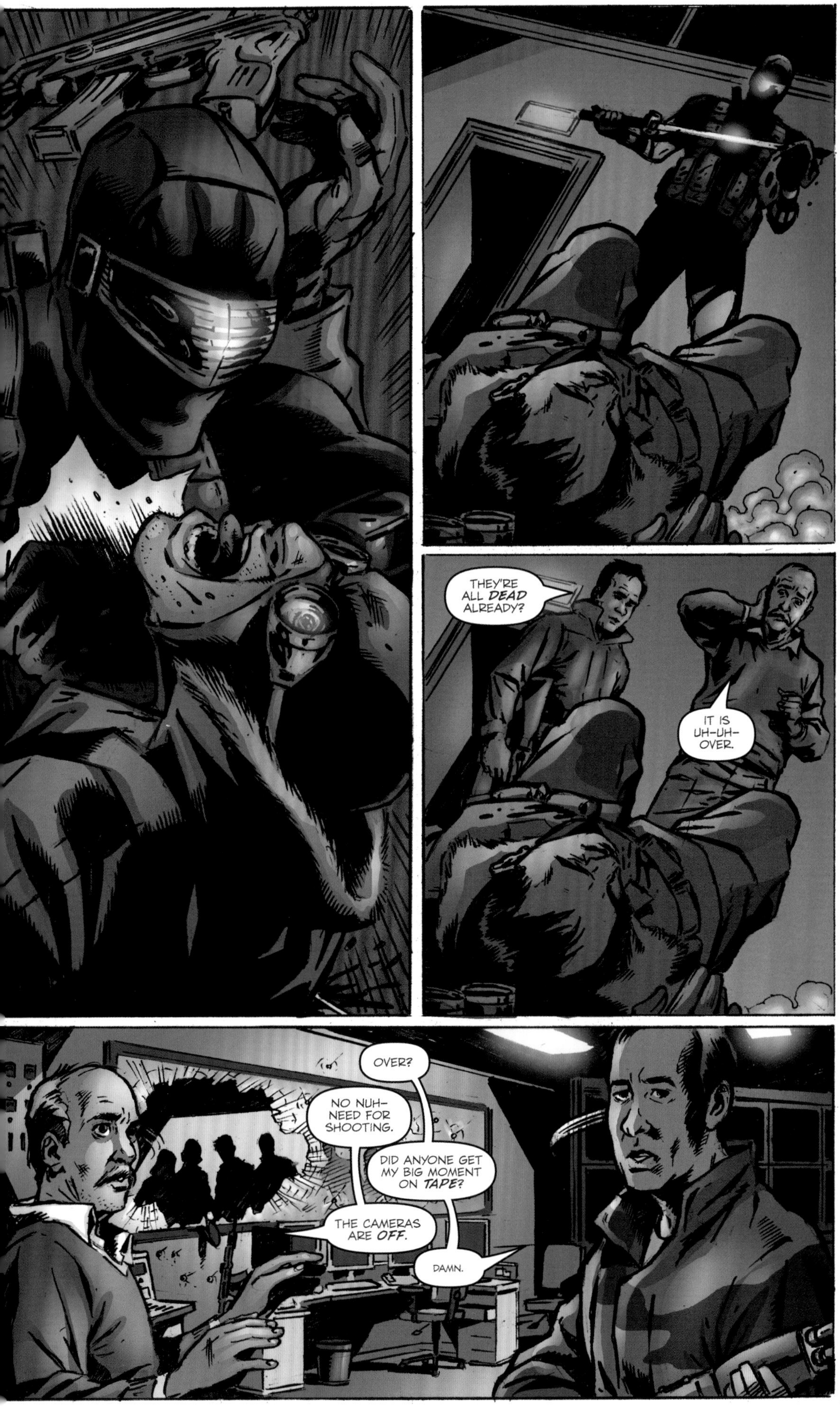
THEY'RE ALL DEAD ALREADY?
IT IS UH-UH-OVER.
OVER?
NO NUH-NEED FOR SHOOTING.
DID ANYONE GET MY BIG MOMENT ON TAPE?
THE CAMERAS ARE OFF.
DAMN.

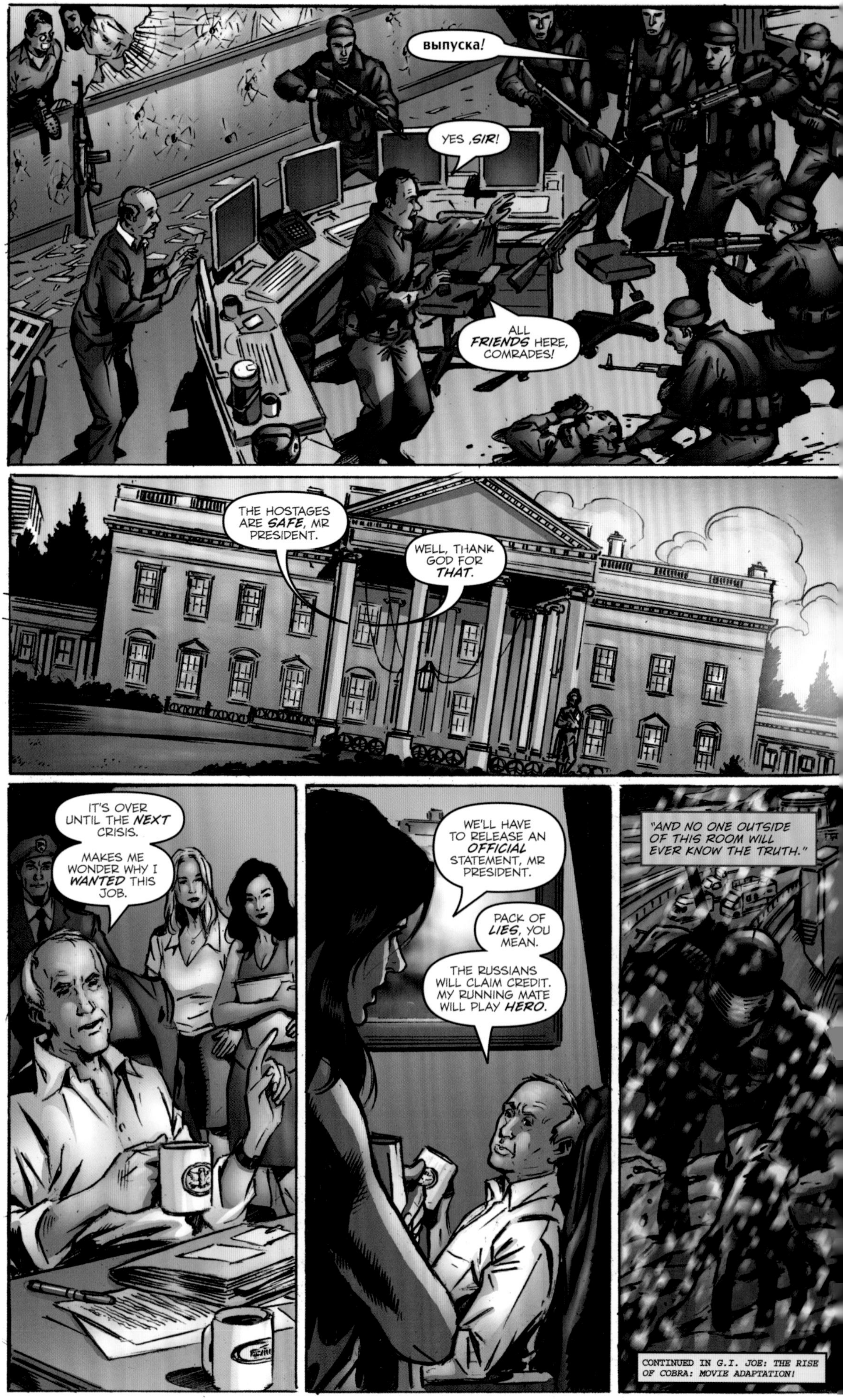

выпуска!
YES ,SIR!
ALL FRIENDS HERE, COMRADES!
THE HOSTAGES ARE SAFE, MR PRESIDENT.
WELL, THANK GOD FOR THAT.
IT'S OVER UNTIL THE NEXT CRISIS.
MAKES ME WONDER WHY I WANTED THIS JOB.
WE'LL HAVE TO RELEASE AN OFFICIAL STATEMENT, MR PRESIDENT.
PACK OF LIES, YOU MEAN.
THE RUSSIANS WILL CLAIM CREDIT. MY RUNNING MATE WILL PLAY HERO.
"AND NO ONE OUTSIDE OF THIS ROOM WILL EVER KNOW THE TRUTH."
CONTINUED IN G.I. JOE: THE RISE OF COBRA: MOVIE ADAPTATION!

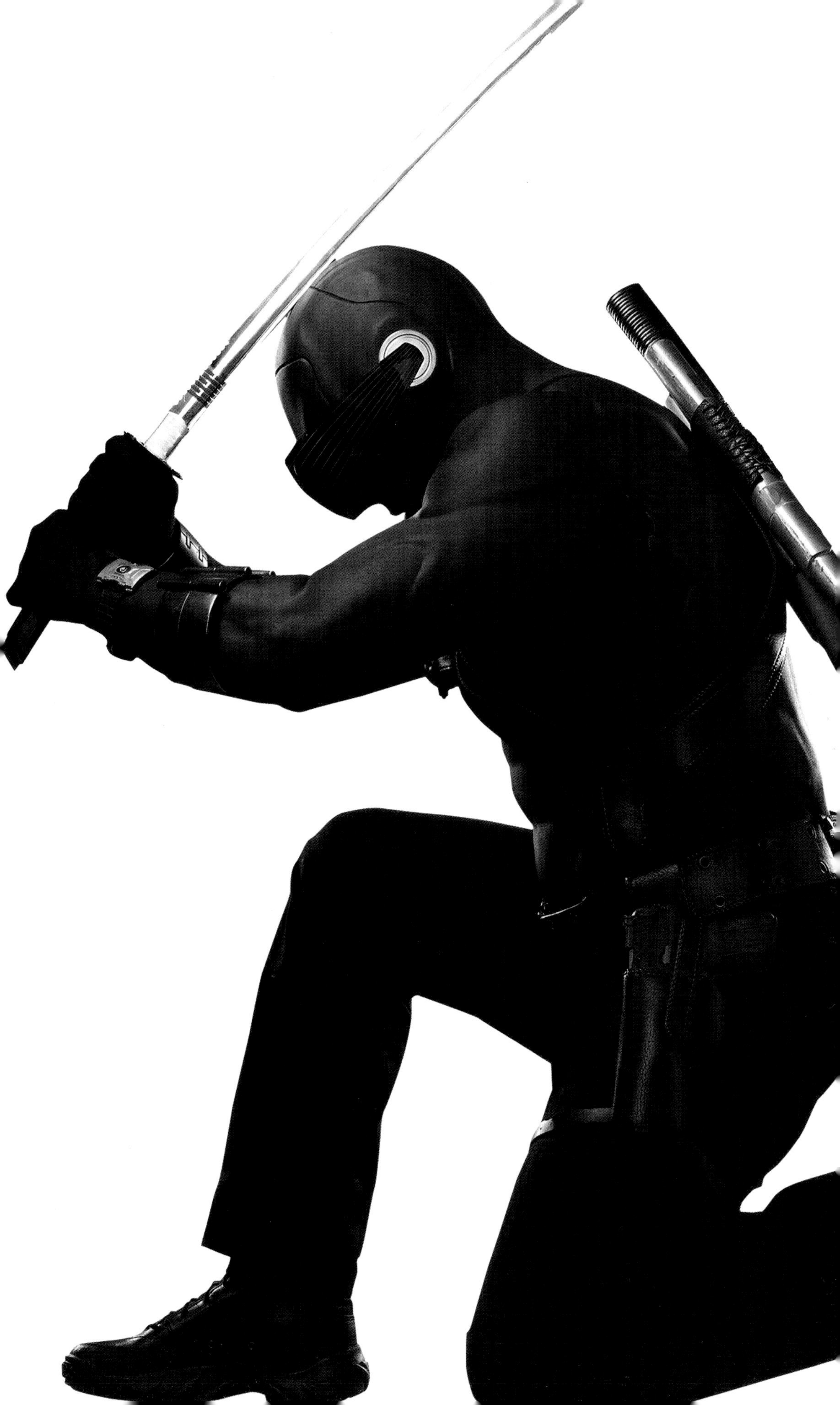

PENCIL PAGES BY
JOE CORRONEY

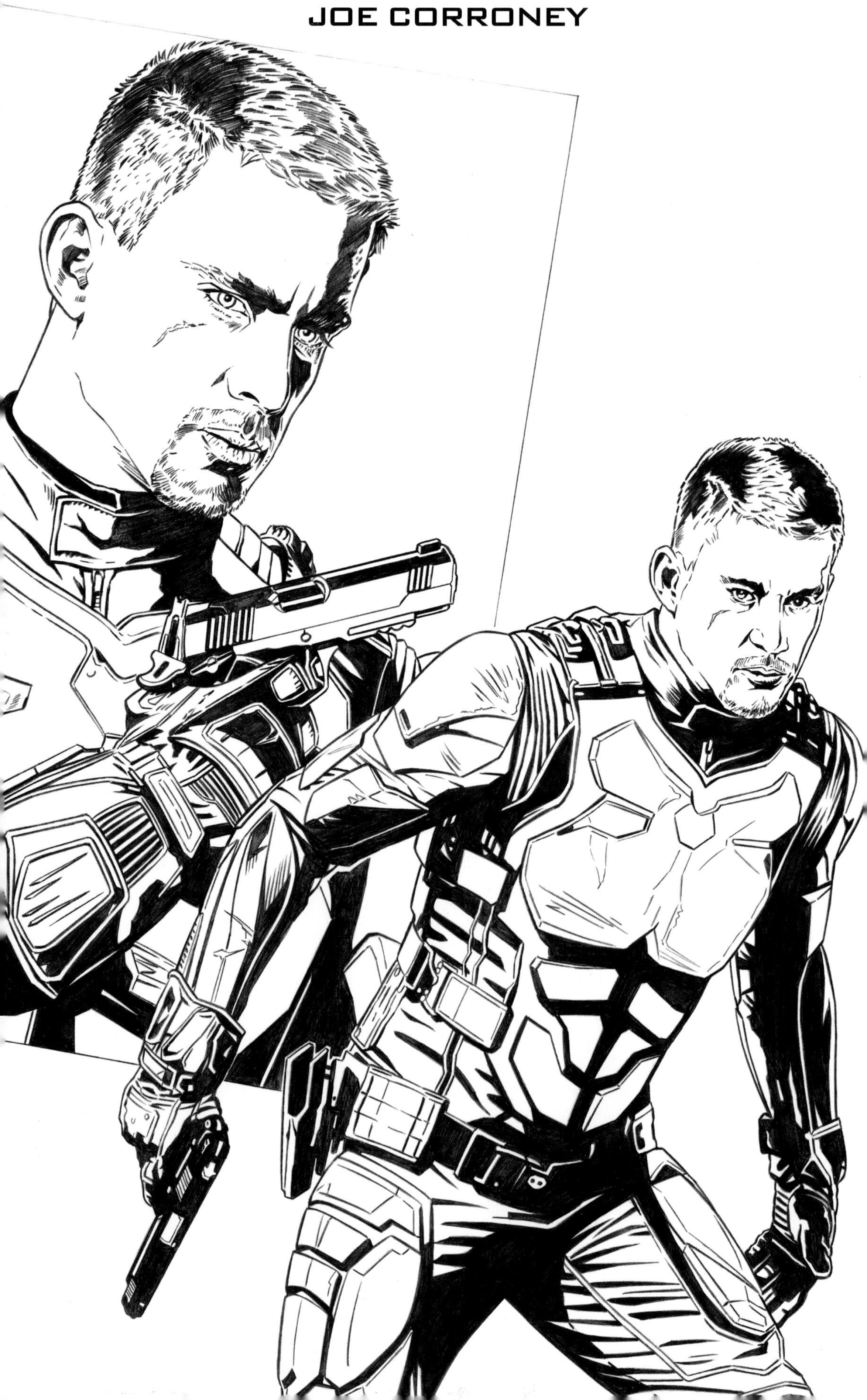

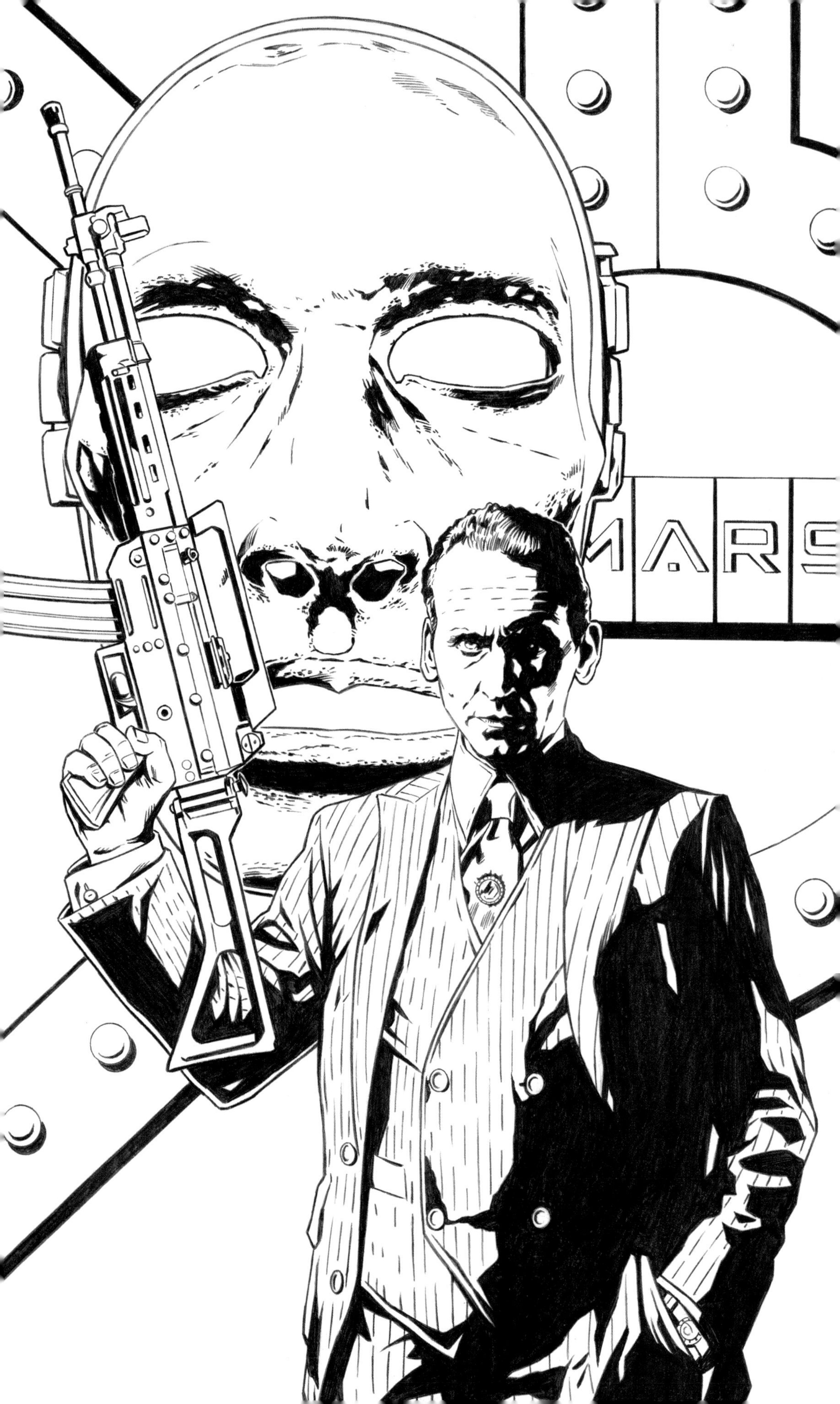
MARS

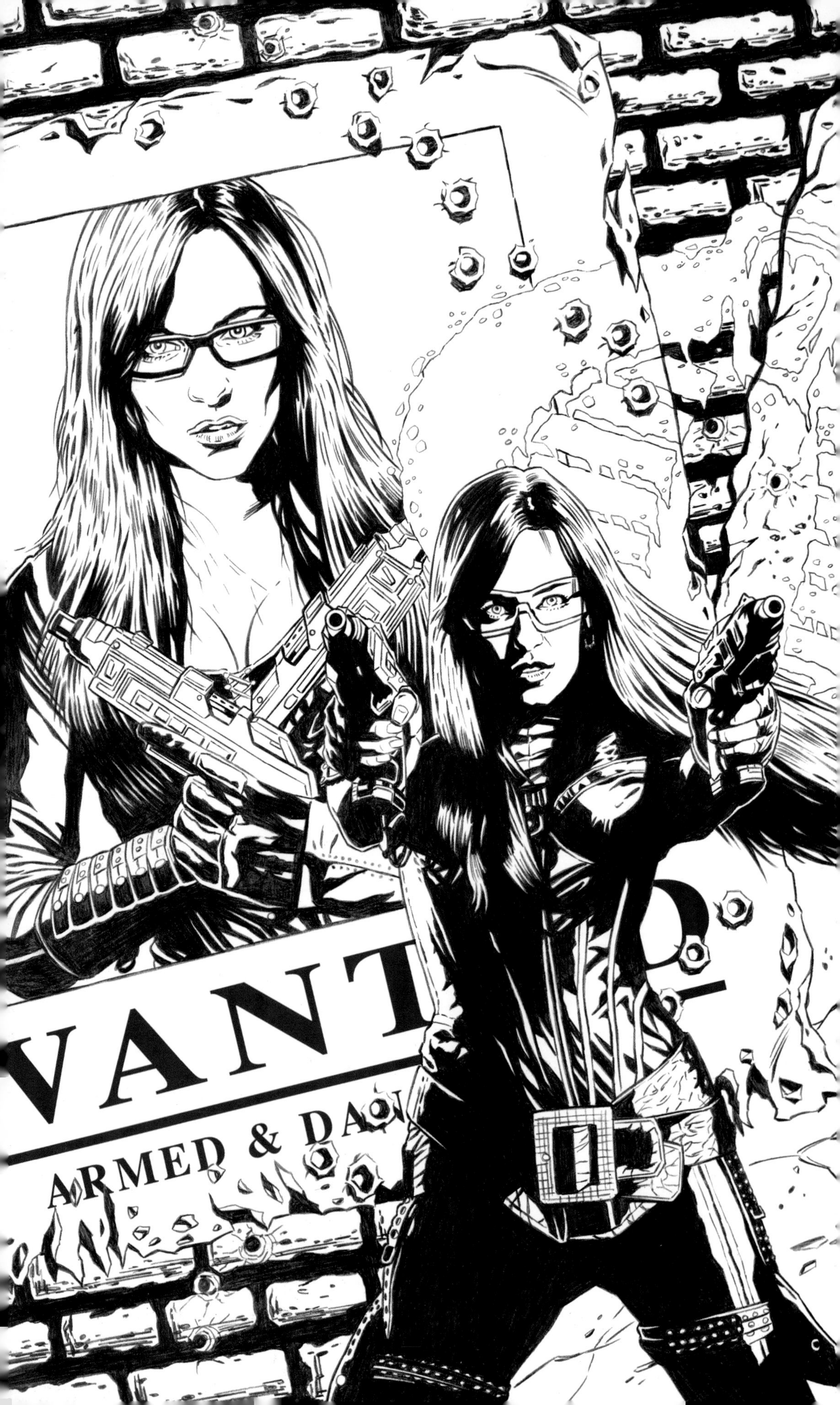
VANT
ARMED & DA

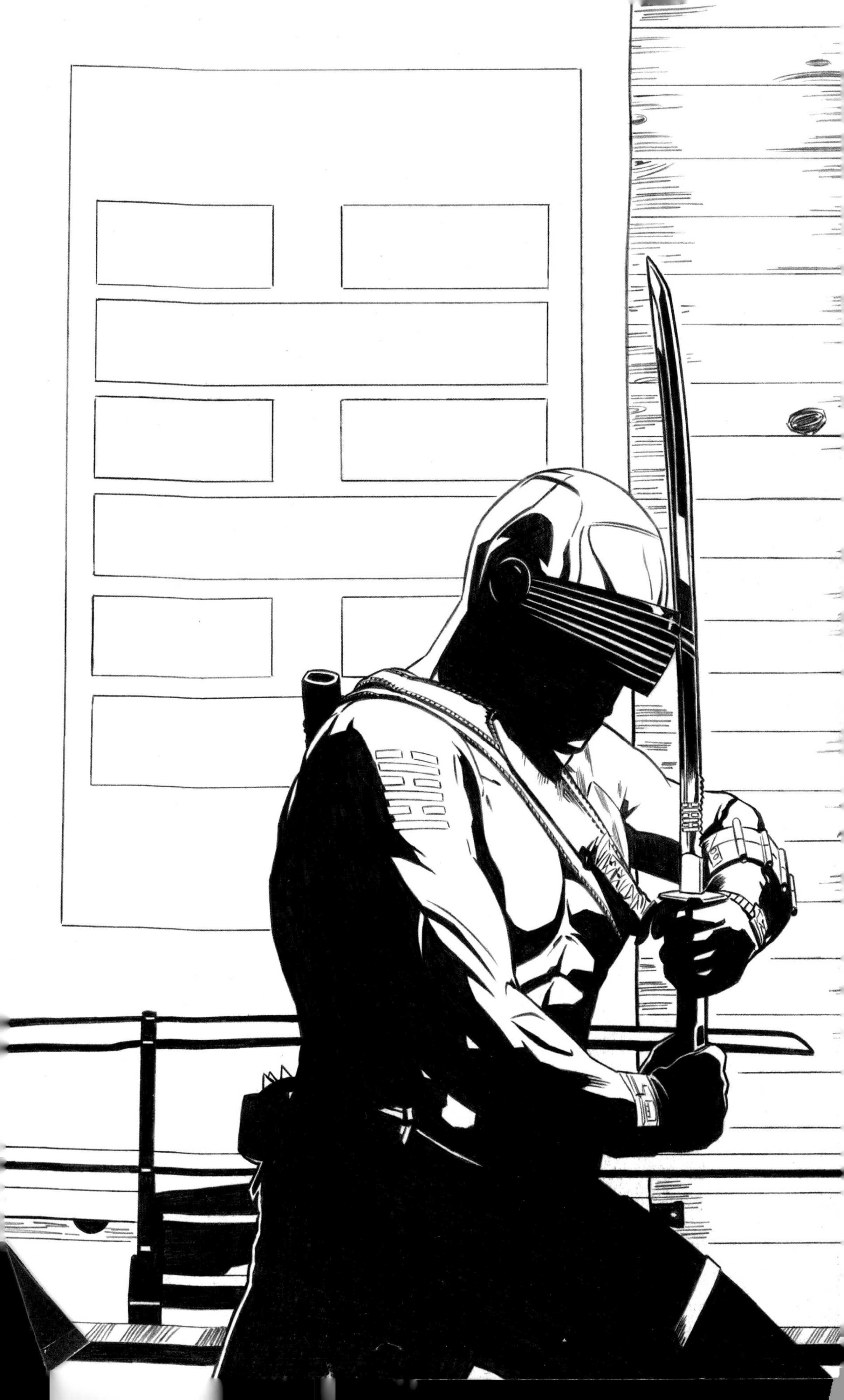